The Clever One

Helena Close lives in County Clare, Ireland with her husband and four children. She has been writing full-time since 2000, and has co-published four novels with her best friend Trisha Rainsford, under the name Sarah O'Brien. Her own first novel, the critically acclaimed *Pinhead Duffy*, was published in 2005, followed by *The Cut of Love* in 2009. Helena is an avid sports fan and a huge Munster and Liverpool supporter. *The Clever One* is her third novel.

HELENA CLOSE

The Clever One

HACHETTE
BOOKS
IRELAND

First published in 2010 by Hachette Books Ireland
First published in paperback in 2011

A Hachette UK company

Copyright © 2010 Helena Close

1

A CIP catalogue record for this title is available from the British Library.

ISBN 978 0340 92020 6

Typeset in Sabon by Hachette Books Ireland
Printed and bound in Great Britain by CPI Mackays, Chatham ME5 8TD

Hachette Books Ireland policy is to use papers that are natural, renewable and recyclable products and made from wood grown in sustainable forests. The logging and manufacturing processes are expected to conform to the environmental regulations of the country of origin.

Hachette Books Ireland
8 Castlecourt Centre
Castleknock
Dublin 15, Ireland
A division of Hachette UK Ltd
338 Euston Road
London NW1 3BH

www.hachette.ie

In memory of my brothers – John and Eamonn.
This one's for you, lads.

One

Results 2007

They call it Bucky and it tastes exactly like Calpol and I can feel it now trying to come back up my throat. Can taste the cloying sweet gloop as it fights for daylight. Their faces float in front of me like bobble heads, their voices high and giggly like cartoon voices. I can't think straight and I want to go home. I force myself to stand up, my legs wobbly and not connected.

I wonder if I can speak. I practise my words in my head. "I'm off so, gotta be somewhere."

But it doesn't come out like that at all. It's a jumbly incoherent mumble. They look at me then and I can see the smirks in their eyes and mouths. Somebody takes a video with their phone. Sophie, I think, but she's merging into Ciara so I can't be sure. I can't be sure of anything, actually, and if this is what drunk feels like they can fucking well have it. They can keep it and go out the bank every weekend and do it until they kill every brain cell in their already depleted stock. I shouldn't have come.

I wave and almost fall over, and then I walk away. My legs move faster and faster as I follow the path along the river. I breathe in air and make myself think logically. Clinically. OK. The alcohol has entered my bloodstream. It will make me feel a certain way for a certain length of time and then it will wear off and I will never do it again. The Bucky's rising again so I stop and lean my head against a tall, ancient oak tree. I feel dizzy.

"Are you OK, Maeve?"

I scream, then see Jamie Burke's face smiling at me. I don't trust myself to speak so I nod, propped against the tree for support. I smile back at him but I know it's a big goofy grin. Jamie Burke. Rugby star. Pin-up boy.

"It's shit, isn't it?" He's still smiling.

I nod again, trying to work out what's shit.

"I never drink the stuff. I stick to cans."

Another profound nod from me.

"You did brilliant, you know. You must be some brainbox."

I shrug this time. Just for variety.

"Ten As. Fuck sake. That's awesome."

"And a B. Ten As and a B in English." My words sound like words this time. And the dizziness is gone. "I'm raging over the B." I don't know why I'm telling Jamie Burke this. It makes me sound like a right ungrateful bighead. But I'm fucking raging over the B. And in English. My best subject. My favourite.

"I got a C on a pass paper. You're lucky." He smiles again and I can smell Lynx and beer and fags. And Bucky.

"Are you going to the gig?" He leans towards me, putting a hand on the tree near my face. I can see a pale shadow of stubble on his upper lip and a little circle of pimples on his forehead, like a tiny solar system. There's a big one in the middle and the others are in a ring around it.

"Naw. I'm going to head home, I've . . ."

He's kissing me. Slowly at first and it's actually quite nice and I feel my body responding, my nipples hardening underneath my silk top and the weirdest feeling in my stomach. Jamie Burke likes me. The hottest guy in school likes plain old Maeve Hogan. He stops suddenly, pulls back and looks at me. Then he holds my head in his hands and leans into me, his body pressed against me. I'm jammed up against the tree and I can feel its knobbly bark pushing into my spine. His mouth is on mine again but now it's different. It's like it's disconnected from him completely, like it has a mind and a purpose all of its own. His tongue pokes my mouth open and invades me, drooling and wet and slobbery. I can feel his erection pressing against my hips, as urgent and purposeful as his tongue, and I can feel the Bucky returning now and I try to swallow it back but his fucking tongue is in the way and his hands are all over me, on my bum, pressing me against him, and up my top and under my bra, his fingers finding my nipples and rubbing them like he's trying to erase them. My head is pounding and I'm trying to say stop, stop it, for fuck sake, and then he's dropping to his knees and pulling up my skirt. Oh, God, Jamie Burke is trying to . . . Jesus . . .

"Stop it," I shout, but he's oblivious. His hands have me pinned to the tree and now he's sticking his finger – Oh, God, I hope it's his finger, I mean, I hope it isn't his . . . oh, fuck, it hurts . . .

And then the Bucky saves me. I puke and it's pink and it's flowing down the top of Jamie Burke's head, down his pretty-boy face. He looks up at me, like he can't believe what's just happened.

"I told you to stop," I say. My skirt is up around my belly button. The smell of vomit is strong in the air and suddenly I burst out crying. Jamie's still looking at the puke. Wiping it off his face and looking at it on his hands as if it's going to make it go away. Pink lumps of it are stuck to the gel in his hair. "I said to stop."

He stands up. "You're frigid." He walks away then, still trying to clean himself up.

"Fuck off," I shout after him.

He turns back and gives me the finger. "Go ride a book, Frigid."

"Hilarious, Jamie. I'd rather ride a book than hang out with a dumbass like you."

He turns suddenly, his face black and mean. He's beside me in three strides and grabs my arm as I try to run away. "Miss Clever Clogs, how clever are you now?"

I struggle to get away, the friction of his tight grip on my wrist causing a Chinese burn.

"Well? How fucking clever are you now? How fucking clever?"

I will myself not to cry and turn my face away from his.

"I could have you now, if I wanted, do you know that, Frigid? I could fuck you stupid right this minute – but do you know something?"

I squeeze back tears, but they escape anyway. Lots of them.

"I couldn't be bothered fucking an Iceberger. A Fat Frog." He laughs and lets go my hand and I'm racing down the wooded path, following the snake of the river, knowing it'll lead me home. I'm racing until my heart is pumping so hard I think it'll burst and my legs are at full stretch, swallowing up the ground, and everything is a green blur I'm running so fast. And I think I can hear him coming after me, pounding the earth faster than me, nearer and nearer, but it's the noise of my heart and my breathing and I run and run until I fall hard into the soft grassy bank of the river.

I gulp in air. Huge lungfuls of warm September air, smelling of river and mud and the day's heat. Fucking cretins. The world is full of dumbass cretins. I search my pocket for my phone and think about ringing Mam. Bad idea. Mark? No. He'd only laugh at me for going in the first place. He'd say, "Junior Cert Results Night – the kiddies' night out."

I sit up, and my breathing is normal again. And my stomach feels grand now since I puked on top of Jamie's head. Oh, fuck, did I really vomit on him while he was trying to . . .? I close my eyes and shake my head, trying to dislodge the pink-tinged picture in my mind. And then I laugh, slow at first but then I laugh so much that tears come again. Oh fuck! Maeve Hogan has discovered a whole new way of giving head. If I had the guts to tell Mark what happened tonight even he'd think that was genius.

And then I hear a voice. Low and deep and coming from the riverbank. My heart starts the pounding thing again and I lie very still in my springy bed. I hear it again now, soft and low, calling something, a dog, maybe. And then there's another voice, higher pitch, foreign guttural sounds, Polish maybe or Russian. I sit up slowly and peer over the bushes. There are two people, men I think, on the edge of the riverbank, calling softly over the water, coaxing and cajoling. I can't see who or what they're calling so I stand up and move a little to the side, for cover. And then I see it. A swan. A beautiful female – I know she's a female because of her smaller beak. She's feet away from the two men, her silhouette reflected perfectly in the still water. She's watching them as they throw bread at her, still murmuring encouragement. A few feet away another swan watches, her mate obviously. He's so still he looks like an ornament.

The female swan glides towards the men, her neck outstretched for bread. She finds a piece floating on the water and gobbles it. The men hold out more and the swan is confident now, edging closer and closer until she's inches from the shore. Suddenly there's a flurry of snow-white feathers and squawking, and one of the men has the swan by the neck, her huge wings flapping and her mate now screeching too. The other man shouts, waving his hands while the wings flap and flap. And then the man holding the swan just snaps her neck really quickly and the other guy laughs as the swan's body falls to the ground, still jerking with the last remnants of life.

I realise I've been holding my breath and let it out in a gasp. My head is swimming again and my stomach is swirling. The male swan is screeching and flapping, like he's going to attack the men, but they ignore him. They're bent over the dead swan and the taller guy, the swan-killer, has a long gleaming blade in his hand. He puts his other hand under the swan and lifts her breast towards him. Then he slices it off, one side at a time, quickly and deftly, like a butcher. I put my hand over my mouth to stop myself shouting, biting down hard on it. Now they're laughing and wrapping the breast in tinfoil. Birds are singing in the trees near me and midges dance in a cluster over my head. The swan looks ravaged, lying still and broken, her breast a red raw wound, blood making her feathers pink. And that's what does it to me, the pinky red mess. I start to puke again, trying not to make any noise and choking in the process. I drop to my knees, vomiting pink into the bushes, huge gobs of it coming in horrible waves. How much vomit before your stomach's empty?

At last it stops and I raise my head and see the men looking down at me. Their faces are wide and flat, eyes small and dark. I have a terrible urge to pee. The taller guy reaches out to me and I cringe away, almost toppling over. He speaks in Polish or Russian or whatever. I shake my head at him. "Leave me alone," I say, my voice croaky.

"You are OK? You want help you?"

"Fuck off," I say, stumbling to stand up. "Leave me alone," I scream. "Leave me alone."

"Is OK, is OK," the other guy says, backing away from me. They walk towards the riverbank and I start running. Running as fast as I can.

It's almost dark by the time I get home. The lights are on in the sitting room, and I can hear the soft drone of the telly as I fumble to open the front door. Mam comes rushing out of the kitchen, mouthing something to me.

"What's up?" I say, glancing at myself in the hall mirror. Jesus, I look wrecked. Like I've been dragged through a hedge and puked on.

Mam doesn't seem to notice. She's pointing to the kitchen and miming something. I roll my eyes and march straight in. My older sister, and I use the term "older" loosely, Fiona, is sitting at the kitchen table, her doe eyes red from crying. She's seventeen and claims to be dyslexic, but I think she's just plain thick and my nickname for her is Attract-a-Knack. Fiona is like a heat missile where knackers are concerned. She'll seek them out, make friends with them, adopt their accents and modes of dress as if by osmosis, and suddenly she's talking in this barely comprehensible Limerick accent, wearing huge Rihanna-like hoop earrings and claiming to be in love with her latest scumbag boyfriend. Dad would turn somersaults in his grave.

Sitting beside her tonight, the night of our joint Junior Cert results, is the wonderful Big. Big is called Big – and this is a real knacker Limerick thing to do – because he's not big. In fact, he's tiny. Think Frankie Dettori. Same kind of look too. Ferrety brown eyes in a long, sharp face. Shaved head but with the fringe intact. An eyebrow piercing and a whole host of tattoos. Every mother's dream for her elder daughter.

He gives me his standard salute – a kind of half-wink, half-nod. "How's it going? Rough night?" He grins at me, his teeth an orthodontist's nightmare.

"Like your outfit," I say. It's the one he's worn ever since his family moved into our cul-de-sac nine months ago. Our first "Regeneration" family. Things have gone downhill since – just as Mark predicted they would. Mark and I now call Limerick's Regeneration Programme the Degeneration Programme. The way we figure it, they took the mess in the troubled areas and spread it around Limerick, like soft butter on hot toast. Anyway, Big's wardrobe is invariably white wife-beater vest (summer only), white Adidas hoodie with black stripe on sleeves, white or black tracksuit bottoms (the stripe on the hoodie sleeve normally colour-coordinates with the bottoms) and Nike runners. Mark and I always wonder why the runners aren't Adidas too – just for symmetry.

"Oh, Big, here it comes again – oh, Jesus Mammy, I'm in agony . . ."

Fiona stands up, her hugely pregnant belly swaying in her tight Playboy T-shirt.

"Breathe, love, breathe," says Big, and you know straight away it's something he picked up from *Casualty* or *ER*. No antenatal classes for our Big.

"Labour, I presume?" I say to my sister.

Mam is standing behind her, rubbing her back. "There, now, you'll be grand, just breathe through it. It's always worse the first time."

I glare at my mother – the first time is enough. Fiona might like all this attention. We could be doing this every nine months. Before the pregnancy we had a Fiona drama every couple of days. Scumbags fighting with her at school, langers drunk and brought home in a squad car, shoplifting, anorexic, overweight, depressed: we've done the rounds with Fiona.

The pain eases. Fiona sits down, her legs splayed in front of her like Humpty Dumpty's. "Three days. I've had pains for three days."

Big is fidgety, dying-for-a-fag fidgety.

"Braxton Hicks," I say, filling the kettle to make tea. I'm suddenly starving, my stomach the emptiest it's ever been. I throw bread into the toaster. I don't want to risk anything heavier. Jesus, I couldn't bear any more pink vomiting.

"Who's he?"

"He, my dear sister, is them. They're false labour pains, kind of like practice ones."

She looks at me, my big dumb sister, trying to work out if I'm playing her or not. "And so speaks Dr Maeve Hogan," she says. Big laughs. Mam butters my toast and gives it to Fiona. She nibbles a corner and Big takes the other slice. I make one cup of tea, squeezing the teabag until it's almost dry. I stir in a heaped spoon of sugar and it tastes lovely. Warm and soothing.

"Who was out?" my sister asks, nibbling at the toast like a pregnant doe-eyed mouse.

"All the usual cretins." I root in the press for biscuits. Mam has gone off to phone the world about the imminent birth – I can hear the drone of her voice in the hallway and snatches of conversation: "Ten minutes apart . . . No, you'd be only hanging around out there for days . . . I'll ring you straight away . . ."

"I hear you're a right genus." Big grins at me.

"Yep. A genus. We're all a genus, actually."

Fiona gives me the puzzled look again, the are-you-joking-or-what look.

"What you get anyway – a rake of As?"

"Yep. A whole rake of them."

"I hope our fella has your brains. He'll be fucked if he takes after me or her," says Big. He laughs, and Fiona laughs with him, like he's given her the nicest compliment in the world. "I didn't even do no Junior Cert – no point. I went for a trade and then the fuckers let me go. Shower of cunts." Big opens the back door and stands outside. I can hear his lighter flicking.

"You look sick." Fiona has finally noticed the state of me.

I shrug and eat a chocolate-chip cookie in one bite.

She smiles at me, stroking her belly. "You were drinking."

"Just trying to catch up with you."

She's offended at that. "I haven't had a drink in weeks."

"Mmm – let's see, that could be because you're pregnant, right?"

"Oh, Dr Maeve again. Why didn't you go to the gig? I was going to go only these pains started."

"Couldn't be bothered. I watched a breast reduction instead – getting in some operating room practice."

Suddenly Fiona's standing up, clutching the table. There's water pouring down her legs, staining her jeans black at the crotch. "Oh, my God, oh, fucking hell, Big, help . . ."

16

Two

It's like there's a United Nations conference on in the Limerick Regional Maternity. There's every nationality floating around, whole tribes of them. We have the biggest tribe, though. Big's family have all turned out for the great occasion. This is the first time I've seen them close up and all together. I've often seen them hanging around outside their house, passing cans of beer on a fine evening, the mother sitting on a wrought-iron garden bench, smoking and laughing with a gaggle of teenagers and children. But much as I wanted to I couldn't really hang over the garden gate and study them intently.

We're all in a waiting room and I have a pounding headache. Mam and Big are in the labour ward and I swear I can hear Fiona roaring. Big's mother, Vonnie, is on her mobile, giving a blow-by-blow account of Fiona's labour. Big's sister, who's around twelve and about three stone overweight, is drinking a bottle of Coke. Every so often she smiles at me and I smile back. Two of Big's brothers – they look around ten or eleven – are flying up and down the corridor outside, shouting and laughing. I need my bed.

"Very warm in here," says Vonnie, to nobody in particular.

She's holding the phone out in her hand like she's expecting it to answer her. I'm wishing Fiona would hurry up so we can go home. "I remember when I had my last one, my Chelsea. Jesus, she nearly killed me, eleven and a half pounds, I was walking like John Wayne for a month afterwards." Vonnie laughs, her eyes crinkling at the corners, deep lines at the edges of her mouth. "Jesus, I'm melting with the heat. What age are you?"

"Sixteen," I say.

"Same age as our Sonya. Do you know her?"

Sonya Walsh. Expelled from the Comp last June. I don't want to know her.

"I know her to see," I say.

Suddenly my aunt Linda bursts into the room, all breathy and perfumy. For once I'm delighted to see her. "Maeve, did she have it yet? I couldn't get a babysitter – Tom's in Madrid – and I just had to be here. Poor Fiona."

"She's in the labour ward." Vonnie is smiling at me and Linda, looking from one to the other, waiting for an introduction.

"Linda, this—"

"Anyway, I'm glad I'm here now. Did the scumbag family show up yet? I told your mother, Maeve, I told her straight out, 'Fiona will grow out this, she'll shun him in a while and that type won't be bothered with custody or maintenance . . .'" Linda stops as she finally notices the look on my face.

I don't know what to do. Introductions would be pretty dumb after that little faux pas. But Vonnie doesn't wait around for niceties. She roots in her huge handbag and takes out a new pack of Marlboro Lights and a silver lighter with tiny jewels inset in it. Then she stands up slowly and looks directly at Linda.

"Don't you know me?"

Linda colours underneath her expensive Mac makeup. She shakes her head.

"Funny, cos I know you. I remember when you were a small skinny thing who always smelt of piss. Married a big shot and lost your memory?"

I smile to myself. Then she walks out of the room, leaving her daughter to mind her bag. The girl drops her eyes, examining her nails, peeling bits of pink polish from them.

"Oh-oh, silly me," says Linda. "I can't remember her at all – your mother does but she's older than me. Why didn't you warn me, Maeve?"

Maybe because you're a motormouth, Linda. "Tried to." I nod at her and then at the girl.

Linda looks puzzled and then the penny finally drops. She puts her hand over her mouth and her eyes are two Os. "Sorry," she whispers.

I shrug. It's no skin off my nose.

"Listen, I've got a huge surprise!"

She waits expectantly for my enthusiastic response. I shrug again.

"Don't you want to know?"

I'm thinking, bought a new outfit/house/appliance/beauty treatment. Something that involves swiping a credit card. "What is it?"

"I booked us all on a holiday." She smiles at me, my mother's younger sister, my aunt. I feel years older than her.

"That's lovely for you, when are you going?"

"For all of us, Maeve. The two families. Tom is taking time off work and the boys will be on mid-term – Hallowe'en in Lanzarote. Fiona's baby will be nearly two months and . . ."

"I can't go – exams."

She gives me her puzzled look, wrinkling her forehead and shaking her sleek bobbed hair. "You just did exams, Maeve."

"I'll have more – I skipped Transition Year so I'm straight into Fifth."

Linda giggles. "It'll be great, Maeve. Your mother could do with the break. I've booked a villa for the lot of us. We'll have a wonderful time."

The girl coughs and Linda walks over to sit beside her. "What's your name?" she says, patting a chubby legging-clad thigh.

"Nicole," she says, barely above a whisper. She keeps picking at her nails.

"Are you excited? You're going to be an auntie."

She nods, still not looking at either of us. Still examining her nails.

Linda gives up being nice and opens her snake-print hand-bag. "Ta-da," she says, handing me a white envelope. "I have one for Fiona too but I'll hold off now until the baby's born."

That would be an excellent idea – inappropriate to hand somebody in the throes of labour a Junior Cert congrats card. "Good idea," I say. "Thanks for the card."

"No problem. We're so proud of you – best result in the country your mother said."

"Nope – some guy on the Aran Islands beat me."

"Your dad would be so proud," she says, her eyes filling. Linda's eyes fill at the least thing so it's no reflection on her love for Dad. In fact, Dad and Linda had little or nothing to say to each other.

"Yeah. How are the boys?" I say, deftly changing the subject.

Linda doesn't even notice. "Wonderful. Oisin takes after you, a clever clogs, and Andrew's full of beans."

I almost laugh out loud at this. Andrew's mad. A six-year-old walking tsunami. And Oisin is weird, like the kid in *The Omen* weird, and he doesn't take after me at all.

"Did your mother tell you that we've applied for Oisin to go to the school for gifted children next summer?"

The school for gifted children. Genius school. The worst thing I ever did in my life. "Are you sending him there?" I ask.

Suddenly Big rushes in, his face wet with tears. "She's had him – he's fucking lovely. Where's my mother?"

I stall outside her room, waiting for the crowds to disperse. How many people are there in Big's family? I peek through the square glass on the door and there's so many bunches of balloons tied to Fiona's bed that I imagine it'll float away, off out of the window and across the Shannon. A nurse comes in and orders people out. They pass me without seeing me, planning a trip to the pub to celebrate. Mam and Linda are the last to come out.

"Why didn't you go in?" asks Mam.

"Too many in there," I reply, but it's not the truth. The truth is that it's always Fiona. It always has to be Fiona surrounded by people, being fussed over, being discussed, being centre stage. My head tells me I'm being childish, a big baby, needy.

Mam looks at me like she knows what I'm thinking. "Go in and see your nephew," she says. "Did you ring Cian?"

It's on the tip of my tongue to tell her that Cian doesn't want to know. That Cian is mortified that his sister is having a baby, mortified that he will now be related to the Degeneration Family. "I forgot."

"I'll ring him, Marie," says Linda. "How's he doing in college? Physics, if you don't mind – we're so proud of him. Tom says physics is a great area."

Mam nods agreement. A great area, like the best side of town.

"We're going for a coffee, Maeve. We'll wait for you outside."

I look in the little window again. It frames my sister like a photograph. She's sitting up in the bed, the baby wrapped tightly – a bullet of blue in her arms. She looks about eight and a childhood memory steals its way into my head. It's Christmas morning and she's clutching a baby doll, the ones that could wet and cry real tears. Dad and I are on the floor with my brand-new *Star Wars* Lego set, totally engrossed in constructing it. Fiona's trying to talk to Dad, trying to show him her doll. He doesn't hear her, doesn't even see her, and she keeps calling him, pulling his sleeve. She doesn't understand Dad. When he's doing something, concentrating hard, he can't hear anybody. She doesn't get that, but I do and I want her to go away. I give her one of my looks, a glare, really, and it works. Off she goes with her doll. Off to Mam.

I take a deep breath and open the door. "Hi."

She looks up, smiling, and when she sees it's me the smile fades. "Oh, hi."

"Jesus, thanks for the big welcome."

She sighs and looks down at the baby again. I stand a bit away, feeling awkward. What do you say to your seventeen-year-old dumb sister when she's just had a baby with a dumb scumbag? "Congratulations" seems all wrong. "Congratulations."

"Thanks."

Her tone is sulky and I bite back a smart comment, swallow it and count to ten.

"Am . . . what are you going call it?" I'm still standing about three feet from the bed. I can see the top of the baby's head, the hair dark wet and matted. There's a tiny streak of blood in it and it looks like it's been highlighted.

"We haven't decided on a name for him. We're thinking of Harvey or Levi."

I swallow another smart comment, harder this time. "Nice names."

"I knew you'd be smart, knew you'd have to have a go."

"Jesus, Fiona, all I said was that the names were nice . . ."

"It's the way you say things, Maeve. It's the way you say them."

"Oh . . . like using words?"

"There you go again."

Silence now. I can hear the baby snuffling. Hospital sounds in the corridor. A toilet being flushed.

"Let's see him anyway," I say eventually. I move towards her and she holds out the bundle. I sit on the edge of the bed, pull the soft blue blanket down from his face. And then the strangest thing in the world happens. He opens his eyes, fat slits, and his fists box the air and he smiles at me. A big, gummy, goofy smile.

"He's smiling, look at him, Fiona, he's smiling at me."

"Wind. That's what the nurse says."

"Can I hold him?"

She nods. I take him in my arms, and he has the nicest smell in the world. I wonder why they don't make perfume that smells like him – they'd make a fortune. He's still air-boxing. I carry him to the window, his slit eyes looking up at me like I'm the most important and interesting thing in the whole world. Fiona's baby doll never felt like this. Never felt like a tiny ball of energy and life, never looked at you like you were a new discovery in a science lab, never smelt so incredible. I touch his cheek, soft and downy. "Oh, my God, you're gorgeous," I whisper. "You're gorgeous."

He stares at me like a wise old man, a fat Buddha, a slug, a beautiful, perfect slug. I almost expect him to say something to me.

I look at Fiona but she's fallen asleep, snoring lightly. I take him over to the chair and sit down, loving the weight of him in my arms. I stroke his face again, enjoying the width of his nose, how far apart his eyes seem to be, his tiny little mouth. His eyelids begin to droop. I can see dark spidery lashes through the fat. My heart is pounding and there's something in my head that's just there for no reason. Something I know that has no logic. No theory. No reason. I love him. I know it, like I know how to breathe.

So we sit, me and him, his breathing rhythmic, eyes scrunched closed. I want to sit there and hold him all night. My phone buzzes in my pocket and Baby gives a startled jump in my arms, opens his eyes for a second and then dozes off again – like he knows I'm there to protect him.

I jump as the door opens. Big and two of his pals arrive in, talking loudly. He shushes them when he sees that Fiona's asleep. His friends, a boy and a girl, are holding hands. She's so skinny that her hip bones stick out and her skin-tight white jeans look like they're going to fall down. Her hair is long and straight and unbelievably blonde. The boy is dressed in "the uniform". Same as Big but different colours. He's tall – although anyone is tall in comparison to Big.

Big doesn't bother with niceties like hellos and introductions. "Give him over here," he says, in a loud whisper. He takes the baby from me. "Feel the weight of him, Jay – seven pounds nine. He's fucking huge, isn't he? Here, hold him, go on, hold him." Big plonks the baby into Jay's skinny arms. Anger bubbles inside me.

"Jesus, man he's a ton, a bruiser," says Jay.

"He's average. The average weight of a newborn baby in Western Europe is seven pounds seven ounces, so he's not huge." I'd it said before I could stop myself.

The three of them look at me like I'm speaking Chinese.

"Here, let me hold him," says Blondie. "Aw, look at him. He's a dote – he looks like my Holly, doesn't he, Jay?"

Blondie looks about twelve and I'm presuming that Holly isn't a dog, a cat or a stuffed toy. Blondie is a mammy too. I wonder if Jay is the daddy but I haven't the nerve to ask.

"He's dotey – I'd love another one." Blondie lifts the baby to her face and kisses him on the cheek. "I love that smell, when they're just born – I love it. Smell him, Jay."

They all take a whiff of the baby.

"You have to see this, Jay – wait till I show you." Big takes the baby and lays him on the bottom of the bed. He unwraps the blanket and starts to pop the fasteners on the pale lemon Babygro. Then he peels back the tabs holding the nappy in place. "There. Look at that, Jay – the biggest shlong you ever saw."

They all stare, and Blondie giggles, and I'm so angry now that I want to thump Big right in his stupid dumb face.

"Look at that for a weapon – he got that from me, didn't you, fella?"

"He hardly got it from Fiona," says Jay, and they laugh like it's the best joke ever.

25

Fiona stirs and opens her eyes. Blondie runs over and hugs her. "Well?" says Blondie.

"I'm fuckin' wrecked, Carrie," she says, in her best put-on knacker accent. "I won't be able to walk for a month."

"You won't be able to do nothin' else either," says Blondie. They laugh, and then Fiona notices me sitting on the chair.

I look at her, straight at her, and then I look at Big and Jay, cooing over the baby. Then I look Blondie up and down, from the top of her too-blonde head to her high-heels and French-manicured toes. I look back to Fiona again and she's glaring at me.

"Are you still here?" she says.

"Obviously. I haven't quite mastered bi-location but I'm working on it."

She rolls her eyes at Carrie. Big rolls his eyes at Jay. I know Fiona wants me to leave and I know I should but I sit there anyway.

"Did you pick out your buggy? I saw a lovely Mamas and Papas one, a BabyBoo thing, you know – Gwyneth Paltrow has one and Myleene Klass. I didn't like the colour, though – burnt orange. That'd go out of fashion very fast . . ." Carrie is perched on the edge of the bed, her long thin legs crossed. She's found a hairbrush in her bag and starts to brush Fiona's hair. The conversation continues between them, Blondie doing Fiona's hair, stopping every now and again, hairbrush in the air, to laugh or exclaim. They look like sisters. They act like sisters. I leave. Nobody notices.

Three

Mr Hynes smiles at me and shakes his head. "It doesn't work like that, Maeve, and that's exactly what I mean when I say that sometimes you miss the point."

"The point is that I deserved an A and I want it rechecked."

Mr Hynes leans back in his chair, arms locked together behind his neck. He smiles at me again and it makes him look young, like one of the boys in my class. He's handsome in a Mr Darcy kind of way – old-fashioned, really. The girls in my class go weak at the knees over him but I can't see why. He's no Russell Brand.

"Maeve, you're very bright, scarily so. You can probably do anything you want at college. If you sat your Leaving Cert in the morning, you'd get a bucket load of points – I've no doubt about that . . ." He pushes his hands out in front of him, steepling them together and cracking his knuckles all at once. My brother Cian does that. A male thing, definitely.

"I feel a 'but' coming, Mr Hynes."

"But – there it is, Maeve – English isn't like other subjects. It's not something you can learn. The cleverest person in the world might not be good at English. You can't measure it the way you can maths or science."

"I know I did two excellent papers."

"True. I'd say you did."

"So I want a recheck. I want my A."

His grey-blue eyes bore into me as he says, "One question."

"OK."

"Why?"

"Why? Because I should have had an A in English. It's my best subject. I want . . . I'm better than, say, Ciara Long and she got an A. She can't spell."

"No, that's not what I mean. Why do you want your A? Why?"

"I told you already."

"No, you didn't. This is a different question. Why do you want your A?"

I look down at my hands and shrug.

"Think about that, Maeve."

Another little shrug from me.

"Will you do something for me?" His eyes seek my face for the answer.

If he asked Sophie or Ciara the same question I know what they'd say.

"Sure."

"I know you like to write. Some of your work is excellent, very well constructed. Beginning, middle, end. I want you to forget all that. Forget everything you've ever read about how to write – and I know you've done your research, Maeve, because that's how you operate . . ."

"Is that a bad thing?"

"Most of the time it's a good thing. But with English, with

writing, you can over-think it. I want you to write from the heart – the first thing that comes into your head, just write it. Forget about structure or what genre it is or if it's poetry or prose or a bloody blog. Just write without thinking. Do you think you could do that?"

I want to tell him it's a ridiculous idea. That it's just drivel and anybody could do that, write a pile of unstructured shite.

"Well?"

"I'll do it. It can't be too hard. But I don't see how it'll help me."

He smiles. "Listen, you're a very talented girl, you know that. You're the best student we've ever had in this school. Try this. See what happens. Do it over a few weeks and I'll read it." He pushes back his chair as if to get up and I know he wants to go home. The last of the students are leaving the building and an eerie quiet settles.

"Hey, how's Fiona doing?"

"Fine." I'm mortified at the mention of her. I have been since this whole pregnant thing started. When your sister's parading around your school, her belly huge in her school-uniform skirt, her scumbag boyfriend waiting outside in his souped-up Honda Civic, you'll be mortified too. I could feel my classmates looking at me sometimes like being dumb and pregnant is catching or a family trait.

"A little boy, wasn't it?"

I nod.

"Is she home yet from the hospital? You must be excited."

"Thrilled."

He looks at me strangely, picking up on the tiny note of sarcasm in my voice. I try to make amends. "She's coming home today."

"How do you feel about it?"

I give the shrug answer. How do I feel about it? I feel my sister is the thickest person I ever met in my life. I feel my mother indulges her. I feel we should bar Big and all belonging to him from our house, and definitely I feel he shouldn't be left within an ass's roar of that little baby. These aren't even "feels" – they're facts. Any intelligent person would know these things. But I can't say any of this out loud.

He gives me the funny look again. "Any time you need a chat just come to me. I remember being your age – most confusing time of my life."

I nod agreement. He's wrong, though. It's not confusing. "Frustrating" is a better word. It's easy to work stuff out, make sense of it all. It's frustrating watching other people, particularly the ones you live with, stumble around in a confused daze.

Mark is waiting for me by the main exit. "Mmm – cosying up with Barry Hynes. Bit of a cliché, though, Maevis, falling for the teacher."

"Shut up, you," I say, punching his arm.

Mark is my best friend. We've known each other since we were in playgroup together. We tell each other everything.

"Saw you on YouTube." He grins at me, his gelled blond hair a work of art. He's got a great face but he's a little too funky for the girls in our year. Skinny jeans, tight T-shirts, weird taste in music.

"I heard about it. Didn't bother to look. How bad is it?"

"Not too bad – you're swaying a bit and mumbling, and there's a small amount of drool involved . . ."

"Bastard."

"What possessed you anyway?"

"Ciara and Sophie texted and I decided here goes . . ."

"A night out with the cretins – Jesus, I'd rather bleed from the eyes. That swan thing was weird, though, Maeve. You must have been freaked."

"I Googled it last night. Apparently people in other countries consider swan a delicacy and there are claims that our swan stock – our fish and fowl stock too – has dropped considerably since EU accession in 2004."

Mark bursts out laughing.

"What?"

He laughs harder, dropping his Rip Curl schoolbag on the ground. He's holding his sides and it's infectious. I grin at him. "What's so funny?"

"Two . . ." He goes into another laughing fit. "Two things. One, you are such a little information Hoover – and the way you deliver it, exactly like Miriam O'Callaghan . . ." More laughing.

I thump his arm. "Wanker."

"A teenage Miriam O'Callaghan. And two, we have another thing to beat the foreigners over the head with – first our jobs, then our women, and now our swans . . ."

Both of us crack up. We're holding each other laughing and then Jamie Burke is standing right in front of me. He's with Colin Ryan, a quiet, studious type, and another guy from sixth year. I feel my face turning red and I wish there was a way to control blushing. I'd spent a whole night on the Internet once hunting for a blushing antidote. No luck.

Jamie has to step over our bags, dumped right in the middle of the footpath.

"Hi," he says, avoiding my eyes. Good: the enemy is scared and on the defensive.

"Hi, Jamie, haven't seen you for a couple of days – sick?" I say, in a bright, friendly voice.

He mumbles something incoherent.

The other two lads are talking to Mark, laughing and joking with him. But I can see Colin half-listening to the exchange between myself and Jamie. My face starts to burn bright red again and I wonder what Jamie's been saying about that night. Telling all his mates I'm a slut, just like my sister.

I look at Jamie – well, at his hair, really. I imagine I see little bits of pink stuff in the spiky gelled-up creation but it could be the sunlight.

He mumbles something.

"Sorry – what did you say?" I ask, dragging my eyes from his hair. The blushing has stopped for the time being.

"Sorry. About the other night. Sorry. I was a bit . . . out of my head . . ." He walks away and the others follow, calling goodbye to the two of us.

"What was that about, Maevis Ravis?"

"What was what about?"

"The little tête-à-tête with Mr Burke, rugby stud?"

"Nothing. And why were you spying on me?"

Mark grins, his hair bouncy and shiny in the sun. "Touchy, Maeve. Methinks the fair lady likes the rugby stud." I try to hit him but he ducks and grabs his bag from the ground. "Let's go – I'm starving and there's a Rustler in the fridge with my name on it."

Mark's parents both work – no, they both have "careers". He's an only child – spoilt rotten but the food isn't great.

"Hey, Fiona's coming home today." We walk towards

Dooradoyle, the Friday traffic beside us a continuous snake of noise.

"I know."

"How do you know?"

Mark slings his bag over his other shoulder. "That'd be telling you."

"How do you know?"

"Big rang me last night – asked me to come wet the baby's head. A nice glass of wine or a refreshing cocktail . . ."

I snort with laughter. "Yeah, right – down by the canal. That lovely al fresco bar he frequents?"

"I was talking to your brother."

"Cian doesn't talk."

"On MSN, you eejit. And you're wrong. Cian has a lot to say for himself."

"Not the Cian I know. So what were ye talking about? Physics? The Big Bang?"

"Music mostly, and college and being an uncle."

"Jesus, we must try that at home – MSN with him instead of real conversation."

"Anyway, Brainbox, back to my original question. What were you discussing with Mr Hynes?"

"Philosophy. Feelings. Pregnancy. Writing drivel – the usual boring old stuff."

Mark laughs.

"So, are you calling over tonight?" I ask him.

"Absolutely – wouldn't miss it for the world. Did they give him a name yet?"

We're just turning into my avenue. I stop, drop my bag and grab his hands. His long-gelled fringe covers one side of his face and his lips are so red it looks like he's wearing gloss. He smells of almonds.

"Guess." I grin at him.

"You are one bitch, Brainbox. OK – Tyrone? Stevie G?"

"Try harder, fool."

"Let's see. Am . . . Joshua, Kelvin, Ronaldo, Richard . . ."

"Richard? Be serious, Mark, please."

"Just tell me, Maevis. We could be here all night."

"Harvey Levi Gerard Hogan."

"Gerard?"

"After my dad."

"Harvey Levi?"

"No idea. Top names in *Now* magazine?"

"What's he like?" Mark takes a pack of cigarettes out of his trouser pocket and lights one up. I love the way Mark smokes. The way he tilts his head to the side as he holds the lighter to the cigarette, then dips it the other way. It's graceful, like ballet. And I love the smell, but only off him. Fiona smokes and the smell turns my stomach. She smoked her way through her pregnancy, lying to Mam and me about it but the stink from her clothes would have knocked you. I'm surprised Harvey wasn't born with emphysema.

Mark holds the fag up to his lips and takes a long drag. "Well?"

"He's grand. He's a baby – you know – wrinkly, baldy, pink."

"Imagine Fiona has a baby – a son. So weird."

"Tell me about it."

"I hope they get married – that'd be a great laugh. Your in-laws, the Walshes."

I punch his arm. "Please."

*

Fiona's home and she's taken to her bed. I peek in at her and she's snoring lightly, her ancient *I love Ireland* teddy clutched to her face. Her room has been transformed into a nursery – changing station, baby clothes, huge boxes of Pampers. And a white crib with a canopy – a present from Vonnie and straight out of *Sleeping Beauty*. I tiptoe over and look in. He's asleep on his side, a fist curled under his cheek. His hair is dark and glossy, his skin velvet and clear. I haven't seen him since that one time in the hospital and my heart does the melting thing again. I remember something my dad told me years ago – that kittens are so pretty just to make us love them. That nature makes babies gorgeous so that we fall in love with them. Harvey stirs in his crib, then stretches out, rolling onto his back, his two fists now above his head. The baby smell wafts up to me. I could stand there watching him all night.

Downstairs Mam is cooking dinner.

"Maeve, can you make a salad? Cian loves a salad with his lasagne." She's busy at the cooker, stirring pasta sauce.

I take out the salad stuff, and start washing and chopping.

"How's school?" Mam asks.

Standard Mam question to me every day. She doesn't really expect an answer.

"I wish I was in Leaving Cert – I'm the oldest in my class and I have to spend another two years with those eejits . . ."

Mam stirs the pot. "That's what you get for being an August baby. They wouldn't take you in school until the following year."

"Hardly my fault. Anyway, I'm having my English rechecked."

She stops stirring and turns to me. "That's ridiculous, Maeve."

I slice a red pepper with vengeance, gouging the chopping board in the process. "Why?"

She shakes her head at me. "You did great. Ten As – that's enough for anyone."

"And a B in English."

"Your sister would have been delighted with even one B. Poor Fiona, sitting that exam and she pregnant. She's a great girl."

"Yeah. Managing to get pregnant – it's very hard to do that."

Mam drops the spoon into the pot and the thick red sauce swallows it. "I'm going to say this once, Maeve. Just because you're smart doesn't give you the right to trample all over people. I expect you to be nice to your sister, support her like a normal sister would."

She picks up a glass of wine, her Friday-evening-after-five drink of choice, and takes a long sip. Then she sighs and goes back to her pasta.

"I wish I had a normal sister."

She drops the spoon again, this time on the white worktop, splattering sauce all over it. "That's a terrible thing to say."

"But you just said it about me."

She glares at me, my mother, the glare that's supposed to stop me but all it does is make me want to keep going, the harder the better. "Don't try your clever tricks with me. I'm sick and tired of your smart comments. Fiona's right about you."

"And Fiona would know – what with her prize boyfriend and her scumbag friends . . ."

She's slapped me before I even realise what's happened. Her hand jerks out and back and then she's crying.

I can feel my cheek beginning to throb. My eyes are watery from the pain. I don't move.

"Go away or I'll say something I regret." She picks up her drink and takes a huge gulp.

"I'm sorry."

She's surprised.

"I'm sorry I told the truth."

She catches up the glass of wine and hurls it into the sink. It shatters. "You're just like him, do you know that? You're just like him and you'll turn out the same as him."

I know straight away she's talking about Dad. "Thanks for the compliment, Mother. I'm proud to be like him."

"Pride comes before a fall, Maeve. Remember that." Her voice is quiet. She reaches out to touch my face but I pull away.

"I'm back," a voice says, from the doorway. My brother Cian, back from college for the first time.

Mam lights up like somebody plugged her in. "Ciany! We missed you!"

She runs over and stands on tiptoe to kiss his cheek.

Cian is mortified. He nods at me and drops a huge bin-bag on the floor. "I brought my washing."

"I'm cooking your favourite dinner. And I made tarts too, one rhubarb and one apple. How are you settling in?"

Cian sits down at the kitchen table, Mam opposite him. He's describing UCC in the usual Cian way, monosyllabic. Yes, no, I don't know. But Mam's face is a picture. She's riveted, like she is when she's watching her favourite soap only more so. It's like she's drinking in his face, his smell, like she can't get enough of him. And I'm invisible.

*

I write about the kittens. It's not what I planned and I have no idea where the memory came from – if it is a memory. Maybe I imagined it but there it is now, appearing on my computer screen as if somebody else is typing.

It was the hottest day of the summer. Fiona and Maeve wore matching pink-cropped trousers and pale blue T-shirts and had been playing in the garden all morning. Tiger, their big tabby and her three kittens, were way better toys than dolls or Lego or even swingball. The sun was a blinding orange disc in the sky, beating down on their backs as they laughed and watched the kittens play with each other. They'd named them earlier, each choosing a name and drawing lots for the third. Muffin, Puffin and Duffin. Maeve didn't like Duffin – she said it wasn't even a word – but Fiona insisted. She said he looked like a Duffin, and Maeve said, "What does a Duffin look like?" but Fiona wouldn't change her mind. Then Daddy came home from work. Came home early, which he never did, and he sat on a wicker chair in the garden, watching them play. Maeve ran up to him the second she saw him. Ran up and threw her arms around him and tried to pull him out of his chair, but he said, no, he was too tired. She was to go back and play and the kittens weren't to come into the house.

And then Fiona sneaked off. Just when the game was getting good she sneaked off with her friend Rosie from the next avenue. Maeve wanted to come too but the friends just laughed and ran away together. Down the garden and out the side gate, giggling and laughing as they skipped off.

Daddy had fallen asleep in the chair and Maeve wondered why he was so tired. The kittens were tired too now, all curled up in a ball of fur. There was no sign of Tiger. Maeve was getting sleepy just watching them and feeling the heat of the sun on the top of her head. And then there was a huge dog in their garden. He came bounding up the path, and Maeve noticed that Fiona had left the gate open. Stupid Fiona. Maeve looked over towards her dad but he was gone indoors. The dog was barking now, barking at the scared kittens. Maeve scooped them up and ran into the house, the dog jumping on her with his big black paws.

The house was dark inside. And cool after the garden. She crept upstairs, holding the kittens tightly, her heart still pounding. She called her daddy but he didn't answer. She went into the pink bedroom that she shared with Fiona. The window was open and the breeze coming in made the curtains flap. She lay down on the bed for a minute, the kittens curled up beside her. They purred, and the purring and the soft breeze and the heat were making her sleepy. She tried to keep her eyes open but they just closed all by themselves.

And then there was shouting. Her daddy standing in the doorway screaming at her.

Screaming, "No fucking animals in the bedrooms – how many times must I fucking well say it?" She sat bolt upright, looking at her father, listening to the terrible curses coming out of him, curses she'd never heard before in her life. She was too scared to say anything. Puffin was trying to climb inside the pillow, the other two kittens were miaowing at her.

And then he marched over to her, all in a blur, his body huge and scary and his face so mad, and he reached out and first she thought he was reaching for her, grabbing her so that he could slap her, but he snatched up the kittens, first Muffin and Duffin, holding them high in the air with one hand, and then Puffin, who'd peeked out of the pillow. Maeve started to cry, and screamed at her dad, "No, Daddy, no, they'll be good and I won't . . ."

He swung his hand into the air, the two kittens squealing, and flung them out the window, just flung them the way Ciany did sometimes with his basketball. Maeve ran at her daddy then. Ran at his long legs as he swung his other arm and poor Puffin went flying through the air like a furry ball. Tears streamed down her face and she was afraid to look out the window. Daddy stood beside her, rubbing his forehead and saying, "Oh, God, oh, God." She took a deep breath and peeked out the window, the curtain dancing against her wet face.

Muffin and Duffin were in the yard below her. Muffin was so still he looked like he was asleep except his legs were all funny. Duffin was beside him, mewing softly. She searched for Puffin, her favourite. She could hear Daddy breathing behind her and mumbling and talking to himself. She was so scared of him and she wished Mammy would come home from town or Ciany would come home from playing soccer. But most of all she wished that Puffin was alive.

Then she saw him. He'd landed on the shed roof. He was miaowing too but his legs looked straight, and she was so glad about that. Daddy had his arms around her neck now and was saying how sorry he was and he loved her and his head hurt. And first she wouldn't turn around and talk to him. First she pushed his hands away and then he was crying too and she turned around and he hugged her and she hugged him back and his crying got worse so she talked to him then. She said, "It's OK, Daddy, it's OK. Puffin is alive, Daddy. You didn't kill them all cos Puffin is on the shed roof . . ."

I read back over what I've written. What a load of tripe. Mr Hynes must be out of his mind if he thinks this is the way to go with English. It won't get me my A1 in the Leaving and I'd bet my iPod Classic that Hemingway or Joyce or even Austen never wrote crap like this. And if Hynes thinks I'm ever going to show him this he'll have a long wait. No wonder he's only a teacher.

There's a knock on my door and I hide the screen immediately, like Cian used to do years ago when he was checking out Internet porn.

"Can you hold him for a minute?" Fiona's standing there with the baby held close to her chest. She looks tired. "I want to have a shower and Mam's busy – Ciany's home." She rolls her eyes at me and we both laugh, knowing that once Cian's around Mam forgets about everything else.

"No problem. Here, give him to me." She hands me Harvey.

"He's fidgety, doesn't want to be put down. And he doesn't even want me to sit down." She smiles at me and as she leaves it strikes me that from the back Fiona looks like a twelve-year-old. Skinny shoulders, tiny bum, narrow waist. Tiny baby bump of fat on her belly.

I walk around my room, Harvey snuggling into me. His eyes roll in his head as he drops off to sleep. Holding him in the quiet evening room, the low sun peeping in the window, makes me think again about that day and the warm cosy feel of the kittens curled up asleep beside me.

Four

Harvey's getting bigger by the minute. It's like somebody's pumping him up on the sly while I'm at school. Now he's bursting out of his newborn clothes, and pastel shades are gone in favour of reds and browns and navy. But nothing prepares me for the Uniform.

It's a Saturday morning, a lovely late-September day, with clear skies and a nip in the air that reminds you of coal fires and stew. Mark's calling for me and we're going to town for the day. I've allowed for the free time in my study plan. I just had to jiggle it a bit, cut out Mr Hynes's drivel-writing, stay up an hour later last night.

Mam is at work, bossing poor Polish people around in Aldi. Fiona's been up since the crack of dawn. Special day today, apparently. Harvey's first trip to town and then a night out for Fiona and Big.

Harvey's wearing the Uniform. Fiona's dressed him in miniature scumbag clothes – tiny white Adidas tracksuit, minuscule Nike runners. There he is in the hallway in his shiny new buggy, sound asleep, oblivious to his horrible attire.

Fiona arrives downstairs dressed to the nines. Skin-tight

white jeans – I'm thinking straight away that this must be the girl version of the Uniform – little belly top, tiny black jacket, hoop earrings, ponytail, lots of makeup. I look her up and down.

"What?" she says, sticking her chin out at me. That's a new thing with her, sticking her chin out in this challenging way. She must have learned it recently. Read a new chapter in the Attract-a-Knack guide to Scumbag Perfection.

"Absolutely nothing," I answer.

Cian comes downstairs and grunt-nods at the two of us. He gets a giant bowl from the press and fills it to the top with Cheerios.

The doorbell rings and Mark and Big are on the step. They look hilarious together: Mark tall, highlighted and metrosexual, and Big small, tracksuited, his newly shaved head shiny in the morning sunlight.

"She ready?" says Big. I can hear his car outside on the road, the engine humming softly.

Mark's grinning at me and I try not to laugh. But the accent would kill you, an exaggerated TV Limerick dialect.

"Fiona, come 'ere I want ya," I call into the hallway, imitating perfectly Big's tone.

Mark stifles a laugh and Big sticks his chin out. So the guys do the chin thing too.

"Very smart, aren't ya?"

"So I've been told." I wink at Big.

"Just tell her come on. Gimme out the baby."

I look at Big, his ferret eyes narrow, his earring glistening. "Gimme out the baby" – like he's asking for a football or a bike. He looks way too young to be driving, and way too young to be fathering children. I go in and roll out the buggy. Harvey's still sleeping. The buggy has so many accessories hanging from it – matching baby bag, colour-coordinated sun brolly and rain cape, little toys and a tiny book clipped inside. A book, for fuck sake. A book for a newborn. Big lights a fag, and holds it in the corner of his mouth as he pushes the buggy with one hand down the path and out of the gate.

Mark and I watch as he tries to negotiate getting through it. He flicks the fag away, then glances at the buggy and his car. He scratches his head and waits for the buggy to fold itself and insert itself into the boot.

"He'll never manage that," says Mark. He has that almondy smell again and I wonder what brand of aftershave it is. It's nice, so not Lynx.

"Wait till he gets to the bit with the car seat," I say, as Fiona comes rushing out, her heels clicking as she flies down the path, all breathy, ponytail bouncing.

The buggy brigade is out in force. Saturday afternoon, September sun almost too warm, the town is busy with shoppers. I remember a few months ago watching a programme about the buggy brigade in England. It was called *Pramface* and now, as I watch the young girls pass me, chatting and laughing and pushing their shiny buggies, I think what a great name that is to describe a whole generation of girls who treat motherhood like the latest fashion trend and eventually a ticket to an income of their own. And there's my sister Fiona, marching down Cruises Street, and she's one of them, ponytail swinging, heels clicking, a fag in her hand. Big is nowhere to be seen.

I'm waiting for Mark – he's in HMV talking animatedly to a guy with eyeliner and very tight jeans. Fiona hasn't seen me yet. A bunch of girls from our school stop and surround the buggy, admiring the baby and the pram and Fiona's earrings. As they move off she finally spots me. "Maeve, can you do me a favour?"

"What?"

"Could you mind him for about half an hour? I made an appointment to have my nails done and Big had to go away and do something . . ."

She pushes the buggy handle towards me. I don't want to do it. I don't want to push a pram around the town and have people I don't know judge me and decide I'm a Pramface too – a dumb young girl with no brain and no future. "OK."

She smiles at me and even through the makeup I can see the old Fiona. The Fiona of just a couple of years ago. Sunny sweet Fiona, always trying to please people.

"I'll text you when I'm finished. There's a bottle in the bag but he's fed and changed."

She's gone, and I'm left holding the baby. The minute Mark comes out of the shop he cracks up laughing.

I glare at him and push the buggy awkwardly down the street. The little wheels seem to have a mind of their own. And I can see the looks, the quick glances from me to the buggy and then to Mark, I can feel them penetrating the back of my head as I pass. Mark must feel it too because he slips his arm around my waist. I giggle and catch sight of us in the window of Brown Thomas – a proper little family – and I notice I have my chin stuck out exactly like Fiona.

We sit in the new skate park – still called the new skate park years after it first opened – and watch the skaters as they do tricks and grinds, the boards making a constant crashing soundtrack. Mark has Harvey in his arms, bundled up tight in a pale green blanket. Harvey's staring up at him, his eyes big and open now, not scrunched-up slits any more.

"He's gorgeous, Maevis."

"I know. You'd just have to love him, wouldn't you?"

Two young girls pass, oohing and aahing when they see Harvey. Or maybe when they see Mark holding him.

"This is good for my rep, isn't it?" He smiles at me, hair floppy and shiny, like a shampoo ad.

"A man holding a tiny baby – it's brilliant."

"It makes you wonder, though – I mean, he's so perfect now, but what'll happen to him? Hard to believe that Big is his father."

I shrug. "I can't even think about it. I'm doing an excellent imitation of my mother lately – you know, it'll all be grand, Fiona'll move on, meet someone else . . . Can I tell you something, Mark?"

"Sure." He doesn't look up from Harvey's soulful eyelock.

"I think it's all going to end badly."

"You don't know that."

"It's just a feeling I have. Like when you're doing a really hard maths problem and you can see a . . . a pattern . . . yeah, a pattern, but not clearly enough to know how to solve it. Or even name it."

Mark laughs softly.

"Don't laugh, Pig."

"Hey, Professor Hogan, you can't solve the world. This guy has his own family to look out for him, haven't you, O Wise One? He looks like a wise old owl. Hey, want to go to my place later? The parents are cruising the Aegean even as we speak."

"Sure, but I promised Fiona I'd babysit tonight – my mother's going to her 'book club'." We grin at each other. The book club should do itself a favour and acknowledge that wine is its only *raison d'être*. My mother will fall in the door tonight in a Chardonnay-induced haze of bonhomie and love.

"Quite the helpful little sister, aren't we? Not like you, Maevis."

"Sure it is."

But Mark's right, as usual. It's not like me and I swore the minute I heard she was pregnant that I wouldn't help – that she could sink or swim and Mam could run around like a blue-arsed fly giving Fiona the soft landing she always got. But I'd been missing part of the equation then. Harvey.

It's raining by the time Fiona collects Harvey. Mark and I walk home. I pull my hood up and Mark says it makes me look like a girl version of Big, which earns him a thump. We play Five Questions as we walk – a game we've been playing since we were tots. You have to think of five really hard questions for your opponent – nowadays we usually glean them from the Internet. I always win except on movies. Mark is such a know-all about movies. I like them but not enough to be able to quote huge chunks verbatim. He knows this is my Achilles heel. I try to pretend I know the answer to his latest offering.

"Oh-oh, there could be trouble ahead," he says.

"Never heard of that movie – thought it was a song."

"Look up, Maeve."

We're near Mark's on the North Circular Road. A long tree-lined avenue with high walls surrounding the upmarket houses. Very des-res but not the place you'd want to be when there's a shower of scumbags walking towards you.

"Oh, fuck, what'll we do?"

Mark holds my hand. "Just act normal. Keep walking and chatting. Answer my question or pay a forfeit, loser."

The scumbags are closer now, so close I can hear their voices carrying towards us. I look past them. Not a sinner around. I can hear the drone of their voices, then a laugh. Our footsteps and theirs draw us together. I laugh nervously but I know this is not funny. Not in the slightest. Mark is rattling on, but I can't hear what he's saying and he's gripping my hand so tightly it hurts and my stomach is doing somersaults as they come right up to us. There's three of them, two around our age and one younger, a little fellow with ferrety brown eyes. They step off the pavement and let us pass. I let out a long sigh of relief and turn to smile at Mark as one of the scumbags jumps on top of him from behind.

"Give us your phone and your money," the guy screams, kicking Mark in the back. Mark is kind of kneeling and puts out a hand to steady himself.

"Stop," I shout, but one of the others catches me around the waist, holds me really tight, lifting my kicking feet from the ground, laughing softly into my hair.

"Mmm, I smell a cunt," he says. Mark is on his feet now, searching his pocket for his phone.

"I'm looking at one," I say. It's out before I can stop it. The guy in front of Mark starts laughing.

"That's fucking brilliant," he says.

My guy doesn't think so. His eyes are narrow and mean and he pushes his face into mine. "Smartarse, aren't you?"

I push him away. "Leave me alone."

Mark and his attacker are talking to each other, Mark's smiling at him and he's smiling back. I move closer to Mark, and he puts his arm around me. He's still talking to the scumbag. "Man, there's no need to kick me or hurt us. Jesus, man, we're just minding our own business – I'm going home with my girlfriend, like. No problem."

My scumbag comes over and boxes Mark right in the face.

"Man, leave him be, for fuck sake. He's sound, aren't ya, kid?" Mark's guy says to him. I can't believe it. Mark has actually talked them into leaving us alone.

Mark's guy grins at him. Mark grins back.

"Now empty your fucking pockets fast, man," Mark's guy says.

"Back to square one," says Mark.

And then I notice that the smaller scumbag is standing a bit away from us, almost dissociating himself from it all. A middle-aged couple approach, and as they see us, they cross to the other side of the road.

"Please help us," I shout over. They pretend not to hear. The scumbags laugh.

"Empty your pockets. The girl too," says Mark's scumbag again.

"Hey, Walshie, come over here and give us a hand, illya?"

Walshie. The minute he says it I know who Walshie is. Big's little brother. Same ferret eyes. Same build. Same uniform.

He still hangs back and now I know why. He's recognised me too. "Your Big's brother, aren't you? I must tell him I bumped into you when I go home."

He doesn't know where to look.

"You know her?" says Mark's scumbag.

"No. Don't know her at all."

Mark says something to me while this debate is going on but I can't understand him and then I realise why. He's speaking in French and he's telling me to run on the count of three. We take off down the road, feet pounding the pavement, one of the scumbags shouting, "Welcome to Limerick," after us, and then we're flying past the middle-aged couple, running and running until we're outside Mark's walled house and he's keying in the code for the gates on the pad inserted into the wall. We run all the way up the tree-lined drive even though we know now we're home and clear. As Mark fumbles with door keys I start to laugh, tears streaming down my face.

Mark's laughing too as the adrenalin subsides, and when he pushes the door open we fall onto the marbled floor in the huge hallway, collapsing in a heap.

"Fucking hell, this town," says Mark, after the laughing eases.

"'Welcome to Limerick' – where the fuck did they think we were from?" I say, wiping my eyes with the sleeve of my sweatshirt. "Was that Big's brother? Jesus, he's starting young, isn't he?"

"And, of course, Mark has to try and reason with them – why did you do that?"

"Well, it nearly worked – and you can't talk – smarty pants – what about 'I smell a cunt'?"

We start laughing again. Mark gets up and puts out his hand to pull me to my feet. "Come on, let's make something to eat."

I follow him along the large hallway and into a huge open-plan kitchen. The units are sleek and white and never-ending, the appliances showroom stainless steel, gleaming and new.

"My God, this is like *Grand Designs* – how do you find anything in here?"

"They had it all redone last month. It's a techie's dream – watch." He presses a button on the wall and a small flat-screen

TV appears under one of the units. He fiddles with more buttons. The lights dim and doors slide open in the corner to reveal a huge well-stocked larder.

"Expensive."

"Dad was always a genius with money."

This must be the understatement of the year. Mark's father isn't a genius, he's more a clairvoyant or a soothsayer. He can predict the future. I swear it, he can. And I've told Mark so many times, much to his amusement. Mark's dad is currently selling off all his property – everybody says he's mad but I doubt it. He knows something's brewing – I'd bet my house on it, if I had one.

"I'm starving. What do you fancy?" Mark grins at me. He has the best smile. Apart from Harvey, that is.

"Can you cook?" I ask, fingering the multitude of cans and packages and bottles.

Mark grins. "Nope. But I can dial." He picks up a phone sitting on a huge granite island. "Domino's?"

"Yes! Loaded meat, extra cheese."

He makes the call and I wander around the huge kitchen, running my fingers along the spotless work surfaces. I feel like I'm on the set of *The OC*. The kitchen opens into a beautiful conservatory with a spectacular view of the manicured gardens outside.

"Fancy a drink?" Mark says. He's standing behind me suddenly and I jump.

"I don't know – I haven't touched a drink since the night of the Bucky. I don't think it agrees with me."

"A real drink, Maeve – a bottle of my dad's finest, come on."

We go back into the kitchen area and he slides open a

white door to reveal a tall fridge. He pulls out a bottle of champagne and studies the label. "This'll do," he says, popping the cork. Then he finds two long glasses in one of the presses and pours. "Now taste that." He sips from his glass, looking at me over the rim.

I put mine to my lips. The bubbles make me want to sneeze. It's delicious. I take two huge gulps. "Oh, my God, it's lovely. It's like grown-up lemonade."

"Let's go into the den." He picks up the bottle and walks towards the door.

The den is a cosy little room just off the kitchen. There's a plasma TV on the wall and an incredible sound system in the corner. The furniture is minimal – long black leather couches and a low, pale-wood coffee-table. Everything is so new and clean.

I plonk down on the couch, still gulping my drink. It's too nice to sip.

Mark uses a remote to switch on the music system and suddenly the whole room is full of the Kings of Leon's "Knocked Up".

"Jesus, where are the speakers?"

"Integral sound system throughout the house. You can listen to this while you have a crap."

"Fucking hell, Mark! Can I move in? It's incredible."

He adjusts the sound and refills our glasses. My head is beginning to swim but nothing like the Bucky night. Much nicer than that. "Hey, if your parents are away, who's here with you?"

"Me."

"No way. You're by yourself?"

He nods, drains his glass and refills it again.

"I don't believe you. You're sixteen."

"Well Katya, the housekeeper, is here too."

"You have a slave? Brilliant."

Mark punches my arm. "She's not a slave – we play chess together sometimes."

"Where is she now?"

"Mass. She goes to a million Masses every week."

The intercom on the wall buzzes.

"That's our pizza – I'll go and get it."

I sit there in the designer room, the Kings singing their hearts out, and try to imagine what it's like to live in a house like this. To have so much space and perfection and order. I think of the sitting room at home, full of baby paraphernalia, the worn couches with barely a spare seat, Cian stretched out in one, Mam and Fiona beside each other on the other, all watching the magic box in the corner regardless of what's on.

Mark comes in with the pizza and another bottle of champagne, and as the room fills with the smell of food I realise I'm starving. We eat noisily and gulp champagne like it's water.

"Are you a virgin?" The question is out before I can stop myself.

Mark pretends to be shocked. "I'm never feeding you again if that's what it does to you. Are you?"

"I asked first."

He helps himself to a cigarette from the box on the table and takes his time lighting up. Then he leans back and has a long drag, blowing the smoke in rings. "Short answer? Nope. Now you." He leans towards me. His skin is flawless and I think that's really unfair – not one teenage pimple. I have enough for both of us. Fresh crops every morning, immune to Clearasil.

"Who was she?"

He grins, a lovely Mark grin that reminds me of him when he was four or five. Big happy smile every time he saw me. "That's not fair, Maeve. Your turn. Are you?"

"Hang on a minute – you popped your cherry and never told me? I don't believe you, Mark."

"I have no reason to lie. I gave up trying to impress you when I was seven."

I know Mark and I know he's telling the truth, and a little ball of something I can't name has formed in my stomach, a mixture of jealousy, curiosity and annoyance.

"So?" His knee is digging into mine.

I shake my head and feel myself going hot red, starting at the neck and creeping up my face.

"Aha – what have we here?" I put my face into my hands and he tries to pull them off. "Come on, little virgin, nothing to be ashamed of." His hands are tugging at me.

"Stop, Mark. Stop it." My voice is choked with tears.

"Hey, Maeve, what's up? Hey, come on, I'm sorry, I was just kidding around, hey, baby . . ." He takes me in his arms and holds me and then the tears really come, fast and noisy and snotty. He strokes my hair, lovely gentle strokes, fingers light and feathery. I lie there in his arms, the Kings of Leon still playing away and the tears stop. I blame the alcohol but, deep inside, I know it's other stuff. It's Harvey and Puffin, Muffin and Duffin, Mam always watching herself with me like she's afraid of me, and Cian like a ghost brother, and Fiona gone because she's gone. And Dad.

"I miss my father," I say into Mark's chest.

"I know. You two were soulmates."

"I miss talking to him and not having to explain myself

and . . . I don't know . . . the others think I'm a smartarse and I want them to – I want them to like me . . ."

He shushes me and kisses the top of my head. I pull away from him and look at him. "I'm giving up drinking. I always end up vomiting."

"Do you feel sick?"

"I mean it figuratively."

"That's a big word, Maevis – the drink does wonders for your vocabulary. We all need to vomit now and again – figuratively, as you say. One question?"

I nod at him. There's a snot-and-tears stain on his fitted white T-shirt.

"How did we get from virginity to this?" His head is cocked to the side, eyes wide and serious. And then we're laughing, holding on to each other, collapsing back into the couch, the room spinning slightly. I close my eyes to make the spinning stop and when I open them he's crouched above me, his thighs outside my legs, the weight of his body supported by his arms. He's still grinning down at me.

"You're great, do you know that?" he says, his voice soft. The Kings of Leon stop singing – like they want to hear what Mark has to say – and the room is eerily quiet.

"So are you." I stretch up my hand and outline his face with my fingers. Soft floppy hair, high cheekbones that any girl would die for, lovely jaw, red lips. I lean my face towards him and touch his lips with mine. He pulls back a little and then kisses me, his lips exploring mine, gentle and light and sexy. My breathing is fast as I push my body into his and hold his face with both my hands, just like Jamie Burke did to me before he was possessed by his erection. Every part of me is tingling and I don't know if it's the alcohol or the hormones or both and I don't want it to stop.

"Oh, excuse me," a voice says, and Mark raises his head. I try to sit up, knocking him backwards.

"Katya, hi. Come in," says Mark. He fixes himself on the couch. I'm still lying there prone, like a big eejit. "This is Maeve, my friend," he says.

I manage to sit up. Katya is standing in the middle of the room. Blonde hair, lovely slim body wrapped in a cream coat. She could be eighteen or thirty. She wears no makeup but she doesn't need to.

"I make dinner, yes? No pizza again?"

Mark grins at her. "No, we're good. We've eaten."

"Your mother, she phone to talk so I tell her to ring later, yes?"

"That's cool."

She sits down then, smiling. "We watch TV? *X Factor*?" she says, taking the remote and switching on the plasma screen. Simon Cowell's voice fills the room, pompous as ever, and Katya laughs at what he's saying. I want to thump her hard in her pretty Polish face. She spoiled the whole thing and something was about to happen and it felt so good, so not like the cretins with their slobbery tongues, their urgent thrusting hips and their cocky behaviour. I look at Mark as he lights up another fag and he gives me the little-boy grin. I don't believe in romantic love, not like Fiona, and I don't know what's going on. All I know is that it feels really good. My phone rings abruptly. Fiona. The big night out.

Harvey's crying again. He's scrunching up his old-man face and opening his gummy mouth and crying like he's in agony.

I've tried everything with him, feeding, changing, playing. Finally I wrap him in a soft blanket and hold him close as I walk up and down our sitting room, singing Kings of Leon very badly. It works. He stops screaming, his tiny body shuddering with little aftershocks of crying and his dark eyes close. He's finally asleep but I keep him on my lap as I watch an old black-and-white movie about a shower of bank robbers taking refuge in an old dear's house.

I wake with a jump, almost dropping Harvey. Fiona's shouting in the hallway and somebody's hammering at the door. "Let me in, bitch . . . I'll fucking kill you, mind . . ."

I put Harvey into his buggy and run into the hall. Fiona's standing there, swaying slightly against the banister. Her face is streaked with tears, running black from her mascara. Big bangs at the front door, screaming for her to let him in.

"What happened?" I whisper.

She looks at me and shakes her head.

Big's voice stops and I can hear the flick of a lighter.

"Are you OK?" I ask.

Another shake of her head, her ponytail flicking. There are mud stains on her pale blue jeans.

"What's up?" Cian appears from upstairs, rubbing sleep from his eyes.

"Where's Mam?" Fiona says, her voice slurring a little.

"She's still at her . . . am . . . book club . . . Are you OK? What happened?"

"It's stupid, just a tiff . . ."

Big starts again but this time he's changed his tack. "Fiona, let me in. I just want to talk to you, that's all," he pleads.

Cian comes down the stairs, dressed only in his boxers. "Does anyone want tea?"

I raise my eyebrows at him as he passes but he doesn't notice.

"Babe, I love you, know that? I fuckin' love you, man. Open the door for me."

Fiona's panda eyes are huge and scared.

"Don't," I whisper. "Don't open the door, Fiona. If he wants to talk to you he can come back tomorrow."

"Please, babe. I can't go home like this, with us fighting. Please, I just want to talk."

She walks to the door and opens it. He doesn't come in, he grabs her by the hair and pulls her out into the porch. "Don't ever fuckin' make a fool out of me like that again. I could break that cunt's two legs this minute. I could kneecap him, know that, bitch?"

"You're hurting me – stop it," says Fiona.

My heart is pounding in my chest. "Leave her alone," I shout, but he pushes the front door closed.

"Cian, help, for fuck sake." I struggle to open the door. I can see their silhouettes through it. Big has Fiona pinned against the glass of the porch.

Cian arrives, with a mug of tea in his hand.

"Do something – he's hurting her." I manage to get the door open.

"Fuck off, this is between me and her," Big says, without taking his eyes from Fiona.

"Leave her alone," says Cian.

Big doesn't even acknowledge him. And I know why. There's no threat at all in Cian's voice. He can't hurt Big in any way and Big knows it.

"Fucking bitch, off talking to that cunt for the night

making me look like a prick – fucking bitch," he screams into Fiona's face.

"I'm ringing the guards – Cian ring nine one one. Cian, are you listening? Ring the guards, he's off his head – he'll hurt her," I scream.

Big slams the door. Cian is on the phone. Harvey's crying. I open the door again. Big has his fist in front of Fiona's face, just holding it there in mid-air, a tiny smile on his lips. She's cowering. Why the fuck did she open the door? It's like she wanted this big scene. Fiona and scenes can't seem to resist each other.

"Leave her alone, you thug," I scream.

Mam is walking – no, Mam is tottering up the path, a big Chardonnay smile on her face. A squad car pulls up outside the gate. Two policemen get out and follow her.

"Hi," she slurs, not noticing the situation or the guards right behind her. Big has dropped his hand and Fiona's wiping tears, leaving streaks of black mascara on her new white jacket.

"What's going on here? We got a call about a disturbance." says one of the guards, a tall guy with a monobrow.

Mam and the two officers are peering at the porch as if it's a stage. Some of our neighbours have opened their front doors to see what's happening.

"There's nothing going on. Just talking, that's all," says Big, staring at Fiona.

The guard looks at her. "Are you OK?" he asks.

Mam hiccups.

Fiona nods.

"You sure?" he says.

She nods again. "We had a tiff, that's all."

"He was threatening her and he pushed her and—"

"We were talking," says Big. "Right, Fiona?"

She nods a third time.

"Cian, you were here, you saw it all – tell them."

Cian has Harvey in his arms and in the middle of the fracas I realise that it's the first time I've seen him hold the baby.

"Am . . . I wasn't exactly paying a lot of attention. Maybe they were just talking . . ."

"That's a funny kind of talking. Tell them, Cian, don't be such a fucking wimp."

"That's terrible language in front of your mother," says Big. He has that tiny smile on his face again. A tiny smile that makes me want to kill him.

"You're only a fucking scumbag," I shout, "a cowardly scumbag who thinks he's a big man. You're a fucking scumbag." I'm screaming now, and everybody's looking at me like I'm the lunatic. Big is shaking his head at the guards.

"Why don't we all go in and have a cup of tea?" says Mam, smiling at us.

I scowl at her. "Yeah, right. We'll all go in and have a nice cup of tea with the scumbag."

"Now, Maeve, don't be over-dramatic. Teenagers!" says Mam, to the guards, as she pushes her way in through the crowded porch. I march in after her. She goes into the kitchen and puts on the kettle, her movements slow and measured, like she's trying to pretend she's sober. "Do you want tea or coffee?" she asks.

Cian arrives in with the baby.

"Ciany and Harvey, my two favourite boys – aw, look how cute he is. Hello, little man – you're wide awake, you wee devil." She takes Harvey from Cian, kissing his fat jaw.

Cian smiles at Mam. "He's heavier than he looks, isn't he?"

Mam laughs, her tinkly wine laugh. "He's a little bruiser – aren't you, sweetie-pie?"

"You don't give a fuck, Mam, sure you don't." I cross my arms.

"Chill out, Maeve – they're young, they think they're in love, what do you expect?" She cuddles Harvey and he gurgles at her.

"I don't expect you to encourage your daughter to go out with a scumbag. I don't expect you to say it's OK for him to threaten her."

She looks at me over the top of the baby's head. "I'm thinking of Harvey. Whether you like it or not, Big is Harvey's dad and we have to make an effort."

"You're a joke, do you know that? The best thing for Harvey is if Big and the rest of his scumbag clan fall off the face of the earth."

"That's a terrible thing to say. I've known Vonnie since I was a child – they lived around the corner from me. Her father and your grandfather fished together."

I've heard the story a million times of how she and Linda grew up in the heart of a Corpo housing estate and how it did them no harm. And if Mam is well on the Chardonnay she'll tell you about how they both bagged two catches – a solicitor and an accountant – like the best prizes on *Winning Streak*. "It's not the place you're from, Mam, it's what you are. He's a scumbag – plain and simple."

I look at my brother, who's buttering toast at the table. "What do you think, Cian? What do you think of our new scumbag relations?"

"Dunno – if that's what Fiona wants . . ."

"Oh, for fuck sake – Fiona's too dumb to know what she wants. She needs a proper mother to tell her what she wants . . ."

"Goodnight, Maeve," Mam says.

I can feel the adrenalin pump again as my temper rises. "Here's a question – where does Big get all his money?"

"Go to bed."

"Answer me. Where do you think he gets money for clothes and a car and, wait for it, he just bought himself a fucking laptop – where does he get the money?"

Mam glances at Cian, who drops his head to examine his toast like it's the most interesting thing he's ever seen. "I have a headache now, Maeve – conversations with you have that effect on me."

"Oh, right – it's me and not the Chardonnay."

She rubs her head, swaying slightly against the worktop.

I take Harvey from her and leave.

I bring him to bed with me. His small warm body folds into mine and I'm sure he's smiling at me as his eyes close. Outside, I can hear Fiona and Big talking and laughing in low voices. I can't sleep so I creep out of bed quietly and walk to the window. They're sitting on the wall, a streetlight above them making them glow a soft amber colour. He has her face in his hands as he kisses her. A long kiss, hardly coming up for air. He stops then and she leans into him, both arms around him. He lights a fag and glances back at our house. Looks straight up at my window and spots me. He does the little smile thing again and chalks an imaginary one up. I give him the two fingers back and he laughs, then starts to kiss Fiona again. This time he puts his hand under her new purple top.

Five

Mark has a girlfriend. He hasn't said anything and I don't want to ask him directly because he might realise I fancy him and, anyway, I don't know if I want to hear the answer. He's here with me now in my bedroom and his phone is beeping constantly. Message after message after message. And he loves the sound of it. I can see the anticipation in his face as he studies his phone before opening a message. I haven't seen him for a full week – he's been off school with flu – and now he's more interested in his phone than in catching up on all the news.

"You shouldn't have bothered calling over," I say, as I boot up my computer. If he can read his messages then I can work on my projects.

"What?" he says, as his phone beeps again. He smiles at me, giving me his full attention, the phone tight in his hand. I know he's dying to read it.

"You should have stayed at home with your phone."

He grins. "Hey, I thought you were going to give me all your notes – the best notes in the country, I bet."

"Yeah – I'm going to charge you for them."

"So, what's the news?"

"Haven't much, really. I went to town with Sophie and Ciara yesterday – thought I'd die with boredom. How many shops can you go into in one afternoon?"

"Did you go out last night?" The phone beeps again. He ignores it but he's itching to open those messages. I know he is.

"No. Babysat. Watched that fool Pat Kenny and a brilliant documentary on National Geographic about leatherback turtles."

"Exciting stuff, Maevis Ravis. Babysitting is the new going out for you – three weeks in a row."

"I know. But I can't face the bush drinking any more. Standing around out the bank in the freezing cold listening to the cretins. It's just not the same without you."

"Glad someone missed me." This time his phone rings. He looks at me for permission to answer it. He points to the door and waits until he's outside to talk.

I look at the icons on my computer and spot the drivel-writing folder. I haven't touched it since that first time and now I have an unbelievable urge to drivel-write. And I know exactly what I want to write about. That night of the fight with Fiona and Big and the way he manipulated the whole show. There's no sign of Mark and, anyway, he's too busy hanging out with his phone. I double-click the icon. The snow-white screen is inviting and taunting at the same time. My fingers start moving over the keyboard like they have a mind of their own . . .

Cian came to the beach even though he hated it and he didn't talk the whole way, and Maeve wondered how he could stay so quiet especially when it was sunny and they were going to Lahinch and Mam had made a lovely picnic. And they got brand-new buckets and spades in the little shop on the prom and Mam said, "Cian, would you like a bodyboard?" and Cian just shook his head and kicked stones with his shoes.

Maeve held Dad's hand all the way across the sand. Dad explained to her that the tide was fully out now and that's why the beach was so big. And then he talked about spring tides and moons, and Maeve listened, not understanding but loving the sound of his voice. They stood in the shallow water, letting the sea nibble their bare toes. Maeve loved the feel of wet sand, loved scrunching her feet into it and then when the waves came the feeling of sinking right into it. There was foam left when the waves went back out. Creamy soft foam like on the top of Mam's coffee sometimes. There was a word for it but she couldn't think of it.

Daddy had stopped talking. She looked up at him but he was staring out to sea. She followed his gaze but there was nothing except a bright orange buoy miles away. He dropped her hand suddenly and started walking straight into the water. She watched his back as he went deeper and deeper, the water making his trousers all wet. What was he doing? Mam'd be cross if he went swimming with his clothes on. She followed him and called, "Daddy, Daddy, what are you doing?" but he didn't hear her. Never even turned around. He just kept walking out towards the bright orange buoy.

Maeve tried to walk faster and faster but the water wouldn't let her and she called him again, "Daddy – Daddy, wait for me, wait for me!" It worked this time. He stood still, the water up to his chest. She half-walked, half-swam towards him.

He turned around to face her. She couldn't see his eyes because of the glare from the sun. But she could hear his voice soft and full of pain. "I'm sick, Maeve, and I can't fix it. Tell your mother I can't fix it."

"Daddy, stop, come on, stop it," she said, holding her chin up so that she wouldn't swallow the seawater.

She had to keep moving her arms in circles to keep her balance. He came towards her in the water, bent down and kissed the top of her wet salty head, talking into her ear like he was telling her a secret – "My clever one, I always knew there would be one. Law of averages." And then he turned away and started the walking thing again, walking, walking until the top of his head disappeared into the blue-grey sea.

She didn't know she was screaming until she saw the people gathering around her, asking her what was wrong and why was she screaming, and she just pointed at where she'd last seen Daddy's head but she couldn't say a word. It was scream or nothing. And then Daddy was there too, swimming towards her, smiling at her. He scooped her up in his arms even though she was way too big for that and carried her to the shore. The foamy beigy bubbles were everywhere now, and then the word came, rolling off her tongue, lovely and warm and surprising.

Cappuccino.

Mam and Fiona were standing in the shallow water. Fiona was crying and saying she thought a shark came, and Mam had her cross face on, glaring at Daddy, and Maeve glared back at her but she didn't tell about Daddy being sick. She knew that he didn't want them to know. But still she hated Mam. All the way home in the car she stared at the back of Mam's head, trying to make it explode all by itself because she'd read about that happening sometimes. She hated her because Daddy was sick.

"What are you up to?" Mark's standing behind me, looking at the computer screen.

I immediately close down the window. "Nothing. Just fooling around." I can feel colour flooding my face.

He leans down and tries to click the computer mouse.

"Fuck off, Mark." I push him away.

"Let me see – an Internet lover is it? Some middle-aged perv in Atlanta pretending he's a teenage boy?"

"Shut up, loser."

He kisses the top of my head, like I'm his favourite pet dog. "Fancy going to the cinema?" he asks. "The new Coen Brothers movie." He's kneading my shoulders as he speaks and my stomach has butterflies and jitters and shudders and all the other things they say in trashy chick-lit books.

I check my watch. "Dunno – I have a biology project to do and we're late for the eight o'clock show . . ."

"Oh, Maevis, shut up. Fuck biology and I got us a lift." He puts his arms under mine and drags me up. "Come on, let's have some fun."

"OK, OK, I'm coming. Who's giving us a lift?" I hastily brush my hair and tie it up in a ponytail. Mark's phone is beeping again.

"Our carriage awaits."

Downstairs in the sitting room, Big is stretched across the couch watching a football match. Fiona is doing her nails beside him, his feet on her lap. Harvey is asleep on the floor in his Carry Tot car seat.

"Where's Mam?" I ask, bending down to kiss Harvey. He sneezes loudly without waking.

"She's gone on the training day with Aldi until tomorrow – Cian drove her to the station. Where are you going?" She doesn't even look up from her nails as she talks. Big lets a roar out of him as some overpaid soccer player finds the net. Harvey jumps and starts screaming.

"Fuck's sake," I say, taking the crying baby out of his seat.

Big and Fiona laugh, and she puts out her arms for Harvey. "It's all right, baby, your team scored, didn't they? You're my little Man U baby."

Big moves his feet and sits up. "Fuck off, ref, you cunt, that was no free," he shouts at the telly.

I stand there glaring at him, arms folded across my chest. I feel like the mammy in the house. He keeps watching the match and scratches his balls through his tracksuit bottoms. He knows I'm looking at him, the little bastard.

"Will you bring us back chips if you're passing Luigi's?" says Fiona. Harvey's snuggled into her chest, still whimpering. Big absentmindedly throws an arm around her and I watch this pantomime of a perfect nuclear family. The 2007 Limerick Regeneration version of love.

Outside, Mark is in the passenger seat of Mam's battered old Toyota. Cian is at the wheel and I'm shocked for a second. I keep forgetting that Cian has learned to drive and even passed his test.

"Is this our lift?" I ask, climbing into the back seat.

"Yep."

As we pass Big's house on our way out of our estate I do a double-take. There's a few teenage boys sitting on the wall, talking to Big's sister Sonya – the one who was expelled from our school. She reminds me of a bitch in heat, the three young guys jostling for her attention. But that's not the reason for the double-take. That's down solely to the horse that's tethered to the garden gate.

Mark bursts out laughing. "Jesus, that's brilliant. Bet the neighbours won't be too happy with that."

"You can laugh – there'll never be regeneration on the North Circular Road," I say.

"Maevis, be nice now about your new relations. I'm still holding out for that wedding."

I wallop the back of his head.

"Ouch – Cian, your sister is a vicious horse-hater," says Mark, rubbing his head, then flicking the rear-view mirror so he can fix his hair. I ruffle it. I know how much he hates that. "Hey, lay off my Nicky Clarke locks."

Cian ignores us, leaning over the steering-wheel, peering at the road like he's reading a newspaper.

"I think I'll run for the local elections," I say, to no one in particular.

Mark guffaws. "Brilliant, Maevis – on what ticket?"

"The Degeneration one, of course. You can plan my campaign and Cian can do the driving. Although he'll have to speed up a little – at this rate we won't reach the cinema until tomorrow night."

Mark's still fixing his hair in the mirror. He grins at my reflection. "I love it, Maevis. I always wanted to be a spin doctor. Now let's see – what are our issues?"

"Horse-shit of all description." I smile at him in the mirror.

"So is that our slogan – 'An end to horse-shit of all descriptions'? Sounds like something from *Father Ted*."

"Yeah – that's why people will like it. Seriously, Mark – what age do you have to be to run in an election? Councillors get a wage, you know – about thirty grand, I think. We could play a blinder on this."

"Cian, there's something wrong with your sister – she's sixteen and she knows that councillors get a wage, and more worrying is the fact that she knows there are elections. No hope for the girl – she'll be burned out by twenty."

"She said her first word when she was eight months," Cian remarks, as he carefully negotiates a roundabout.

"I didn't know that. How do you know it? Were you there? What did I say?"

Cian laughs – it's a long time since I heard him laugh. Or maybe it's a long time since I noticed.

"I was three so, no, I don't remember. Mam told me. She said it was the weirdest thing ever – a bald gummy baby saying a perfectly formed word."

"She must have been mistaken. Maeve was never a baby – she was born a know-all old woman."

"Shut up, Mark. Mam never told me that."

"She said Dad was so proud that his baby could talk, he told everybody. And Fiona was almost two and still couldn't speak and you could."

"Yeah, and she still hasn't shut up, have you, Maevis Ravis? Anyway, back to the campaign – the creative ideas are flowing. Could we use the baby-talking thing in any way?"

"I never knew that, Cian." I look at the back of my brother's head as he concentrates on his driving.

"Yeah – well, it's a fact, apparently. You were a genius even when you were a baby."

"It was probably a fluke – baby garble."

"No. Mam says it was as clear as day. You were in your high chair and she had an apple in one hand and a banana in the other and she couldn't decide which to give you."

"So I said, 'I'll have the banana thanks very much and could I have fries with it'?"

Mark claps. "I've got it. 'Don't vote for the same old dogs – give the young bitch a go.'"

We both ignore him.

"Apple. You pointed at the apple and said it as clear as that. 'Apple.'"

"No way."

Cian chuckles. "Mam dropped the fruit and ran out of the kitchen. She said she thought you were possessed."

"Lovely. She still thinks I am. So that's why she's been giving me those weird looks for as long as I can remember."

We finally pull up outside the cinema.

"Thanks, Cian – see you next weekend," I say, waving as I get out of the car.

Mark links me as we walk through the doors and then Cian comes flying up behind us. "Anyone want popcorn?" he says, as he joins a long queue at the tills.

"Why is he coming with us?" I whisper to Mark.

"Because he loves the Coen Brothers, because he has to stay home and keep an eye on you lot while your mother learns the Aldi Way and because he's a really nice guy."

I burst out laughing. "That's some other person you're talking about – Cian's a nerd. If it isn't science it ain't sexy."

"Listen to who's talking! Hey, there's whatshisname over there – Colin Ryan. Now he's hardly a Coen Brothers fan."

Colin Ryan is with a girl from my year. I can't remember her name but it's one of those made-up ones phonetically manufactured by silly mothers everywhere. He catches my eye and smiles at me. I know Jamie Burke has told them all that I'm the Chief Slut at school. Why else would the likes of the *über*-cool Colin Ryan be bending over backwards to salute me? I'm delighted to see that he goes bright pink. I hold Mark's hand

71

and smile up into his face, blinking and looking dumb. I'd seen Sophie and Ciara do that a hundred times.

"I get it, Maeve – you're not dazzled by my good looks, you've the hots for Colin over there."

"Don't be stupid."

But my heart sinks a little. I want to ask Mark straight up about his girlfriend, and if Cian wasn't with us I think I could. The three of us sit down in the dark cinema, the surround sound deafening as it belts out very bad ad jingles. And as Mark and Cian chat, heads bent together, Cian laughing softly as they share a tub of popcorn, I hate my brother. I hate him for stealing my best friend. My only friend, really. I barely speak for the rest of the night.

Six

I'm at a party. It's not a party I'd choose to be at because the music is gangsta – lots of talking and swearing. I can hear people laughing and I must be drunk because I can't open my eyes. And there's a baby crying and I try to work out in my foggy head why there's a baby at a party at all.

I sit bolt upright in bed. The music downstairs is blaring and Harvey's crying in the next room. I jump out of bed and pull on my jeans and a balled-up T-shirt I find on the floor. Harvey's screaming his head off, kicking and waving his arms to high heaven. "Come on, little guy," I say, picking him up. His nappy is soaked so I change it quickly and carry him downstairs. The music is thumping out from the sitting room and I can hear voices.

Manoeuvring Harvey onto my hip, I open the door. Big is sitting on the couch with two of his scumbag friends. I know them to see, the usual scumbag heads, small eyes, dodgy hair, bad skin. The Uniform. Fiona is stretched out on an armchair, her head lolling back, a small smile on her face. She looks out of it. There are beer cans strewn everywhere, and two empty Bucky bottles. But it's the white powder set out in three neat rows on Mam's new coffee-table that freaks me the most.

"Get the fuck out of my house and take your drugs with you," I say, looking straight at Big.

He grins. "Mammy's home."

His friends crack up and Fiona's smile widens. Then her eyes roll in her head.

"I'm calling the guards."

Big takes a tightly rolled ten-euro note from the table, bends down and snorts some of the coke. He sniffs loudly and winks at me. "Call them if you want, Mammy. But how'll ya explain all the dope stashed in your house?"

Big's buddies guffaw this time.

"Get out." I try to make my voice sound assured. In my head I'm debating whether he has stashed drugs in the house.

"Fuck yourself," he says.

"Fiona, tell those bastards get out. I'll ring Mam."

They all laugh at this. Big shakes Fiona by her shoulder but her head lolls forward, blonde hair forming a curtain over her face. "Fiona, your sister's going to tell Mammy you're a bold girl." He pushes her hair back and her head flops back too. Her eyes are closed but she's still smiling. "See? Happy as a pig in shit. Gimme over my baby." Big stares at me, challenging me with his eyes.

Harvey nuzzles my shoulder, his mouth searching for food. I walk out of the room, take a bottle from the fridge and stand it in a pot of water to heat. I know Big's behind me: I can smell him and feel him. He watches silently as I take the bottle from the bubbling water, jigging Harvey to soothe his whimpers.

"Gimme my baby."

I ignore him, shaking the bottle and murmuring to Harvey.

"Gimme him now."

I walk out and as I'm passing he grabs my arm, pinching it tightly.

"Leave me alone, get out of my house."

Big lifts the baby from my hip and snatches the bottle from my hand.

"Go to bed and mind your business." He walks off with Harvey.

I run upstairs and bolt into Cian's room. "Cian, wake up, you've got to . . ." Cian's bed is empty. I run into my bedroom and look out the window. The car's gone. Where is he at this time of night? Fucking fool of a brother, and Mam leaves him in charge. I lie down on my bed, still in my jeans, staring at the ceiling as the music thumps downstairs. I wish Dad was here. He'd never tolerate any of this – scumbags taking over our house and my sister, Mam off on her Aldi nights, Cian out in the middle of the night doing God knows what. The tears come then, hot and wet and loud. I bury my head in my pillow, trying to block out the music. Horrible thoughts keep popping into my head uninvited, with pictures of Fiona drunk and beaten, and poor Harvey growing into Big. That's the scariest thing of all – a gorgeous tiny baby growing into one of those wasters.

It's as if last night never happened. When I get home from school Fiona's cooking dinner. Goujons and chips. Mam is at the kitchen table telling her about her great Aldi weekend. I dump my bag in the hall and march into the kitchen, glaring at Fiona. But I know from her face she doesn't remember a thing about last night.

"Hi, Maeve, you hungry?" says my sister, smiling brightly at me.

She's as fresh as a daisy. Drugs must agree with her. I give her a withering look. "Enjoy yourself last night?"

"We stayed in and watched a movie."

"It wasn't *Trainspotting* by any chance?"

She scrunches up her eyes like she's trying really hard to understand me. I know my dig is way too subtle for her. We're talking Dougal here with knobs on.

She looks at Mam and Mam smiles at both of us. "Did Ciany keep an eye on you two last night? He promised he would. I feel sorry for him going back to Cork today. He hates his course, you know."

"So why did he pick it?" I take a plate from the dishwasher and dump oven chips and chicken goujons on to it.

"Because, Maeve, sometimes people make mistakes. Did that ever occur to you?" Mam and Fiona exchange a knowing glance.

"Pretty big mistake to make. But that seems to be a family strength in this house, right, Fiona?"

She sticks her chin out at me and rolls her eyes. "Here we go again. Give it a rest, Maeve, and get a life for yourself."

"I have a life. And I'd like to keep it scumbag-free."

"Maeve, stop it now. We don't want to hear any of that. I'm off for a shower, Fiona, I'll check on Harvey on the way."

Fiona starts to clean off the table.

"Don't ever let that happen again," I say.

She drops a plate on the table and puts a hand on her hip. The chin is out again. She could be Big's sister Sonya. "What ya mean?"

"How come the scumbag accent always appears when Mam walks out the door? Can't you speak properly?"

"Fuck off, Maeve. Who do you think you are? God? I'll do what I like – you're just jealous."

I snigger. "Am . . . right. Let me see . . . jealous of your career choice? Check. Jealous of your future? Check. Oh, yeah, and the biggie, if you'll excuse the pun. Jealous of that handsome devil of a boyfriend of yours?"

Fiona narrows her eyes, which makes her look like a complete stranger. "You'll never get a boyfriend. They laugh at you in school – do you know that? They ask me what it's like living with a freak."

"I'm a freak? Why? Because I don't go round opening my legs for the first scumbag or cretin in the queue? Cos I want to go to college and make use of my brains and not my tits? Please, spare me."

She flicks her long poker-straight hair. "You can't have fun. You're a robot. That's what they call you – the Robot."

"Gee, I'm deeply hurt. I'd rather be called that than Big's woman – now that'd be the pits."

"You're a fucking bitch, Maeve. A cunt."

"Mm – nice to see you're learning their language too. Won't be long now before you graduate – qualified scumbag."

Fiona's crying. Small tears at the corners of her eyes. She walks out and bangs the door so hard the pictures on the wall shake. I play with my food, feeling mean and guilty and lonely. How I always feel when I have any prolonged contact with my sister.

Mam comes back into the kitchen, in a worn pink dressing-gown. Her hair is very wet. She glares at me. I ignore her and pretend to eat my dinner.

"What was that about, Maeve?"

"A fight. The usual."

"The usual? Calling your sister a scumbag?"

"I had good reason to – do you know what went on here last night?"

"Actually I do. I spoke to Cian this morning. Fiona and Big and a couple of friends got together – I don't have a problem with that."

"They got together with a little stash of drugs – have you any problem with that part?"

She looks at me, and I think of what Cian told me about my first word. How she thought I was possessed. I imagine she's looking at me now exactly as she did way back then.

"Cian said everything was fine. I believe him."

"And not me?"

"Cian doesn't want to make trouble for Fiona – it's all you seem to do lately and I won't stand for it. She's just had a baby, she needs us and that's all there is to it."

"A baby with a scumbag . . ."

"Shut up, Maeve. Big is Harvey's dad, and the last thing we need to do is drive him away or make an enemy of him." She's standing over me now, her hair dripping on to the collar of her dressing-gown.

"Maybe that's exactly what we should do – for Harvey's sake." I hold her eyes.

"Sometimes Maeve, for all your cleverness, you miss the obvious things. Harvey's the important thing here. We have to do what's best for him."

"Shoot his father."

I know she's mad now, so mad she holds her hands tightly together in front of her to stop herself striking me.

The doorbell rings. Mam sighs and goes to answer it. My aunt Linda arrives, weighed down with shopping bags. She waltzes into the kitchen and bends to air-kiss my head, talking non-stop all the time. Andrew the tsunami follows her, grinning.

"Where's the baby? Andrew's dying to see him, aren't you, Andrew?"

Andrew doesn't answer because his head is in the fridge.

"Can't stay, can't stay. Oisin has rugby training and Tom and I are going to the golf club AGM. Now . . . where's your mother gone?"

"To get dressed."

"Well, I booked us all on flights last night. Tom said, 'Just do it, Linda, while the flights are cheap.' All of us, including Cian. It'll be great, Maeve. The villa sleeps twelve so we'll have acres of room, and it's air-conditioned . . ."

I'm struggling to work out what she's talking about. Lanzarote for Hallowe'en. There's no way in hell I'm going on that trip of a lifetime.

"Am . . . Linda . . ."

"Tom says it'd be perfect for the families – a complete rest, he says – and the shopping's great there. We'll have a ball. There you are, Marie – ah, look at the little fellow. He's gorgeous."

Mam's come in carrying Harvey. He's just woken up, his face puffed from sleep. My heart does a little flip when I see him. He burps and everybody laughs. I instinctively put out my arms for him and Mam frowns at me as she hands him over, reminding me of our previous conversation. Harvey smells delicious, baby shampoo, milk and the X factor all mixed together.

He stares up at me and I notice that his eyes have changed colour. They were navy blue, just like Fiona's, and now they're a rich black-brown, just like George Clooney's – and Big's. I make a note in my head to look up eye colour on the net later. Can a baby's eye colour change like that? And, if so, can it change back again?

Linda's bossing Mam around the kitchen and Mam is agreeing with everything she says. Flights, Shannon Airport, all of us together, a big mad family holiday, dress-up costumes for everyone – Tom got them at work – a surprise party for Cian's birthday on Hallowe'en night. I haven't the guts now to say I'm not going.

The tsunami comes over to look at Harvey and then, grinning at me, sidles out of the door. Linda is so busy convincing Mam that the holiday will be a panacea for all that's wrong in the world that she doesn't notice his disappearance. I listen anxiously for the sound of tsunami destruction – my computer flying out of the window or water flowing where it shouldn't. I'm just about to get up in search of Andrew when he's flying back into the kitchen. "Mam, come and see, cops and robbers – come and see . . ." He flies out again and we follow.

I hear the sirens as we reach the front door. Outside a crowd has gathered but I can't see anything. And then they come into view. At first I think there's nobody in the car, that the police are chasing a self-propelled or remote-controlled vehicle around the oval green area in front of our house. Big's mother Vonnie is in hot pursuit of the car chase, screaming at the top of her lungs. And as the car passes the second time I see the driver in a blur, his baby face grinning with glee, his head barely above the dashboard. It's Big's kid brother – the one I recognised a few Saturdays ago.

"She's wearing pyjamas," says Linda, incredulously. She obviously hasn't noticed that a child is driving the car.

Andrew is jumping up and down, giving the speeding cars the thumbs-up and shouting, "Cool!" at the top of his lungs.

The car chase does another high-speed circle of the green. Parents are calling their gaping children in off the road. Mr Higgins, an elderly retired guard, is standing at his gate next door to us, shaking his head continuously.

Vonnie gives up her canter and stands on the footpath in front of us, wiping her forehead. She takes a cigarette from behind her ear and asks poor Mr Higgins for a light. He pats his pockets for a lighter even though he's never smoked in his life. The cars zoom past us again, and the tiny driver waves cheekily at his mother. Vonnie screams at him. "I'll fucking kill you, Joey – I'll murder you when I get you home."

But Joey's gone in a blur, off around the green again.

"I feel like I'm in an episode of *Shameless* – you know that series on TV, the rude one," says Linda.

"They shouldn't chase him – they're only doing what he wants and they'll make him crash," says Mam.

No sooner has she it said than Joey goes straight onto the green and crashes into the ornately carved wooden sign displaying the name of our housing estate, Swallow Park.

The cops screech to a halt but Joey's out of the car and down the road before his mother or the guards know what's happening. Vonnie leans on our wall as one of the cops pursues him on foot. The other surveys the damage to the car.

Vonnie's found a light somewhere. I can see a spiral of smoke floating over the top of her head as she watches the guard. She turns and shrugs at us. "Boys – they're deadly, aren't they?" She's speaking to my mother. Harvey's dropped off to sleep in my arms, unfazed by his uncle's antics. "I'll brain him when I get him home." She takes a long drag from her cigarette, and flicks her platinum-blonde hair.

"They'd break your heart, wouldn't they? How's the little fella? Ah, look at him . . ."

She opens the gate and comes towards us, cigarette waving in the air. Her pyjama bottoms have tiny pink hearts on them. Linda's gaping at her, open-mouthed. Vonnie peers down at Harvey in my arms, and pulls back his blanket a little to see his face. "An angel sent from God – I hope he isn't a little terror like Joey when he grows up." She takes another long drag from her cigarette, and flicks ash into the potted plant outside the porch.

"Now, my Big – as good as gold, always did what he was told – he'll kill Joey over this."

I struggle to keep a straight face. Big is obviously a saint in his mother's eyes.

"You're Linda, aren't you? I remember you from the Boro. You and Marie, the two glamour pusses, I always knew you'd bag yourselves the good fellas. Look what I got – the fucker ran as soon as the babies started coming."

Mam smiles at Vonnie.

"I'm minding him Saturday night, aren't I, love? I can't wait."

My heart sinks at this news. I always mind him on a Saturday night. Every Saturday night since he came home from the hospital. Now stupid dumb Fiona is allowing him up to that madhouse. Up to the Joeys and Sonyas and Vonnies of the world.

The guard at the crashed car beckons Vonnie and she stubs out her cigarette on the footpath. "Never a dull one with my lot," she says, as she leaves.

We all watch her walk over to the guard, talking and gesticulating madly to him. I notice that our estate sign now reads "low Park". Good name, that.

*

Saturday night. I stupidly agreed to go out with Ciara and Sophie. I'm pretending to drink. We're in Sophie's house because her parents are gone to Kilkee for the weekend. Her seventeen-year-old brother is "minding" her. Except he's comatose on the couch in the study. That's what a naggin of vodka does for you. And he'll wake up in the morning laughing and joking about the great night he had that he can't remember. I think I'm slowly becoming a teetotaller – although Mark's dad's champagne might be the one exception. Anyway, I'm bored out of my tree and I keep thinking I could be at home snuggling up to Harvey with the house to myself. Like it's my house and my baby. I watch Ciara, unsteady now in her high heels, swallowing shots with a crowd I barely know from our school. Sixth years. They're egging her on, laughing at her, but she's oblivious. And obliterated.

I'm dumping my vodka into the sink and filling my glass with water. It's working a treat and as everyone gets langers they don't even notice that I'm stone-cold sober. I don't even have to pretend I'm drunk. I see Colin Ryan out of the corner of my eye, sloping into the kitchen, a can of Bavaria in his hand. His hair is a credit to Nicky Clarke – all spritzed and gelled and waxed. Must have taken him hours. He nods at me and I nod back. I can see him debating in his head whether to come over, but I turn my back and start chatting to Sophie and her boyfriend Ray. I mean, it's not like Colin and I are friends or anything. He just thinks he's on to a good thing after listening to Jamie Burke's version of the night. Not the real version with the slobbery kisses and the pink vomit. And Colin is one of the It crowd so it's certainly not my friendship he's after. And, anyway, he's a dumb cretin. I laugh at something

Ray says, which is really a drunken mumble – I have to because everybody's laughing.

I can smell Colin Ryan before I see him. Good old Lynx – a dead giveaway.

"Hi."

"Oh, hi." I turn to face him. He's playing with the ring pull of his can.

"How're things?" he asks, still looking at his can.

"The finest. You?"

"Grand."

There's a silence between us and normally I wouldn't bother to fill it but I'm supposed to be steamed up and having a great time. I try to think of something funny and original to say. "Great party." I grin at him.

He smiles back and picks at the ring pull again. Jesus, what's his problem with it? "Am . . . did you like . . . am . . . the movie?"

I'm trying to follow his conversation. The Coen Brothers movie.

"Loved it. You?"

"Am . . . Danika wanted to see some love shit but I like the Coen Brothers so I got my way."

Danika. That's the made-up name I couldn't think of in the cinema.

"So where's Danika tonight?"

"We split up. Nothing in common, like."

Could have fooled me, Colin. "That right?"

"She . . . she doesn't like the Coen Brothers."

"Yeah – that's a real deal breaker."

He laughs at this, ignoring my sarcasm.

Ciara's standing on a worktop, dancing to the Killers. A

group of guys are standing around clapping and shouting, "Off, off, off."

I don't like where this is leading.

"Am – Maeve . . . am . . ." Colin is rolling the beer can around in his hands now like it's a cup of hot tea.

The crowd is more boisterous now and Ciara is doing a sexy dance, rubbing her body with her hands in a very sad imitation of Paris Hilton on some YouTube clip or other. Fucking idiot, Ciara. No sign of Sophie and Ray. They're probably upstairs testing out her parents' super-king-size bed.

"Am . . . I was wondering . . . am . . ."

The crowd up their chant. "Off! Off! Off!" Ciara's not that stupid. She's just laughing and teasing.

"Am . . . would you like to . . . come out with me some time . . . I mean . . ."

Ciara is that stupid. She's seductively pulling up her top, revealing a bright purple bra. "Ciara!" I shout, but she doesn't hear me over the music. The crowd's in a frenzy as she whips her top off over her head. She's tottering now on the granite island right in the middle of the kitchen, her thin, narrow shoulders and small, purple-clad breasts young and girlish in comparison to the sexy-stripper dance she's trying to perform.

"So . . . am . . . what do you think?"

I look at Colin's lovely pretty-boy face – as hard to maintain as Fiona's. "I don't know what Jamie Burke's told you about me but it isn't true. I don't give blow-jobs, I don't wank people off and I certainly don't fuck them. Not at the moment, anyway, and definitely not any of the lame dumb excuses for boys that currently attend our school. Clear?"

Colin's jaw has dropped and his eyes are round with

disbelief. There's a roar from the middle of the kitchen as Ciara begins to slide her skinny jeans down her hips.

"Oh, fuck." I run over and pull her arm.

She smiles and tries to push me away. The crowd jeers at me. I ignore them and catch Ciara's arm again. Somebody's filming her with his phone – John Quinn from my applied-maths class. A fool with a good memory instead of brains.

I push him aside, accidentally on purpose, and he stumbles drunkenly, landing on his butt.

"Oops – sorry," I say sweetly. Then I grab Ciara again and manage to pull her down, but she falls right on top of me so I'm on the ground with a half-naked girl.

"Lesbo action!" shouts someone. I drag Ciara to her feet and pull her into the hallway.

She giggles and hiccups and giggles again.

"What are you up to, you fool?"

She stares at me, eyes round, then bursts out laughing.

"You're going home, Ciara. Where's your coat? Or, more importantly, where's your top?"

She laughs again, and then her face goes green.

"Oh, no, please don't," I say, trying to haul her into the loo in the hallway. There's somebody in there and I rap on the door. "Hurry up, there's someone being sick out here."

There's more giggling, inside the loo now, and I bang on the door.

Shuffling and whispering.

"The Law," I scream, and the door flies open. Sophie's young sister comes out, her top skewed, followed by Jamie Burke. He winks at me as he passes, his big dumb rugby head wobbling on his fat neck. "Fucking cradle snatcher," I say, as I push Ciara through the door of the tiny loo. "Fuck sake, Ciara,

Sophie's sister's, like, fourteen – ridiculous," I say, but Ciara is busy vomiting and missing the toilet bowl by at least a foot. I hold back her hair and aim her face directly over it. The smell is disgusting and I turn away as she heaves the contents of her stomach and then some into the loo. The party outside has revved up a gear. Time to go home. I'm already looking forward to stealing Harvey from his cot and snuggling up with him in my bed.

"Ooh ... dying ... going to die . . . Help me die, Maeve . . ." Ciara tries to stand up but slumps to the floor in a heap of sick, drunken, half-dressed girl.

Nothing for it – I'll have to bring her home with me. I ring a cab from the loo. Engaged. I flush the toilet and try another number. No answer. Fuck sake. Then I have the bright idea of phoning Cian – he went out in Mam's car so I know he's not drinking.

"Hi. Are you busy cos I need a lift home?"

"Am . . . it's a bit—"

"Cian, I can't get a cab and Ciara's drunk and the guards are coming any minute."

"OK. Where are you?"

"Sophie's."

And it's as if the guards are listening in because now I hear sirens outside.

"Hurry, Cian, the cops are here."

I drag Ciara into the hallway, through the kitchen and out of the back door. Colin Ryan is standing on the deck outside, smoking a fag. I remember then that he actually asked me out during Ciara's strip. Thinks I'll show him a little action.

"Hey, Maeve?" he says, as we pass.

"I'm off. The cops are coming," I say, struggling to hold

Ciara upright. I pull her down the garden and through the back gate. She can barely walk as we make our way to the bottom of the road. She's shivering – no surprise when she's only wearing a purple bra on top. A paddy-wagon passes and I pull her behind a tree. She's almost asleep. Where the fuck is Cian? And then I see Mam's car chugging up the road. There's someone in the passenger seat and I think for a second that maybe Cian finally found a girl. But it's Mark. They pull up beside us and Mark hops out to load Ciara into the back seat.

"What are you doing here, you sneak?" I ask him, as I climb in beside the sleeping Ciara. I'd begged Mark to come out with me earlier but he'd said he had to go to dinner with his parents.

"I bumped into Cian walking home so he gave me a lift," says Mark. "Good night?"

"Does it look like it? Horrible night. Cretin party."

"Told you so, Maevis."

"Where does Ciara live?" asks Cian.

She's snoring now, her head on my lap, Mark's jacket thrown over her. "I'll have to bring her home. She'll be grounded for ten years if her parents catch her like this."

Another cop car flies past us on the road.

"Saturday night in Stab City – lights, camera, action," says Mark. "Apparently there was a stabbing outside the Chicken Hut. It's grand, though – nobody died." He and Cian laugh.

"How was dinner with your parents?" I ask.

"Short and sweet. Was out of there in an hour." He grins at me, but I get the feeling he's not telling me something. "So what did you do after that?"

"Maeve Hogan, ace detective. A guard wouldn't ask me that. And, no, I wasn't outside the Chicken Hut stabbing people."

Another squad car zooms past, blue light flashing.

"What's going on?" I ask, watching the car streak ahead of us.

"That's turning into our avenue," says Cian.

Straight away I have a bad feeling. Harvey in that madhouse. That little prick Joey set the house on fire. Stole the baby. "Hurry, Cian."

"What's the rush?" he says, keeping to his usual steady pace.

My heart is hammering as we drive around the corner into our road. I scan the street for the squad car but there's no sign of it. It must have cut through our road to get somewhere else. The relief makes me giddy. We pull up outside our house and it's in total darkness. Mark and Cian carry Ciara between them and I open the door and flick on the lights. Nobody home. Which means no Harvey. The lads carry Ciara up the stairs and put her into Cian's room. I quietly open the door of Fiona's room and creep over to the crib. Harvey's sound asleep, his little fists under his chin. I steal out of the bedroom and go downstairs.

Cian's in the kitchen. "Fiona's in the sitting room, Maeve. She's very upset." Cian looks at me like I'll know what to do. "Mark's talking to her."

The lights are off in the sitting room. I switch on the lamp. Mark and Fiona are on the couch, his arm around her shoulders. She looks up at me and I nearly die. Her face is covered with scratches and weals. "Jesus Christ, what happened to you?"

She shakes her head and tears stream down her face.

"What the fuck happened?"

Mark glares at me. "It's OK, Fiona. You can tell us."

She shakes her head again.

"Are you in trouble? What happened, for God's sake?"

There's blood on her jeans. Long streaks of it. And marks on her scalp where her hair has been tugged out.

"You're safe now, Fiona, it's OK." Mark pats her shoulder. Her head is bent, her hair covering her ruined face.

"I . . . there was a fight and . . . I didn't do anything . . . just talked to Tony, you know Tony from the next avenue . . ." She stops and sniffles, looking at Mark. "I was just talking to Tony and a girl came up behind me, Big's ex . . ." More sniffles.

Cian's come in and is sitting in the armchair opposite us.

"And she jumped on top of me and Tony . . . Poor old Tony . . . tried to take her off me . . . and then Big came out of the Chicken Hut . . ."

"Oh, please, no," I say.

Both Mark and Cian glare at me this time.

"There was a knife . . . I don't know what happened . . . Everybody was fighting and screaming and the girl was tearing my hair . . ." She looks up then, dark hollows under her eyes, angry red scratches across her cheeks like tribal markings.

"Did the guards come?" Cian says.

"Dunno. Big pulled me up and we ran."

"Where's Big now?" I ask.

She ignores me. "We ran and ran, and then he pulled me into a laneway . . ."

Tears start down her ravaged face again. "He said it was all my fault. He said I was coming on to Tony – I mean, coming on to Tony Collins? And he said I called his ex a slut in the Chicken Hut."

"The usual Saturday-night fight? Fucking typical scumbag." I can hear Mam arriving in the front door, doing her

slow, deliberate, look-how-sober-I-am-really walk in the
hallway.

"I wasn't even in the Chicken Hut. He knew I wasn't. So I
can't understand why he blamed me."

"I can – he's a no-brain scumbag. His night out wouldn't be
complete without a fight – a bit of drama and excitement . . ."

"Stop, Maeve. Let Fiona talk," says Cian, for the first time
in his life assuming the big-brother role.

"And then there was a squad car and loads of noise . . . I
just ran – ran away from Big . . . from all of them . . . got a taxi
. . . got Harvey before Big could . . ."

"Could what?" I ask.

"Yoo-hoo," says Mam, from the doorway. Her eyes are
glazed from too much wine and her makeup has left the print
of her lashes under her eyes. She's grinning – a drunken, numb
grin. "Are ye all home – that's great so— Oh, my God, Fiona,
what happened to you?" Mam rushes over and almost elbows
Mark out of the way. Fiona throws herself at Mam, bawling
her head off like a little girl. Mam listens to her mumbled
jumble of a story, pats her back and tells her it'll be grand.

I watch the two of them together, thinking all the time
about the great night out that Fiona had described and how it
wasn't true that Big craved the excitement and adrenalin of a
fight. Fiona liked it too. She's crying and protesting now but
she likes drama. Always has. Fiona's sobs finally ease.

"Come on, let's all go to bed, it's been a long day," says
Mam.

"I'll drive you home, Mark," says Cian, jingling the car
keys in his pocket.

"Sleep tight, Maevis," says Mark, kissing me on the
forehead.

And then there's a huge crash and Fiona screams and Mam clutches Cian as the glass in the living-room window explodes around us.

"Get on the floor – gun shots," shouts Mark, pulling me down.

Seven

I can hear Mark's heart thumping in my ear as he covers my body with his. Someone's crying – Mam or Fiona or both of them.

"Stay down," says Cian. "Don't raise your heads."

A cold breeze blows through the shattered window. Harvey's screaming now upstairs. I want to go to him, hating the sound of his distress. And then I hear it. A great line that will go down in the annals as the ultimate way of claiming your child: "Gimme out my baby, you cunt."

Big's standing outside the window, net curtains billowing in his face. He's like a mad scumbag ghost. "Gimme him now, Fiona. I don't want to cause no trouble, like. I just want my baby." He doesn't have a shotgun in his hand and I scan the debris on the floor. Three rocks lie in the middle of the shattered glass.

I stand up and face him. "Leave her alone."

Big eyes me up and down, as if considering whether he should answer me or not. Then he comes closer, sticking his head through the jagged hole in the window. "Gimme my fucking son and I'll go away. I don't want no trouble."

"Mam, ring the guards. Go home – you've caused enough trouble for one night, scumbag." I hold his eyes, challenging him to deal with me. Harvey's still crying.

Big points at me. Says nothing, just points his finger at me. Mam is on the phone but the guards are on their way already. The sirens are blaring outside the front door. Big walks backwards, still pointing his finger at me, then turns and runs down through the garden and over the back wall.

I race up the stairs to Harvey, Fiona at my heels. His fists are flying up in the air, like he's boxing, and his body is stiff from crying. I pick him up and he calms immediately, his cries reduced to shudders. "There now, baby boy." I kiss the top of his head, and rock him gently in my arms. Fiona's standing there watching me, her face scratched and swollen. Harvey's mother. I hate her at this moment, absolutely hate her – not for getting pregnant but for getting pregnant with Big. The guards are downstairs. I can hear deep voices talking to Mam.

Fiona puts out her arms for Harvey, then drops them by her side. Like she's afraid to take him from me. I keep rocking him, loving the weight of him in my arms.

"This has to stop."

She looks away when I speak.

"I mean it, Fiona. This has to stop before something bad happens. He stabbed Tony Collins – didn't he?"

She bites her manicured nails. Purple with tiny diamonds on the tips.

"The cops are downstairs. You'll have to make a statement about what happened. What if he's dead?"

She's crying then, huge fat tears rolling down her battered face. She looks so helpless. My anger melts and I pull her down to sit on the bed. She leans into me, crying softly. I put my arm around her while she sobs. Harvey's asleep again, and as she cries her heart out, I feel like I'm sitting there with two babies.

Finally she stops. "Tony's not dead – he was stabbed in the leg."

"Who stabbed him, Fiona?"

"I . . . there was so many . . . I . . ."

"Do you want it to stop, Fiona?"

She nods, picking at the diamonds on her nails.

"No – really, do you want it to stop? Do you want to show him that it's over? That you're finished with him?"

"I want things to change."

"So make it happen, Fiona. I'll help you."

"What'll I do? I don't know how to change it now."

"Tell the guards what you saw tonight. Tell them the truth."

She starts crying again. I get up and put Harvey back in his crib, planning to steal him when everybody's gone to bed.

I kneel in front of her and take both her hands in mine. "I'll help you, Fiona. I promise I'll help – all of us will. Look, you're going back to school next week, aren't you?"

She nods.

"So, Harvey'll be in the crèche during the day when Mam is working, and I'll be with you – twenty-four seven, if that's what it takes. You can do this, Fiona. You have to for that little baby's sake."

She nods again, a curtain of blonde hair hiding her eyes. I push it away from her face. "I swear on Dad's grave I'll support you, Fiona."

"Really?"

"Yes, really. I'm not afraid of Big – not one bit."

There's a gentle knock on the door. Mam opens it. "They

want a word with you, Fiona," she whispers. "About what happened at the Chicken Hut."

Fiona's eyes are round with fear. I stand up, still holding her hands. "Come on, I'll be with you – it'll be fine."

It's late when the guards leave. Mam puts Fiona to bed, having swabbed the cuts on her face with disinfectant. And just as Mam closes the door Harvey wakes up for his night feed. I rush past Mam and pick him up, delighted with his timing. I've been looking forward to this all night. It's back to our usual Saturday routine. Just Harvey and me, safe and cosy in bed together.

But bodyguarding isn't as easy as it sounds. By week two of guarding Fiona, Mark and I are feeling the strain, and it doesn't help that Big lives on the same street as us. He's being very clever too – playing a blinder, in fact. Didn't come near Fiona for the first week, just sent his mother down with a sob story and a huge bunch of flowers in the shape of a heart. They looked like a wreath and, of course, I said as much and got a Mam-glare for my trouble.

So I'm not surprised when we're walking home towards the end of the second week and Big kerb-crawls us in his boy-racer Civic. He's just driving along and looking soulfully at Fiona. Mark and I shield her so she can't look back but I know there's a change in her. Very subtle, but definitely there. And the next day he's on foot. Walks behind us the whole way from school and just as we're going up our garden path he says her name very softly. *Fiona.* Almost a whisper. I give him the finger and push her in the front door. She runs straight upstairs. Mam comes out of the kitchen carrying Harvey. He's so big now –

the huge brown eyes are saucers in his chubby face. I grab him from Mam and kiss his fat jaws over and over.

"You have him spoiled rotten, Maeve. Where's Fiona?"

"Big was hovering outside and I think she's a little upset by it." I hug Harvey tightly, not wanting to let him go.

"Poor Fiona. She misses him." Mam rubs the spiky hairs on top of Harvey's head in a vain effort to tame them.

I can't believe what she said. She's meant to be Fiona's mother and want what's best for her. "You're not serious, Mam, are you? He's a waster, a scumbag, she's better off without him."

"She's sad."

"Yeah – cos she messed up. This is for the best. She needs to stick to her guns. And we need to help her. We – not just Mark and me, you too – need to make sure she does what's right for her and for Harvey."

Mam shakes her head. "What's right is to let it run its course, Maeve. That's the only thing that'll work. I think the plan you and Mark've hatched will only make it worse in the long run."

"How can you say that? So what do we do? Let her get beaten every weekend? Dragged into Scumbag Land and not fight for her?" I'm beginning to shout so I lower my voice in a conscious effort to stay calm. "That's why she's in this situation in the first place – you sat back and left her off, left her to mess up at school, hang around with knackers . . ."

Mam points a finger at me, her eyes glinting with anger. "Don't you dare start the blame game, Maeve. You're sixteen – you know absolutely nothing about life. And you can't learn it in a book – so shut up now this minute."

I march upstairs and Mam goes into the kitchen banging

the door noisily behind her. And I'm supposed to be the teenager! How is my mother so dumb? At least now I know where we got Fiona from. I go into my room, Harvey still in my arms, and jump when I see Fiona staring out the window. There's a tiny tear at the corner of her eye. She's child-like in her navy blue school uniform, faint scratch marks still on her face. The room is cold and I shiver as I walk towards her. And then I see what she's looking at: Big sitting on the wall and staring up at her. His Montague to her Capulet. Spare me.

"Don't, Fiona . . ."

"Please go," she whispers.

I look out at Big, straight into his eyes. He looks back at me and we eye-wrestle for a few seconds, but I win. I know I do because I have his baby in my arms. I sweep the curtains closed with one hand. "It'll get better, Fiona."

She looks at me, her eyes huge, exactly like Harvey's except for the colour.

"It'll get worse," she says, taking Harvey from my arms.

"Come on, Fifi, that's not true." I surprise myself – I haven't called her Fifi since we were kids.

She smiles down at Harvey, but her shoulders sag and now she looks like a worn-out old-woman schoolgirl.

"Hey, would you like to come out with Mark and me on Saturday night? We'll do something fun." This is very generous from me. On the rare occasions that Fiona and I meet socially it's always been embarrassing to say the least. And I can't compete with Big in the fun department – no lines of coke and impromptu fights.

She nods. Not very enthusiastic.

"Mam'll babysit. She's said so already. The book club isn't until next week – or they've run out of wine."

Fiona smiles weakly at my attempt at a joke.

"And, Fiona, I meant to say it to you but if you need any help with your school work, just ask. OK?"

Another little nod. I don't blame her for that, though. Any time I ever tried to teach her stuff I ended up fit to strangle her so I know teaching certainly will not be on my CAO list. In any shape or form.

We're going to Mark's. It beats bush drinking down by the river – much warmer, the bathrooms are better and I don't want to risk going to town with Fiona when, chances are, we'll meet Big or some of the knacker friends. Anyway, I hate the pubs in town with screechy drunken girls and leering guys. Mark's will be a laugh. I try to get Fiona enthused about it and drag her into my room so that we can get ready together. This is a new experience for both of us.

"You should straighten your hair," says Fiona, standing behind me as I sit brushing my long straggly locks. I'm planning on whipping it all up in a go-go once the knots are untangled. "I'll do it for you, if you like." She doesn't wait for an answer, just goes off to her room and appears back with her beloved GHDs. Her prize possession, her if-the-house-was-burning-down-what-would-you-save item.

I sit at the dressing-table mirror as she begins to straighten my hair. She takes small sections and moves the irons down really slowly. She's biting her lip as she concentrates, a curtain of her own blonde hair hooked behind her ear. We don't speak and I start to enjoy the experience in spite of myself. Her hands on me, gentle, almost loving. The shiny silkiness of the just-straightened hair. The feeling of closeness without having to talk.

I'm amazed at the results. I barely recognise my new hair, all sleek and shiny and grown-up. She smiles at me in the mirror, and tilts her head to the side, examining her work. "Hang on one tick," she says, flying out of the room again and coming back with her makeup bag.

"No way," I say. "I hate makeup. The whole idea of it is ridiculous – colouring in your face to make yourself pretty for men . . ."

"Shut up, Maeve, and chill – here, close your eyes for me."

I do as I'm told. Her fingers work my face like an expert's, the little brushes and wands, highlighting, flicking and filling.

"There, have a look."

I swivel my chair back to the mirror. "Oh, my God, I look like a woman!" I stare at a kind of grown-up version of me. "Jesus Christ."

Fiona smiles, the first real smile in days. "Amazing, isn't it?"

"Unbelievable. You're really good at this makeup shit."

"I like it, and when you like something it's easy."

Cian drives us to Mark's and I can hear Fiona low-whistle in the back of the car as Cian expertly punches in the gate code. "Is this, like, just one house?" she asks, as the car crunches to a halt in front of the huge Georgian façade.

Mark's standing in the doorway, grinning at us. I can't wait for him to see my makeover. "Thanks, Cian, see you later." I jump out of the car and run up the steps to Mark.

"My God – you are hot," he says, holding me back by the shoulders to have a better look.

I grin, my stomach melting with delight. He kisses me on the forehead. "Come on in and let's party," he says.

Fiona and Cian follow us into the massive hallway. Fiona's mouth is open but Cian isn't a bit perturbed by the lavish surroundings. He gives Mark a bundle of CDs. "Burnt these for you, man," he says.

Mark takes the gift and flicks through the titles. "Movies, too? Cool," he says, as he waves us into the kitchen. I wonder why Cian's hanging out with us again. I mean, it's bad enough having Fiona around constantly but my nerd brother as well? All we're short of is Mam and Harvey.

Mark throws a CD on the music system – Fionn Regan: I love him but he's way too romantic and poetic for my siblings. He pops a champagne cork and fills glasses with the bubbly froth. It tickles my nose as I drink it. Fiona slugs back hers in one go. "That's the nicest drink I ever tasted," she says, as Mark pours her some more.

The doorbell rings and Mark goes out to answer it. I give Fiona a quick tour of the conservatory.

"Wow – our whole house could fit in here. Where's his family? Are they away?"

I shrug. "His parents are in – let me think – Denver on business or something."

We wander back towards the kitchen, which is now buzzing with new arrivals. Sophie and Ciara are there and already Ciara's glugging beer. She smiles and waves, ignoring my remember-the-last-time-you-drank frown. Somebody's dumped Fionn Regan in favour of Kasabian and upped the music a few notches as well. More teenagers arrive and the place is hopping now. Fiona seems to like the buzz – she's happy chatting and even flirting. Mark's surrounded by girls, talking and laughing. I watch from the doorway, feeling like an outsider.

Cian's flicking through CDs on the floor near Mark and

every so often they have this mad conversation together, Cian talking up to Mark, Mark leaning down towards him, both laughing. Suddenly the room feels claustrophobic despite its size. The noisy voices of teenagers competing against each other to be heard and seen. The beer bottles mounting on worktops and tables. The girls' high-pitched shrieks. The numbing boredom of it. Fuck Mark, with his stupid party. We could have gone to the cinema. Fiona might have enjoyed that.

I sneak into the den, the cosy little room where Mark and I kissed for the first and last time. But Katya's beaten me to it. She's curled up on the couch watching *The X Factor*. She smiles at me and pats the cushion beside her. "Come sit. Simon is so mean tonight."

So I watch *The X Factor* with a pretty Polish woman while the party raves without me. When it's over Katya pats my hand. "You love that Simon, yes? He is so sexy, yes?" She beams.

I shake my head. "No. He's ugly. Russell Brand is sexy."

"Who is this Brand? In *The X Factor*?"

I grin at the picture that comes to my mind – Russell Brand sitting beside Louis and Sharon, listening to would-be pop stars on a Saturday evening.

"Your brother is Cian?"

"Yes. How did you know? Please don't say I look like him!"

She laughs. "He is a nice boy. He comes to watch the movies with Mark. All weekend they watch the movies."

I smile at her but I'm furious. How fucking dare Cian steal my friend? How dare he come here and hang out with Mark whenever he feels like it? Weirdo can't find friends of his own, not even in college in Cork – two cities of potential friends to choose from – and he has to take mine. I march out of the den and into the kitchen. determined to say something. But what do you say and who do you say it to? I scan the room for Cian but spot Colin Ryan instead, heading straight for me. The icing on the cake of a shit night.

"Am . . ."

Here we go.

"Am . . . you look . . . am . . . nice."

Wow. Nice. I look nice. Riveting. "Thanks." I try to locate Mark in the midst of the crowd. I have a plan in my head that maybe I can get him on his own somewhere and maybe we can get a little drunk and maybe something will happen. A lot of maybes.

"I was looking for you . . . thought you hadn't come . . ."

I smile at Colin and keep scanning the party. Fiona's chatting to a guy from our avenue – Robbie, that's his name. She sees me and gives me a beer-bottle wave. And then Mark is beside me, arm around my waist, staring into my face like I'm the most interesting person ever. "How's my favourite girl? Hope I'm not interrupting anything?" He smiles at Colin, who doesn't smile back.

"Fionn Regan got thrown out of the party and I'm blaming you, Mark."

"Fionn isn't exactly up for the laugh, Maevis."

"How dare you speak about the saint in that tone? Favourite song ever?"

"'The wolves come on the radio . . .'" he sings.

"'. . . transmitting through a portal . . .'"

"'. . . in the snowy Atlas Mountains . . .'" he answers.

Both of us laugh and Colin rolls his eyes. Like a girl.

Somebody puts on the Kings of Leon and people start to dance. A tiny redhead in a skin-tight black dress hurls herself at Mark, dragging him onto the sticky kitchen floor. He shrugs at me as if to say, What can I do? I want to kill the little redhead with my bare hands.

"No need to be jealous," says Colin, reminding me that he's still standing there.

"Jealous? Jealous of what?"

"Of her. There's no need." He takes a slug of his beer.

"Don't be stupid."

"He's not interested in her."

I wonder if Colin's drunker than he seems. "What are you talking about?"

"He's not interested in her. Or in you . . ."

As Colin talks I catch something out of the corner of my eye. A face at the huge picture window towards the back of the kitchen. A face with tiny ferret eyes, mean and clever and quick. Big. He's staring straight at me and I lose the plot. I make a run towards the French windows, pushing dancers out of the way as I barrel through the kitchen. I fling open the doors and stand on the deck. Nobody there. It's a gorgeous night, lovely crisp air and a show-off starry sky. I walk to the edge of the deck and look down on the beautiful, subtly lit garden. No sign of him. Maybe I imagined it. No, definitely not.

I go down the steps and along a lovely paved path towards a small fountain. The music and noise from the party fade as I move further away from the house. It's cold – I can feel goose-bumps on my bare arms. "Bastard," I say to myself, as I turn to go back to the house. I hear a rustle in the shrubbery to my left and I stand still to listen. "Who's there?" I whisper, the hairs on the back of my neck standing on end. My heart pounds a loud, noisy rhythm in my chest.

Silence.

I start walking again, forcing myself not to run and humming Fionn Regan's "Snowy Atlas Mountains".

Someone grabs me from behind, clamping a hand so tightly across my mouth that I can't breathe. Then I'm lifted through the air into the shrubs.

"I don't want no trouble," Big says, into my ear.

I struggle but his grip is vice-like, considering he's so small.

"Listen to me, fucking know-all. This is a warning. You mind your business between me and Fiona. You're interfering in my life and I want you to fuck off out of it."

He's still holding me up against him, his hand across my mouth. I nod, even though he can only see the back of my head.

"I'm going to leave go your mouth. Don't fucking scream. I just want to talk, like. Come to an arrangement."

I nod furiously.

He lets go slowly and turns me around to face him, gripping my arms hard.

"Don't be frightened. I just want to talk."

I take a deep breath, and eye-wrestle him. "I'm not afraid of you."

He laughs. "I know that, and I don't give a fuck. I want to sort this out with Fiona. I want you to go in there and get her for me. Tell her it's all right."

It's my turn to laugh this time. "No way."

"So – what are you going to do? Fucking stay glued to her for the rest of her life? I just want to talk to my girlfriend. The fucking mother of my child."

"She's scared of you. Do you know that?"

He guffaws this time. "Scared of me? That's a great laugh."

"She's terrified of you and she wants you out of her life."

His face is deadly serious now and he pushes it right up to mine, so close I can smell his faggy breath. "For someone that's got loads of brains you're very dumb, ja know that?"

I will myself not to step back from him.

"Cos it's you she's scared of. You're a fucking bully, a cunt. And another thing. She doesn't want me out of her life – you do." He's smirking at me like he's won. "Watch this," he says, taking out his phone. He speed-dials a number. "Babe. It's me . . . Outside in the rich cunt's garden. Near the fountain . . . Yeah. That's right. How's the baby? I want to see him, man. Soon, like . . ."

I know he's talking to Fiona. Even though she'd changed her number she'd had to get in touch with him. Had to text. Stupid, stupid girl.

"Come out, Fiona, baby. I miss you, like . . . Come on, she won't know you're even gone. It's a fucking party." He closes the phone. "See? I can do it anyway. But it'd make my life a whole lot easier if you mind your business. Are we understood?"

I fold my arms across my chest, giving him a glare Mam would have been proud of.

"When she comes out looking for me will you give her something?"

I up my glare, narrowing my eyes.

He leans towards me again and I think he's going to slap me. But I don't flinch. Not a millimetre. And then he kisses me. Right on the lips – hard and animal and scary. And then he's gone, running along the side of the garden and scaling the back wall as quick as a cat.

I wipe my mouth, staring at the wall. When I turn I bump straight into Colin Ryan.

"Am . . . I . . . Sorry . . . Came to see if you were OK – didn't realise I was interrupting something . . ."

I ignore him as my sister comes down the garden path. "You are one stupid lying bitch," I scream at her.

She sticks out her chin and puts her hands on her hips. "I didn't lie to you – and, anyway, who do you think you are?"

"I'm trying to help you, Fiona."

She's right in front of me now, eyes glassy with alcohol. "You fucking well kissed him, I saw you, you bitch. Fucking jealous is what you are . . ."

I guffaw. "He kissed me and told me to pass it on to you, if you want to know the truth." I wipe my mouth repeatedly with my hand. "Disgusting bastard."

"Shut up, Maeve. I'm sick of you bossing me around. He loves me."

Another huge guffaw from me. "He wouldn't know what love was if it jumped up and bit him in the arse. He's a waster, a scumbag, a—"

She throws herself at me, punching me hard in the head. I put up my hands to defend myself but there's an angry knot of hatred burning inside me. So I thump her back and suddenly we're wrestling on the damp grass. She's trying to rip my hair out so I do the same to her. She manages to sit on top of me and tears stream down her face. Then Colin Ryan is pulling her off but there's no need, really, because I know from looking at her that the fight has gone out of her. She wipes her eyes on her sleeve, spreading mascara all over her face.

Colin offers me his hand and pulls me upright. "You OK?" he says.

"Yeah." I pull twigs from my matted hair, watching my sister as she tries to clean her face. My heart is still pumping from the adrenalin rush of the fight and a parade of thoughts competes for notice in my head. Like how the scumbag mentality is invading our family – me included – when the only solution to a problem is to tear into each other. I can see how it could become a habit – a default way of dealing with life. And the adrenalin rush – I almost enjoy it.

"I'm sorry, Maeve," she says then, out of the blue.

"I know you are," I say. And it's true.

"Something just goes off inside me sometimes . . . It's all so hard . . ."

"I know."

Colin is pretending not to listen to us.

I hug Fiona tight – I'm almost crying too. "It'll be grand."

"I only texted him about Harvey, that's all. I sent him pictures and I told him I didn't want to see him or talk to him unless it was about Harvey."

"I know."

She smiles at me then, her face grotesque in the eerie light from the floodlit fountain. "You were right, Maeve. As usual. Once he had my number he never stopped. I nearly gave in yesterday – and here tonight, after a few drinks . . ."

"But you didn't give in."

She shakes her head, her silky blonde hair falling across her face. "It's too hard."

"No, it's not. He'll move on – he'll get tired of this."

Another shake of her head.

"Am . . . it's starting to rain . . ." says Colin.

We look at him, then at each other, and burst out laughing.

We hold onto each other as the laughter turns into hysteria. Colin Ryan shakes his head at us, which makes us laugh harder.

So Big ups the ante even more. A bunch of flowers arrives for Fiona on Monday evening, just as we come in the door from school. The card reads *Love you loads, babe, your little Biggy* and I burst out laughing when I read it. Fiona whips it from my hand and marches out of the kitchen, banging the door after her.

"You shouldn't have, Maeve," says Mam.

"Shouldn't what? I didn't say anything."

Mam empties the dishwasher, banging plates and cups into presses, her mouth a hard line.

I make a bowl of cereal and plan my night's study in my head. Applied maths for two hours followed by physics. As I sit down at the table to eat, Mam's plate-banging gets louder – always a message that she's angry and/or wants to let you know about it. I ignore it, and when I catch her eye every now and then I smile innocently, munching my cornflakes. The banging is so loud now that I think the plates are going to smash.

"You'll drive her back to him, Maeve, with this carry-on. You'll make her choose and she'll pick him." Mam's voice is quiet. She wipes her hands on a blue tea-towel and sits opposite me. I expected her to be angry with me, shouting, arguing – our usual mode of communication. I notice new lines around her eyes, and puffy bags under them. Not Chardonnay bags because she hasn't been out all weekend.

"Mam, I'm doing the right thing. I can't stand by and watch her destroy her life."

"Just let the thing run its course. If you try to keep them apart it'll just make the whole thing go on and on."

"Mam, trust me, he'll manipulate her, she'll get pregnant

109

again, he'll get her into trouble. This isn't some nice boy from down the road being a bit wild, it's completely different. I'm going to save her and Harvey and—" I stop. I'm ranting and Mam is silently crying. I reach out and touch her hand. It's strange and dry in mine, and once I've done that I'm lost for anything else to say or do. "It'll be fine, Mam," I say eventually, hating myself for the simplistic platitude.

"I wish your dad was here."

Her hand is still and lifeless in mine.

"I miss him so much too. I'm so lonely without him."

"I wish he was here because then I could walk out and close the door behind me." She looks straight at me and I know she absolutely means every word. My usual Mam knot of anger nags in my head. It becomes a small tight fist that's dying to punch somebody. I count to ten, desperately trying to control my feelings, to analyse them as they occur. I don't say anything at all. I gently pull my hand away, take my bowl and put it in the empty dishwasher. Then I leave the kitchen and go upstairs, risking Fiona's anger for a cuddle from Harvey before my study.

He's lying on her bed, kicking his legs in the air. Fiona's sitting beside him, her phone in her hand. Harvey smiles and kicks harder when he sees me, his bare legs flying up and down like he's cycling an imaginary bike. And then her phone beeps a message, just as I bend down to kiss him, and when our eyes meet we both know that Big's at the other end. I go into my room and sit at my computer – just sit there in the dark, all thoughts of physics and applied maths gone for now. I switch on the computer and as the screen flickers to life I'm crying. I open my physics folder and stare at the jumbled theorems and numbers. None of it makes any sense. Then I click my drivel-writing icon and the second the blank page opens I'm off, the white blemish-free page like an invitation to vomit it all out.

He drew it for her in a diagram. He used her new Magic Markers – the ones with the really bright colours that Ciany said were called fluorescent. Maeve loved the new word. Fluorescent. Loved the way it rolled around in her mouth and off her tongue. And she knew teacher was impressed when she'd put it in her essay at school today.

Daddy used her favourite colour – pink – to draw it. She was in the middle of learning her mountains and he just sat down and took a page from her sum copy and she was going to stop him cos Ms Sheehan would ask her about the missing page and he started drawing. Swirly lines and circles in circles and then a tiny circle in the middle of the drawing and all the time new words, too many so that she couldn't remember them all, and she really wanted to remember them because of the essay competition at the end of the month. They came too fast for her, intracranial, cerebral, anterior. Glioblastoma. Words she'd never ever heard before. He pointed at the drawing when he said them. And when he pointed to the tiny circle, the one he'd coloured in with the pink marker, he said a word and the minute he said it she knew it was bad. It sounded like what it meant. She just knew this even though nobody had ever told her. Malignant. A bad word. A black, dirty word that could only describe bad, dirty things. And she knew in her head what the picture meant. She knew that he'd drawn his brain but she didn't want to think about it. Instead she tried to remember all the new words but the only one she could remember easily was malignant.

And then Mam and Fifi came into the kitchen. They'd been at Irish dancing and Maeve wasn't in it because she hated it so much. She didn't know she was crying until the brain picture started to melt in front of

Helena Close

her. And then Mam screamed at Daddy, "You told a child about it, a child, for God's sake," and Fiona was crying too, and Daddy slammed the table hard with his fist and all the Magic Markers rolled off and now Mammy was crying and screaming at Daddy. And then Fiona got Maeve's hand and pulled her out of the kitchen and they sat on the third step of the stairs. Fiona put her arm around Maeve, really tight like Daddy did sometimes, and she said she'd mind her, and Maeve whispered then, her voice tiny. She whispered to Fifi that she'd wet her knickers and not to tell Mammy. And Fiona laughed and said she'd get her clean ones and nobody would know. And Maeve put her arm around Fiona and hugged her back . . .

I stop typing and notice my hands are shaking. And those stupid tears are back. I close down the page, not even bothering to save it and open up my physics and lose myself in that lovely logical world where everything adds up and makes sense.

The hours slip by and I can't believe it's midnight when I finally check the time. I go downstairs in search of food. The house is in darkness and I debate whether to sneak into Fiona's room and steal Harvey. I make a cheese sandwich and head back upstairs. As I brush my teeth something hits the window-pane with a loud crack, like a bullet. I duck down on the bathroom floor and then another shower of cracks but this time at Fiona's bedroom window. I run into her room just as she opens the window.

"I just want to see him, Fiona. I want to see my son, like," Big shouts up at her, from the front garden. He's slurring his words. Drunk or doped up or both.

"I love you, like. I don't care about you making the

statement to the law, I don't care about nothing, only I know I love you, like . . ."

"Close the window, Fiona, he's drunk."

She looks at me, then back at Big.

"Fiona, just show me him, just so I can go home happy."

I go to the window, almost pushing Fiona out of the way. "Go home, you fool," I shout.

"Why didn't you tell me the cunt was there with ya, Fiona?"

"Go home – you'll wake the neighbourhood," I tell him, banging the window closed.

Fiona shivers next to me.

"It'll be fine – he's drunk, he'll go home. See? He's gone already."

She looks out of the window, still shivering in her light pyjamas. "He'll come back, Maeve. Maybe I should just go down and talk to him, bring Harvey downstairs and let him see him for a minute . . ."

"No, Fiona. He's drunk, he's capable of anything – he could snatch Harvey."

Fiona shakes her head vigorously. "One thing about Big, Maeve. He'll never hurt his family. Never."

"Did he ever hurt you, Fiona?"

She looks away, like it's a trick question, and I suppose it is, really.

"Did he ever hurt you?"

She takes her dressing-gown off the bed and wraps it around her. Then she looks me straight in the eye. "You won't believe me. If I say he didn't then you won't believe me."

"I will. I promise."

"He never hurt me."

Harvey stirs in his crib and Fiona goes over to check on him. He's crying now, tiny half-asleep bleats. She bends down and picks him up, stroking the top of his head as she cuddles him. "You don't believe me, Maeve. I know by looking at you."

"It's hard to believe because I saw stuff with my own eyes."

"No, you didn't." She jiggles Harvey in her arms and his crying is reduced to a whimper.

"Yes, I did, Fiona. I saw him threatening you and—"

"You never saw him hurting me, though—" There's a huge crash outside in the garden. "Oh, my God, what on earth was that?"

We run to the window and pull back the curtain. Big is suspended in mid-air, like a drunk, insane Superman.

Eight

Big is in a cherry-picker, the basket wobbling all over the place. The machine is being driven by his younger brother, the kid from the car chase. And Fiona has the window open and she's talking to the swinging Big like it's perfectly normal.

"Gimme out the baby for a cuddle," says Big, his arms outstretched. A small crowd of neighbours is gathering in the garden, including Mam and poor Mr Higgins next door.

The basket does a huge wobble and jerks up into the air.

"Fuck sake, Joey, will you steady it – what the fuck's wrong with you?" Big shouts at his young brother, who's smiling gleefully, obviously delighted to be back in the driving seat.

"He's a child – maybe that's what's wrong," I say, but Big doesn't even acknowledge me as he balances himself in his shaky perch.

"I love you, Fiona," he says, and Fiona stares at him doe-eyed, the baby asleep in her arms. Like *Romeo and Juliet* but a warped, insane Limerick version. "Gimme wan cuddle offa him," Big says, stretching out his arms again. There's a siren in the distance. Somebody, thankfully, has called the cops.

Fiona glances at me.

"Don't you dare – don't you dare hand the baby out to him," I say, trying to close the window. But Big has caught it and is hanging on for dear life as his tugging sends the basket into a spin.

"Tell the cunt leave us alone," says Big.

"Get down here this minute or I'll brain you. I swear it Big, I'll brain you." All of us look down to see Big's mother Vonnie standing next to the cherry-picker, hands on hips, clad in a bright pink satin dressing-gown. The little girl, the chubby one who was in the hospital the night Harvey was born, is at her mother's side, wearing a tight yellow sweatshirt over pyjama bottoms.

"Mam, go home, will ya? I'll be down in a minute – I'm just talking to my girlfriend, like."

"Get down from there right now – making a show of me in front of everyone. I'll brain you, mind – and you, you little scut, get out of there now." Vonnie reaches into the cab of the cherry-picker and drags out a screaming Joey. Then she leaps in herself and fiddles with the controls until she finds the lever.

The guards have arrived and the crowd has grown larger. I keep thinking it's all so surreal that maybe I'm dreaming. Maybe I've spent too long studying physics and now I'm hallucinating. I'm imagining this macabre version of *Romeo and Juliet*.

Vonnie touches the lever just to get a feel for it and then, once she's confident with her wrist action, she jolts Big up and down in the flimsy basket until he's begging for mercy. Mr Higgins next door, the poor retired guard, looks positively scared. The two fresh-faced guards haven't a clue what to do as Vonnie ignores their shouts and hand gestures.

She finally lowers the basket to the ground and Big gets

out, his face green. As the guards approach he's gone, running down the road, his young brother in hot pursuit.

So, Vonnie ends up in our house for tea and toast and a read of the children. Mam opens a bottle of wine and as I try to fall asleep I can hear them laughing and talking, the voices getting louder as one bottle becomes two. I can hear Mam's laughter and Vonnie's low voice. Doing the talking. Telling the stories. And every now and then I can hear Fiona crying in the next room. It lasts a long time.

Big's in jail. This is the headline news around our breakfast table and it's delivered as if we're being told he's gone to Tesco or Castleconnell. It's Saturday and Mark has a surprise planned for me. I don't know what it is and I'm really excited in spite of myself. I've even put on some makeup – badly, I'll admit – and Fiona's let me borrow her new leather boots, the ones with a little kitten heel that she got last week. So we're all there tripping over each other at breakfast. Mam and Fiona are going to town on a pre-Lanzarote shopping trip – a Penneys blitz: eight outfits including shoes for fifty euro. Vonnie's taking Harvey – an arrangement she somehow wangled out of a tipsy Mam the night of the cherry-picker. Cian is back from college but very down in himself, according to Mam. He doesn't look it now as he tucks into the huge fry-up she's just cooked for him.

And then the doorbell rings. At first I think it's Mark and I'm cursing myself for not being ready, and then Vonnie's in the kitchen. Filling the space with her bleached-blonde hair and her loud, non-stop talk. "I'm here for the child – Nicole's so excited. She can't wait to take him out in his buggy." She pauses and for a second I think she's going to take out her fags and light up but, if she was, she decides against it.

"Sit down there, Vonnie. Would you like a cup of tea? I just made a fresh pot," says Mam.

Vonnie sits next to Cian. "Thanks very much. Anyway, it's a pity Big's gone in – he'll miss Harvey now but sure he'll see him next week."

Mam pours tea for Vonnie, ignoring the "Big's gone in" comment. Cian's still buried in his fry but the minute I make eye contact with Fiona I know something's up. She's avoiding my gaze, eating her toast with incredible concentration. So, of course, big-mouth Maeve has to ask the inevitable. "Gone in where?"

Vonnie looks at me like I'm the dumbest person she's ever met. "Inside. He volunteers to go in every so often to clear the summonses and the fines. Sure you couldn't be paying those. So 'twas bad timing but if you have to go you have to go."

Mam hasn't a clue what this conversation is about. I know by the way she's smiling at Vonnie and nodding at her.

"So he's in jail?" I say.

Vonnie doesn't answer me. Stirs two spoons of sugar into her tea and continues talking to Mam. "Take your time in town now and don't be worried about the child – we're only thrilled to be minding him. Is he ready?"

"He's asleep in his buggy in the living room. I've made extra bottles and there's a change of clothes in his baby bag." Fiona rushes off to sort out Harvey but I know she's avoiding Mam's questioning, shocked face.

Vonnie finishes her tea and leaves with Harvey. Mam calls Fiona into the kitchen. "Jail?" she says.

"It's not what you think, Mam," says Fiona.

I snort – I can't help it. Fiona throws me a filthy look.

"So he's just helping out there, is he? Work experience, something like that?" I say.

"Oh, shut up, Maeve, making a big deal about nothing," says Fiona.

I laugh this time. "No, it's not a big deal – going to jail is a little holiday, a break from routine . . ."

"You're a fucking bitch, Maeve," she screams, her eyes full of tears. "Everybody does it – instead of paying your parking fines you go in for a few days, do the time and you save money. You're twisting it into something completely different, Miss fucking Perfect." She has the chin out now and the hand on the hip.

"So it's just a little recession-busting trick, is that it? Oh, that's different and sure if everybody's doing it then it's fine. Now, do you mean everybody in Limerick or just everybody in Scumbag Land?"

"Stop it, Maeve. Leave her alone," says Mam.

"Her boyfriend's in jail and she thinks it's cool and you're telling me to stop it? I just can't win, can I?"

Fiona storms out of the kitchen, nearly taking the door off the hinges.

"Now look what you did," says Mam.

"Yeah, right," I say, and leave.

My mood gets worse when Mark arrives. He's standing there smiling at me, a large wicker picnic basket at his feet. "Did you carry that all the way from your house?" I ask.

"Don't be silly, Maevis Ravis – I got a taxi."

"So, what are we doing? I'd ask you to come in only we're all fighting with each other and I wouldn't like you to get caught in the crossfire."

"No problem. What's the news?" He grins at me and my heart does a little drum roll in my chest.

"Oh, stop. I told you about Big and the cherry-picker – well, now he's in jail and everybody thinks it's normal, like he's gone to Kilkee for the weekend."

"Whoa, Maeve, jail? For, like, what? For the cherry-picker Juliet's-balcony thing?"

"You're joking, Mark. Nope, Big isn't gone to jail because he deserves it, he's gone in to save a few bob on traffic fines. It's one of his innovative solutions to a tight budget."

Mark guffaws.

"I fail to see the funny side."

"Oh, come on, Maeve. It's funny. Hilarious, in fact. So he goes in for a few days to clear his fines. It's genius."

He's beginning to annoy me.

"Mark, it's very easy to find this funny if you're living outside it. You're doing the typical rich-boy thing now – look how funny and endearing the scumbags are when you don't have to live with them or the consequences of their actions."

"Chill, Maeve. I don't need a Miriam O'Callaghan lecture." Mark leans against the porch, one foot resting on the picnic basket.

There's an awkward silence that I end. "How are we going to carry that yoke?" I ask, toeing the basket.

He takes out his phone and speed-dials a number. "This way."

And then Cian is coming out the door, his face cross. He nods quickly at both of us and heads to Mam's car.

Mark lifts one side of the picnic basket. "Take the other handle and help, for fuck sake."

I do as I'm told, mainly because I'm too stunned to do anything else. "He's not coming, is he?" I say, as we lift the basket into the boot of the car. "Jesus, this weighs a ton – what's in it? A dead body?"

"He's our driver for the day." Mark climbs into the back seat and I follow him. I couldn't bear to sit in the front with Cian. Particularly when he's in such a bad mood.

"This is not going to be fun," I whisper to Mark.

He holds my hand. "Yes, it is. I promise."

I can almost feel his tongue as he speaks and a delicious thrill runs through me. Maybe it is going to be fun after all.

We go to the Cliffs of Moher. It's a beautiful still October day and we pass the small knots of tourists and walk up about a million steps to the tower. Cian's trailing behind and I've given up making monosyllabic conversation with him. The cliffs are spectacular. "Wow, I'd love to see them when there's nobody else here. They're so cool."

Mark hops over a low wall and stands near the cliff edge, pretending to fall in.

"You're such a fool," I say.

He leaps back over the wall and runs on ahead. I'm out of breath by the time I catch up with him.

"Look at this Maeve," he says, pointing to a sign on a low wall. It's an ad for the Samaritans.

"I read all about this, Mark. It's a suicide black spot. They come here in droves to top themselves."

"Hardly in droves, Maevis Ravis."

"No, seriously. And the weird thing is that in the Second World War when there was a twenty-four-hour guard here – you know, guarding the coastline – there wasn't one suicide."

"Trust Maeve to have all the facts and figures." Mark grins at me, grabs my hand and we start running back down the steps, a mile a minute. We find Cian at the bottom, listening to an old man busking. He's playing the tin whistle and it's a lonely, sad sound in the midst of the happy camera-clicking tourists. I root in my pocket for a euro and drop it into his cardboard container. We go back to the car to collect the picnic basket and then we set off along the cliff edge away from the main attraction. Cian and Mark carry the basket between them and after a while Mark signals us to stop. "Turn back and look," he says.

We turn and see the cliffs but from the reverse. Rising out of the water, guarded by the sea stacks, the tourists like tiny insects swarming around at the top.

Mark opens the picnic basket. "Here, give me a hand laying out the stuff."

I go to help but Cian gives Mark a deadly look and watches us, his hands in his trousers pockets.

I roll my eyes at Mark and he does the same back. Then a tiny giggle escapes from me and then one from Mark, and before we know it the two of us are cracking up, laughing so hard that tears are streaming down my face and Mark has dropped the plastic plates and forks.

"Fuck sake," says Cian, and stomps off down the narrow winding cliff path.

"What's up with him?" I ask, but that just makes us laugh more. We finally get the plaid rug laid out and Mark pops a bottle of champagne. He even has glasses, plastic, but glasses all the same. And the nicest food I ever saw. As he lays it all out I'm stunned at the spread in front of us.

I look at him with narrowed eyes.

He laughs. "Katya."

"I knew it. It's fabulous. I don't know what to have."

Mark piles a plate for me. A taste of everything. Homemade bread, coleslaw, potato salad. Thick slices of ham, cold spicy sausage. We eat in silence, savouring the food and the surroundings.

"Being outdoors makes everything taste nicer," I say. "There'll be none left for Cian."

Mark shrugs. "That's what he gets for being in a strop."

I shiver a little as the sea wind picks up.

"Are you cold? Hang on a sec." He clears the food from the rug and wraps it around me, sitting behind me, with his arms around me. Heaven. We sit like that for a while and the sun even makes an attempt to come out. I feel warm and comfortable and safe. Mark rests his chin on top of my head and we're there like that for ages.

"I'm sorry about earlier," Mark says eventually.

"Why? What did you do?"

"I laughed about Big and prison, and you're absolutely right, Maeve. It's not funny when you're in the situation."

"That's OK. Don't worry about it."

"No. What you said made me think about it – you know, the whole situation with Fiona and Harvey and all – and do you know something?"

"What?"

"I think you should butt out. Me too. I think both of us should stop trying to watch Fiona around the clock. We should just let it play out. Maybe your mother is right." He's playing with my hair as he speaks, picking up strands, stroking them, picking up some more.

"She's not your sister. If she was you'd feel different. You'd want to help her. Especially if she'd asked you to."

He kneads my shoulders gently with his hands. Where did he learn to do things like that? "I see your point. But Fiona's going to go back to him. The only thing that's stopping her at the moment is your disapproval."

I turn to face him, almost toppling him over in the process. "You see, that's the problem. Mam doesn't disapprove and Cian doesn't, so I have to do it."

"No, you don't. You're a kid. You might think you're grown-up and clever and all that, but you're a kid. Too young to drink, too young to drive . . ."

"That makes two of us."

He grins at me. "*Touché*, Maevis."

Our faces are almost touching and my hand sneaks up, like it has a mind of its own, and I touch his lips lightly with my fingers. He closes his eyes. I lean forward and I'm just about to kiss him, to bloody well take the initiative once and for all, when I hear a little cough above me. We jump apart and Cian is there. "Sorry, am I interrupting something?" He stares at the two of us, standing over us, arms folded, like a cross teacher.

I'm sick of him. "What in the name of God is wrong with you today, Cian? What exactly is your problem?" He gives me a dagger look and begins to fill a plate with food. He shakes the empty champagne bottle and glares at me again, as if I'm solely responsible for drinking the lot. I glare back, hating him for coming, for arriving back just at the wrong moment, for ruining the day with his sulky, moody head. "Why the fuck did you come at all, if you were intent on spoiling the day out? You're a selfish bastard, Cian. A spoiled little shit."

Mark's shaking his head at me, but I'm on a roll now and I couldn't stop if you paid me. "You're behaving like a two-year-old. And I'm sick of it. I hate you."

The second I say the hate-you bit I know I don't mean it. I put my hand to my mouth, like I'm trying to take back the words. Cian's crying. He's sitting cross-legged, a plate of food on his lap, and tears dropping onto the coleslaw and sliced ham. "Jesus, Ciany, what's up?"

Mark's gone. I can see his retreating back as he ambles down the cliff path.

"What's wrong? Tell me."

He wipes his eyes with the sleeve of his coat.

"Come on, Cian, I don't want to play Twenty Questions with you. Is it college?"

He shrugs.

"Is it a girl? That's it, isn't it? You're in love."

He shrugs again but looks at me this time and I know I'm right when I see his eyes. "Cian, it can't be that bad. Reason it out. I always think that if you can work the stuff out – you know, in a logical cause-and-effect manner – then it's way easier to live with."

"That's not true."

I smile at him. At least he's speaking now. "Yes, it is. There's an explanation for everything. You should know, you're studying physics. Who is she anyway?"

He picks at his coleslaw with a plastic fork. "Just someone. It's complicated."

"Talk to her. Try to work it out."

"What age are you, Maeve?"

"Sixteen."

"So how many times have you been in love? How many times have you been so attracted to someone that it consumes you completely to the extent that you can't eat or sleep or study or live?"

His face is furious as he speaks and I'm scared of him. "I

hope that never happens to me, Cian. In fact, I guarantee it won't because I won't let it."

He bursts out laughing. "Typical Maeve. You're so intelligent you can control the world."

"I can control sentiment and bullshit. I can control this whole dumb idea of romantic love. Just look at Fiona – 'I love Big, I can't help it.' It's all bullshit."

I realise I'm shouting and Cian looks away. We sit in silence for a while.

"I'm leaving college."

"What?"

"I'm leaving college. I hate my course, I hate Cork, so I'm going to leave. I'm looking for a job in Limerick first."

"Mam'll go mad, Cian. You can't do that."

"I have to do it. I hate it down there."

"Yeah, but you'll lose the grant for next year, you'll have to pay fees and—"

"So what? I'll work this year and have a think about what I want to do. Maybe I won't go back to college at all. Maybe I'll just get a job in River Island with a twenty-five per cent discount on my clothes. Maybe I'll go on the dole and become a bum. The possibilities are endless." He grins at me for the first time today.

He doesn't know it but I'm fuming. I'm more upset about this than anything else he's said. Another fucking eejit in the family, throwing away his life. "It's because of her, isn't it?"

He doesn't look at me.

"It's because she's in Limerick and you're throwing everything away to be near her. That's so stupid, Cian. You'll probably end up hating her in a few months and you'll have fucked up your whole life."

126

"Maeve, I'm not you. My studies aren't my life." He stands up and brushes crumbs from his trousers.

We stop in Lahinch for chips on the way home. My legs ache from all the walking, and Cian's sulking seems to be contagious because now I'm the one who's silent and moody. I know in my heart that what Cian said about my studies being my life is a load of horse-shit. That he said it to justify in some way the silly thing he's about to do with his own life. Living for the moment. *Carpe diem*. Bullshit. Bullshit. Bullshit. We get chips from Enzo's takeaway and sit on the prom wall, watching surfers brave the cold October sea. The chips are warm in my hands, the vinegary smell making me hungry.

"Hey, Maeve, remember the day Dad walked into the sea here?" Cian nudges me and points down the beach. "Right over there. Stupid bastard – freaking us all out like that."

"How do you mean, walked into the sea?" Mark asks, as he lowers a fat, greasy chip into his mouth.

"Look at the new lifeguards' hut – it certainly isn't a hut now," I say, attempting to change the subject.

"He was at the edge of the water with Maeve, fully dressed, and he took her hand and walked into the sea, then let her go and kept walking until he was gone."

Mark bends forward on the wall, peering around Cian so that he can see me.

"That's weird, Maeve. What happened?"

"I was glad. I wanted him to keep going." Cian's staring at the sea as he says this.

"That's horrible, Cian," I say.

"It's the truth. He gave me a hard time that day – don't you

127

remember, Maeve? He made Mam cry before we even left Limerick."

"Stop inventing stuff. I was there too and I don't remember that."

"Course you don't. You only remember what you want to about Dad, Maeve."

"Isn't that true of everybody? Selective memory – we all suffer from it. Anyway, time to go – I'm tired." I jump off the wall, wiping my greasy hands on a paper napkin and stuffing it into my pocket.

"If I was to think of one word to describe him it would be 'bully'." Cian looks at me, waiting for my reaction. I ignore him. He turns to Mark. "A bully of the worst kind. An intellectual bully."

"Shut up, Cian, you don't know what you're talking about." My voice is shaking.

Cian smirks at me. "I think I do, Maeve. You know I do."

"Oh, please, Cian. Grow up. What would you know anyway – a guy who gives up his studies, his career, to chase some girl like a lovesick puppy?"

I can see the hurt in his face as my words hit home. And again I regret them and want to take them back. Mark looks questioningly at Cian, waiting for him to explain.

"Thanks, Maeve," says Cian, and walks towards the car.

"Wait a sec," I say, as I run after him. "I'm sorry. I was way out of line there, I'm sorry, Cian, really I am."

He doesn't answer me, just opens the car door and climbs in, staring straight ahead.

I get into the back and try again. "Look, I was upset over what you said about Dad and I lashed out at you and—"

"Rationalising it won't take away the hurt, Maeve."

128

"I'm sorry. What more can I say?"

Cian slips a CD into the player and Fionn Regan's plaintive lyrics fill the car. Mark gets into the back beside me. A tear escapes my eye, running down my cheek, but only one. I swallow the rest, gulping so that the lump in my throat disappears. Mark sneaks his hand into mine, like he knows I'm crying and I lay my head on his shoulder as Fionn's soft voice caresses me to sleep.

> *The girl who collects shells has gone back to the*
> * coast*
> *Hearing voices in car parks*
> *Pull a diamond from your sleeve*
>
> *Hey Badger*
> *You're punched out*
> *Your mouth is around an aerosol can*
> *They want you to sink but you stood up*
> * and swam . . .*

"Hey, Maevis, wake up. We're back in Stab City."

I open my eyes, and I'm looking up at Mark's face. My head is on his lap.

"Jesus, what time is it?" I sit up and rub my eyes, trying to focus. Cian is rigid in the front seat. I can feel the anger and tension held in his body, like tight muscles.

"Hey, Maevis, come on home with me. I'll get you a taxi later on. We can watch a movie." Mark smiles at me beseechingly, but there's absolutely no contest. I can't think of anything else I'd rather do. And the sooner I get away from my brother the better.

"I'd love to," I say, as I get out of the car. It's night now and drizzling lightly. I shiver on the pavement while Mark gets the hamper out of the boot. Cian speeds off immediately, Mam's poor old Toyota screeching with the effort.

Mark looks at me. "Fuck him – let's have some fun."

"Yes! I'm choosing the movie cos you'll force me to watch some French shit otherwise."

Mark keys in the code on the gates, and as they slowly open we carry the picnic basket between us up the long, tree-lined drive.

"Your French, Maeve, is flawless so what's your problem if you have to watch it in French?"

"Dark, meaningful films, with loads and loads of dial-ogue. I'm too tired."

"OK, you choose – see what a lovely reasonable person I am?"

We're halfway up the drive. The rain is heavier now, sheeting down as the wind picks up. It feels nice on my skin. "I'm just glad you didn't invite him to come – I couldn't bear him through a whole movie. He seems to have a lot of stuff going on. Did he tell you?"

Mark shakes his head. He's lying. But why?

"That's really strange – the front door's wide open . . ." Mark drops the picnic basket and dashes into the house. I follow, leaving the basket sitting on the step.

The smell is the first thing I notice. The smell of excrement. The smell of shit. And then I see it. Daubed across the pale cream wall in the kitchen.

Mind your busness.

Spelt incorrectly and written in shit but still as clear as day.

Nine

I want to be sick. It hits me in waves as the smell permeates through every pore in my body. I'm shaking uncontrollably and my legs seem to be buckling, like I'm too heavy or they're made of liquid. I lean against the black granite island in the middle of the kitchen, my eyes closed and my body swaying from the effort of trying not to be sick. *Oh, God, what have I done what have I done?* The mantra starts in my brain.

I open my eyes but the havoc is still all around me. The writing on the wall, the trashed kitchen. Presses emptied, glasses broken. Plates, bottles, photographs. But the smell is the worst thing. The smell and the colour of shit and the idea that somebody could invade your home to that extent. Another wave of nausea comes and I close my eyes again and shout weakly for Mark.

I steady myself and try to calm down. I take deep breaths, like Mr Hynes taught me before my Junior Cert English exam. It's beginning to work. This mightn't be what I think at all. It might be just a random burglary. The shaking stops and my legs feel like they're mine again. I walk slowly from the kitchen. I can hear a TV in the study and *The X Factor* signature tune draws me to it. The door is open and I go in. Simon Cowell is on the plasma screen – a close-up shot of him talking. He makes me feel safe in some strange way and there's no damage in here. No awful smell. And then I hear it. Behind the large black leather sofa. Tiny whimpers like a small hurt animal's.

My heart belts in my chest as I walk around the long sofa. Katya's sitting on the floor in Mark's arms. He looks up as I approach, his eyes dark with sadness.

"No, no, no." I say. "Please no. Please."

Simon Cowell's voice drones on, oblivious to the horrible scene unfolding here. "Is she . . . was she . . . is she hurt?"

Mark keeps staring at me. Katya keeps making the tiny animal sound. Simon Cowell keeps talking. Nobody needs to say it out loud.

I kneel down next to Katya and hold her hand. It's all I can think of to do.

"Have you called the guards? I can do it."

"No police . . . please . . . no police . . . You make promise of no police, Mark . . ." Katya's voice cracks with fear.

I look at Mark for instruction but he shakes his head. "I'm sorry, Mark."

Another shake of his head.

Somebody on the TV is singing a very bad version of Coldplay's "Yellow". I want to do something to help, call the guards, make tea, clean up. Anything except sit here listening to Katya's whimpering.

Eventually she stops crying. She wipes her eyes and gets to her feet. "I clean it," she says.

Mark jumps up. "No, you don't, Katya. Why don't you go upstairs and have a shower?"

Katya nods at him and, straightening her top, walks slowly out of the room, turning off the TV on her way.

"Mark . . ."

"There's nothing to say, Maeve. It's not your fault." He gets up and walks out to the kitchen, with me trotting after him. He takes a bucket from under the sink and fills it with hot water. Then he pours in disinfectant, the smell mingling with the stench of the shit. He roots in the press again, finds a small brush and begins to scrub the writing off the wall.

"Don't do that – the cops will want to see it. You are calling the cops, Mark, aren't you?"

He keeps scrubbing and scrubbing, the letters disappearing one after another.

"We have to call the guards – I mean, if Katya was . . . you know . . . was . . ."

He stops scrubbing and turns to me, eyes blazing. "Raped. Say it, Maeve – raped. If Katya was raped."

Tears sting my eyes and slip down my face.

He turns back to his cleaning, lifting paint from the wall he's scrubbing so hard.

"I'm sorry, Mark, I got you into this – but we need to get the guards—"

"We need to do what they told Katya to do. We need to pretend it never happened. We need to mind our own business and pretend this never happened."

"We can't do that."

"That's exactly what we're going to do, Maeve. Because if we don't they'll hurt us again. They'll get Katya or my parents or—"

"It's my fault. Big ordered this to scare us. To scare me. He couldn't hurt me directly because of Fiona so he does this. Mark, I'm so sorry I dragged you into all of this."

"You didn't. You said something to me this morning, Maeve, about being outside the situation – remember? Well, I'm in it now and I don't like it and I never want to be in it again."

"So call the guards."

"For fuck sake, will you stop saying that? Will you stop being so stupid?" Mark shouts, making me jump.

"I only . . . I want to do the right thing."

His eyes are on fire now and he's scaring me, this angry, bitter Mark I've never seen before.

"I think Katya's upset and she might want to press charges when she—"

"Fucking hell, Maeve. Don't you get it? She's deeply religious. She says she wasn't raped and if she was – which is my guess – she'll deny it anyway. The shame is too great for her."

"You think she was?"

"She pressed the stupid Eircom panic-button thing and when the phone rang they ran off – didn't even bother to rob the place, just ran off."

"Cowardly bastards. You can't let them away with it, Mark, you can't!"

"Watch me. I know when I'm in over my head and you need to learn that too. Let Fiona sink or swim. You can't take on these people."

Tears are running down my face but I don't feel like I'm crying. "Will I let Harvey sink or swim, Mark? Will I let Harvey down too?"

He pats his shirt pocket for his cigarettes and lights one.

His hand shakes as he takes a long, deep draw from the fag. "There's nothing you can do about it."

"There has to be. There is – I know there is. I just have to think of it. I have to think of something really clever – I have to be cleverer than him."

"Maeve, learn from this. You'll cause more hurt than you'll ever fix."

I search for something to wipe my face and find a box of tissues on the windowsill. I take one, dry my tears and blow my nose.

"Why didn't the guards come?" I say, still swabbing my running nose.

"Because we didn't call them maybe?"

"No, Mark. Why didn't they come when she pressed the panic-button thing?"

"They ring first apparently to make sure it's a genuine call. So as the scum were running away Katya took the call and told them all was well. Imagine that."

"Jesus."

Mark flicks his cigarette end into the sink. "I want to get this cleaned before she comes back down."

"I'll help. Are there rubber gloves anywhere?"

Mark continues the scrubbing and I start picking through all the broken glass and cups and plates strewn all over the kitchen. And it feels good to get stuck into something physical. To take out my anger and frustration on inanimate objects. When it's all finally swept away I wash the kitchen floor, scrubbing on my hands and knees so every corner is disinfected. Mark has finished the wall and it looks perfect except for flaking paint here and there. And the horrible insidious smell is finally gone.

Katya doesn't come back downstairs. Mark brings a sandwich and tea up to her room. I'm hoping he'll ask me to stay the night because if I see Fiona I'm liable to punch her in the mouth, to say and do things I never thought I was capable of. The anger inside me is white hot, small and rock hard. Diamond anger.

But when Mark comes downstairs I know from looking at him that he wants me to go home. That his subconscious is telling him to get away from me. That I caused all of this. "I'm tired, Maeve. I'm going to hit the sack. I'll call a cab for you."

I nod. We stand at the front door, waiting to buzz in the taxi, and for the first time ever there's an awkward silence between us.

"How is she?" I ask, and the minute I say it I'm sorry. Like I'm reinforcing the thing between us.

"She's OK. Worried about the kitchen. I told her we cleaned it up. She's worried about Mam and Dad but I told her they'll never even know."

The taxi arrives and pulls up noisily on the gravel drive. I look at Mark, waiting for a kiss, a hug, some show of affection. He gives me a wink and turns to walk inside. I touch his shoulder with my hand and when he turns around I hug him tightly. His body is stiff and unyielding in my arms. He watches while I climb into the cab, then waves at me as the taxi pulls away. I'm bawling my eyes out before we even reach the gates.

I fight the urge to stop at Big's house and scream at his mother or sister or anyone related to him. The taxi driver is watching me in his rear-view mirror. He's asked me a few times if everything's all right and I bawled that everything was fine, thanks very much. My anger is full blown by the time I get home.

Mam and Cian are in the kitchen. I can hear Mam's voice, animated and non-stop – a sure sign the book club was on. I stand outside the kitchen door trying to do Mr Hynes's deep breathing for the second time in one night and then I march in, like a bat out of hell. Mam looks shocked when she sees me.

"Maeve, what in the name of God happened to you? Is everything OK?" She jumps to her feet, her eyes glassy and slightly unfocused.

"Everything is wonderful. Mark's house was broken into by Big and they shat in it and then wrote on the walls with the shit and scared the life out of the housekeeper but apart from that everything's just A-OK"

"Maeve, what are you talking about?" She's swaying slightly on her feet and I don't know if it's the shock of what I've just told her or the alcohol.

"Where's Fiona?" I look at Cian, thinking he might be a little more with it than Mam.

"She's gone to Carrie's for a girls' night – I'm minding Harvey. Where's Mark now? Is he OK?" Cian's voice is full of concern.

"He seems to be. We tidied up the place and . . ." Tears start again and my whole body shakes.

"It can't be. Big would never do that. He doesn't even know Mark," says Mam, almost smiling as she delivers this piece of information.

"Did ye call the guards? Was anybody hurt?" Cian says. I look at him and I know he knows the answer without me saying a word. "Fucking hell," he says.

Then Mam's face lights up like somebody flipped on a switch. "It can't be true. Big's in jail," she announces.

"Mam, please – less of the Chardonnay logic."

She stiffens, as if holding herself tightly will make her less drunk. "It makes sense to me."

I hear a key in the front door and my heart begins to thump – so loudly I can't even hear what Mam's saying. And then Fiona comes in, her blonde ponytail swinging.

She stops as she sees my tear-streaked face. I have an incredible urge to catch her by the hair and swing her around the kitchen. Instead I smile sweetly at her.

"Your boyfriend surpassed himself tonight. He got his cowardly little henchmen to break into my friend's house." My voice is icy calm and I notice that I'm doing Mr Hynes's breathing but a mental version of it.

"What are you talking about?" Fiona's jaw is jutting and the hand is on the hip. Already on the defensive.

I wonder if she knew something like this was going to happen. That Big was going to get me off their case and had said as much to her. "You heard me, Fiona, and I think you knew something about this before you came in that door."

Fiona laughs, but I can hear a nervous edge. "Listen to her, Mam – she's losing the plot. 'I don't know what you're talking about.'" She's grinning at me now, hand still on hip.

My mental breathing is failing to control my temper. Cian looks ready to run out the door. "Your scumbag boyfriend and his thug friends terrified a poor woman tonight. They destroyed Mark's house, they—"

"What are you on about? Big's in jail – tell her to stop, Mam. She's making up lies so that everyone will think Big's a scumbag."

I burst out laughing now. "We know that already. What we don't know is just how big a scumbag he is, if you'll excuse the pun. I know he was behind it."

"You know nothing. He wasn't even here."

"That didn't stop him, you dumb bitch."

"Maeve, don't speak to your sister like that."

"Yes, I will. She doesn't even have to try – she's just naturally dumb, born dumb, the thickest, dumbest fool I ever met."

Fiona launches herself at me and finally I get to do what I've been waiting all night for. I don't even see her face as I start punching and scraping and pulling, just white light like a snapshot of the tornado of fury inside me.

I don't realise I'm screaming until Cian pulls me off her and drags me out of the kitchen. I sob in his arms, my voice hoarse. I can hear Mam consoling Fiona. And then Harvey starts to cry upstairs and I go to run up to him. Fiona barrels out of the kitchen and launches herself at me as I climb the stairs. She drags me back by my hair, screaming and spitting into my face.

"Leave him alone, you fucking bitch. Don't ever go fucking near my child again, do you hear me? Don't fucking touch him!"

Cian tears her off me and she pounds upstairs to Harvey. I sit in a heap at the bottom of the stairs, tears streaming down my face. I can taste salt blood in my mouth or maybe it's tears. My head is sore where she pulled my hair, and my heart is pounding so hard I think it's going to burst. Cian lifts me up and carries me into the kitchen.

Mam is fanning herself with a magazine. "Cian, what am I going to do with the two of them? Thank God you were here

139

tonight. Maeve, you know better than to provoke your sister like that."

"Mam, get real. She behaved like an absolute knacker there and I'm to blame? No wonder she's with that pig of a boyfriend and you didn't—"

Mam throws the magazine down on the table. "I'm not listening to this shit again, Maeve. Fiona's vulnerable, young—"

"I'm a year younger."

Mam gives me her glare. "You don't have a baby and—"

"Oh, for fuck sake – did you ever think she has a baby because of what she's been allowed to get away with?" Now I have my hand on my hip and the adrenalin is kicking right back in again.

"Oh, blame me and I trying to do my best for you lot. Out working all day and then facing this tension all the time. And do you know something, Maeve? It's only in the house when you're here."

I step back from her like she's slapped me. I'd have preferred it if she had. A nice hard slap has only one interpretation. More tears sting my eyes, but I squeeze them back. I'll be damned if I'll let her make me cry.

"That's unfair, Mam. That's lousy on Maeve." Cian is surpassing himself tonight in the big-brother stakes. He's never done that before, stuck up for me. My heart stops pumping and fills with something else.

Mam looks at him like he somehow grew another head in the last five minutes.

"Maeve's right, Mam. She's right about Fiona. You make allowances for her because she isn't the cleverest and you only make it all worse in the end."

"So you're against me now too, Cian? I'm there killing

myself, paying for college, school, food and this is how you thank me?"

"That's a separate issue, Mam. I'm just saying that Maeve has a point." He goes and gets the first-aid kit from the press and makes me sit on the chair. Then he starts to clean my face with damp cotton wool, turning the soft balls pink with the blood. Mam watches for a minute then stalks out of the door. I can hear her climbing the stairs and then the low murmur of voices as she and Fiona talk.

"You OK?" Cian asks, as he swabs my lip with disinfectant.

"Ouch – you'll never be a doctor."

He laughs. "True. Anyway, for what it's worth, you're trying to do the right thing, Maeve – I know that."

My eyes fill with tears for the millionth time tonight. They spill out and down my newly cleaned face. "So why don't you try to talk to Mam? Or Fiona, for that matter?"

He holds my face in his hands searching for more cuts. "Because I'm a horrible cynic. We can talk until the cows come home but Mam will never change – she'll never do the hard thing." He pats my tears with a clean cotton-wool ball.

"What do you mean, Mam will never do the hard thing?"

He shrugs. "So, how's Mark? Is he, like . . . you know . . . Is he upset?"

I nod. I can't speak because Cian's trying to shove a wad of cotton wool into my mouth.

"There, you're as good as new."

"Thanks, Cian."

"You're welcome. Now, I'm sneaking out for a while so I have the car – just in case Mam wakes up from a wine fog and wonders where it's gone."

I stand up, my legs shaky. "Where are you going?"

He grins. "Nosy parker."

"It's your wan, isn't it? The girl you told me about today."

He tips my nose with his finger. "My God, you really are nosy, Maeve. Go to bed – you must be shattered." Then he does a surprising thing. He takes me in his arms and gives me a big man-hug, and I can smell Dad and Lynx and hair gel – a Cian–Dad hybrid. The tears come again. Jesus, will they ever stop? I sob now and he stands still, holding me so tight I can barely breathe, but it's the best kind of tight in the world.

"It'll be OK, Maeve, you'll see. It'll be grand and soon you'll be off to college studying medicine and you'll be the best, I know you will." He's murmuring into my ear, exactly the way Dad used to, and I wonder does he know that he's so like him in some ways.

"What if she means it? What will I do, Ciany, if she means it about Harvey? If she won't let me touch him or mind him or . . ."

He pulls away and looks at me. "That won't happen, Maeve. You know what Fiona's like. She never holds a grudge. She'll want to be friends, especially with you."

"Especially with me? She hates my guts – I think she always has."

"Do you know something? For such a clever girl you can get things so wrong sometimes." He smiles at me. "Off to bed. We'll talk in the morning." He picks up the car keys from the table beside him.

"Thanks, Cian. Thanks for tonight."

"Don't mention it."

I climb the stairs suddenly weary.

142

"Hey, Maeve," Cian whispers loudly, from the open front door.

"What?"

"Can we have a moratorium on the fist-fighting?"

I smile to myself in the dark hallway. I stand outside Fiona's door listening for Harvey sounds. The new gurgly laughing ones he's started to make recently. Chuckling away to himself in his cot. I'd love to sneak him into my bed but I'm not that stupid. I know Fiona'd kill me. So I climb into bed alone, waiting for sleep to come. It doesn't for a very long time. Everything else pays a visit instead. The cliffs, Cian and his split personality, Mark. The wonderful picnic that Katya had packed. Katya on the floor like a small hurt animal, that smell in my hair and my clothes and my very pores. And Fiona. Me and Fiona fighting like . . . well, like scumbags. And the insane adrenalin rush from solving things with your fists. And how you could get to like it. And how, really, there's a little bit of scumbag in all of us. If we let it.

Ten

A fucking B3 in my English paper. I have to look at it twice before I actually believe it. And then I think maybe Mr Hynes has missed something, totted up my marks wrong. I go up to him after class and plonk the paper down in front of him. "A B3?"

"Hello, Maeve, how are you?"

"This is bullshit. You're marking me twice as hard as anyone else. Mark got an A2 for a pile of shit—"

He holds up his hand to stop me talking. It doesn't work.

"—and he did no research, none at all. Diddly squat, as he says himself. And look at my bibliography – Mark says he doesn't even know how to spell 'bibliography', let alone compose one and . . ."

Mr Hynes smiles at me.

"What's so funny?" I say, chest out in Fiona fashion.

"The bibliography part. It's funny."

"Why?" I glare at him.

"Because, Maeve, it was a creative-writing exercise. You didn't need to research it. Didn't need a bibliography."

"Everything needs a bibliography. A framework to show how it came to be—"

He holds up his hand again to stop me talking. Some hope of that.

"—and Mark writes a pile of rubbish off the top of his head, fifteen minutes he spent doing it, so that's creative writing? Throwing down any old crap – no references, no nothing?"

"OK. One question, Maeve. Did you try the writing exercise we talked about?"

He's looking straight at me, like he can see into my brain. I go bright red. I can feel the warmth of it surging right to the top of my head.

"You did, didn't you?"

I do a kind of half-shrug thing. My face is on fire.

"Bring it in and I'll have a read. I'm telling you, this will really help your writing. I'm delighted you wrote. The next step is to let somebody read it." He smiles at me, his head tilted to one side like he's just asked a question.

I do another half-shrug thing.

"So, tomorrow?"

"Am . . . well . . . am . . . my printer is broken and I need to look at the stuff and fix it and . . ."

"The whole point, Maeve, is that you don't look at it. You don't fix it. Don't make a big deal about it. Just bring it in, OK?" He shuffles papers on his desk and beams a goodbye smile at me. He bends down to get his briefcase and starts to put books and pens and notes away.

I stand there watching him.

"OK, Maeve, what is it?" He lifts his briefcase from the desk, like he's gauging the weight of it.

"I can't let you read it. It's rubbish."

"I'll decide that."

"And I'd die if anybody saw it. I'd die in agony."

He smiles at me. "No, you wouldn't." He looks at his watch. "I've got to go – I've an appointment with a golf course."

"No problem."

He walks out, then stops at the door, turns and points at me. "I've got an idea."

"Oh?"

"There's a competition, a creative-writing competition, coming up soon. How about you submit something? I won't read it if you don't want me to and you'll be just another anonymous contestant. I'll get some of the others in class to submit too." He winks at me, like he's just solved a Middle Eastern crisis.

I nod agreement and he whistles as he leaves. I sit down at a desk in the silent twilit classroom. A bird sings outside and a lone basketball player is throwing hoops, the rhythmic thud of the ball mesmerising and soothing. The whiteboard has bits of words left on it after somebody's half-hearted attempt at cleaning it. I think about what Mr Hynes just said. About the competition. I think about my drivel-writing and what I could do to bring it up to scratch. Give it a beginning, a middle and an end. Make it into a short story. Put a short-story structure on it. That shouldn't be too difficult. I can research short-story structure. I smile at the whiteboard. Smile because I'm thrilled about the competition. And then a thought comes to me that makes me smile even more. All the drivel-writing needed was a focus. And now I have it. But, logically, that makes me right and Mr Hynes wrong about writing. I know it does, and I'll argue that with him when I straighten it out in my head.

I arrive home full of enthusiasm. Mam and Linda are in the living room with a new set of wheelie suitcases.

"Maeve, there you are. You take the smallest one and Fiona can take the big one because she has Harvey's things."

Linda smiles at me, and bats her too-long eyelashes. Are they false? They must be. I don't ever remember her having curly lashes like that.

"Excited?" she asks.

For a few seconds I think she's talking about the competition and I'm just about to tell her how excited I am and all the plans I have, then put two and two together. Suitcases. Holiday. Lanzarote. Excited is the wrong word. "Yes, can't wait," I lie, and dash upstairs to my computer. I can't resist a peek in at Harvey, though. I open his door really quietly, in case Fiona's there. She's still mad at me and barring me from touching him, but I just wait usually until she's out and then I take my fill of him, compensating for the missed hours. He's in bed with her and they're both asleep, him propped into the crook of her arm, a tiny little smile on his face. His skin is golden – he has Big's sallowness, but a healthier, sunnier version of it. Almost Spanish compared with his father's yellow-tinged skin. Fiona opens her eyes and smiles first, like she's glad to see me, and then I can see it dawning in her face that she's actually not talking to me.

"Get out of my room," she whispers, her voice venom and ice.

I close the door, go into mine and boot up the computer. My old friend the computer. Never spits venom at me. Only ever helps me. I Google "short-story structure" and, sure enough, there it is in front of me. Reams and reams of information. I settle down for a long session, delighted with the task in hand.

After dinner I open up my drivel-writing folder, armed now with my newly acquired information and eager to try it out. I stare at the blank page, waiting for the usual to happen. For the drivel-writing to take over and dictate literally until words swarm the pages, almost too many to keep up with. Nothing happens. I close my eyes and open them, but the pristine screen is still blank. It's gone. The drivel-writing thing won't work any more. Just when I bloody well needed it to. I sit there in front of the blank screen for God only knows how long but, no matter how much I will myself to write, nothing happens.

Mark's coming to Lanzarote. He's not staying with us, he'll be with his uncle who has an apartment in the old town. Cian's able to tell me this at breakfast. Mark forgot to mention it all week in school. Cian cops I'm mad that my best friend hasn't seen fit to tell me and jumps in straight away to defend him. All lies, of course.

"He only decided last night, very late last night, and we were talking on MSN and he checked the flights and, well, that's it, really. No big deal. He's flying out with us in the morning. He paid a bit more – a lot more – but sure money's no object there . . . Are you all right?"

"Fine. He could have said something, that's all." I butter toast as I answer him, not bothering to look up.

"Well, it was two in the morning, Maeve, and you hardly expected him to ring you up at that time."

"I said OK. Mark's coming. That's great."

Cian looks at me – he must have heard the not-great bit in my voice. Mark's been so distant with me lately – since the night with Katya, if I'm to pinpoint an exact time. And fuck Cian. Of course I'm hurt that somebody I consider my best friend hasn't mentioned the Lanzarote thing to me. I didn't even know he was considering it.

"What's up, Maeve?"

"Nothing. I don't want to go. Mam will be langers all the time and Fiona hates me and Mark . . ." I'm crying and I'm disgusted with myself for it. Disgusted by how easily I cry lately. Yesterday I cried because Harvey smiled at me when I came into the kitchen. I had to run out of the room before Fiona saw the big fat tears running down my cheeks.

"Hey, Maeve, come here." Cian is up and hugging me and the lump in my throat triples in size. "Listen to me. I'm going to talk to Fiona, OK? We'll straighten all of this out before we go. How's that?" He hugs me close and I swallow so the lump goes away.

"It'll be great, Maeve. It'll be a total blast. And Mark's coming too. We'll have a mad laugh, you wait and see." He pulls back and looks at me. "OK? I'll talk to Fiona."

I nod.

"We'll have the best time ever, Maeve."

Mam comes into the kitchen then and asks Cian if he wants a fry. I watch as she fusses over him and all I'm thinking is that Cian thinks he's the cynic but I know I am. Lanzarote is something to dread, not look forward to.

I'm in the middle of accepting reality and actually throwing summer clothes that I hope still fit into a suitcase when the doorbell rings. Everybody's gone out, a kind of last hoorah before the big trip to the Canaries. It's just Harvey and me, back to our usual Saturday routine since Cian kept his word and spoke to Fiona. I run downstairs, afraid the bell will wake him up. He'd been cross earlier, colic apparently, and I was a good hour settling him.

I open the door and Big's in the porch, his foot in the door-jamb so I can't close it on him. "Listen to me—"

"Fuck off, you scumbag, fuck off – I'm still not afraid of you, you bastard – how dare you? Take your foot away from the door, you scum—"

"Shut up a minute and listen to me."

"I've nothing to say to you, only that you're a bastard."

"Yeah, yeah, change the record, love. Listen to me. I know nothin' about what happened in your posh pal's house but if I did then I broke your man's leg – jew get me? Jew get what I'm saying? The cunt's on crutches. That was way wrong, man."

I look at Big, at the ferrety brown eyes Harvey inherited, his Frankie Dettori head, standing there almost pleased with himself. Self-satisfied. "Are you joking me?"

"No. Broke the cunt's leg in three places. He'll be outta action for a long while. They had to put two metal pins in it. That'll fuck him up good in the airport. Them metal pins are a fuckin' curse."

"You're serious, aren't you? You think I should be glad that you crippled some scumbag friend of yours because he raped – yes, raped – a poor girl?"

He flinches at the word "rape". Jumps back like I've slapped his face, but keeps his foot in the door-jamb. "I only done what I thought was right. He fucked up and he got pun-ished. That should never have happened. I'm trying to make it right. That's all." He nods at me and marches away down the path, leaving me speechless at the door.

My body's shaking and I want to do something. I don't

know what – maybe break Big's legs in three places. I watch him climb into his car, listen to him revving the crap out of it before he screeches off down the road, beeping as he passes me. Bastard.

I'm about to close the door when a car pulls up outside the gate. My aunt Linda climbs out, then opens the back door and the two boys stumble onto the footpath, in Spiderman pyjamas and dressing-gowns. What the fuck is going on? Have we all got the flight times wrong? She locks the car and the three of them walk up the path. She's been crying. There's mascara ringed under her eyes and her always perfect foundation is streaked.

"What's wrong? Are you OK?" I ask, as they crowd into the hallway.

"Boys, I want you two to go straight up the stairs and into bed – you can sleep in Maeve's room. That's all right, isn't it, Maeve? And brush your teeth."

The boys look at me. I nod at them and they slowly go upstairs, the smaller one clutching a fat-cat soft toy under his arm.

The minute they're gone Linda bursts into tears, trying to stifle the sound with her beige silk scarf.

"What happened, Linda? Is there something wrong with Tom? What is it?"

She runs into the kitchen, still bawling. I don't know what to think or do. I mean, this is so not my aunt. I wish Mam would come home. Or Fiona. She's better at this kind of shit than I am. Linda's sitting at the kitchen table her head in her hands, sobbing uncontrollably. I eye my phone on the window-sill and consider calling Mam.

"Where – where – oh, what am I – what will I do?" she bawls and hiccups.

"Tell me and we'll see—"

"Where – where is – your mother?"

"Book club. Her phone's switched off."

"I tried to call her – and then I didn't. I didn't know what to do and I just jumped in a cab after I hit him . . ."

"Hit who, Linda?"

"He fell against the kitchen island . . ."

I'm putting two and two together and I'm getting eleven. Panic is rising in my chest, and already in my head I can see the *Prime Time* programme about the woman who killed her husband with a granite island. "Tom's not dead, Linda, is he?"

She stops crying for a second, looks me straight in the eye and then starts wailing again. "A – a single parent . . . me – a single parent?" She hiccups.

Great. That's all we need in the family. A murder.

"How about a nice cup of tea?" I say, and almost laugh at myself. Mrs Doyle, eat your heart out. I fill the kettle for something to do besides thinking about Linda and the murder trial.

She takes out a pack of cigarettes and lights one between tears and hiccups.

I've never seen Linda smoke before. The fag doesn't calm her down, though – if anything, it makes her worse. I'm almost relieved when the doorbell rings although I can't imagine who it could be. Big? Mark? Mr Higgins next door? All of them? I run out to answer it, vowing to drag whoever it is into the kitchen to talk to Linda.

I open the door. "Jesus, what are you doing here? I thought you were dead."

Tom's standing there, a white bandage wrapped around his head like a rugby player. "Maeve, can I talk to her?"

"I'll have to ask Linda."

He nods and I go back into the kitchen but he's followed me in. "Linda, can we talk about this?"

She tries to pull herself together. She straightens up, wipes her eyes and sniffs back the next round of tears. Then she gives him a Mam glare. Says nothing, just glares.

"I'll leave you two alone—"

"No, you won't, Maeve. I want you as a witness when I take him to the cleaners in the divorce settlement."

"Now, Linda, there's no need to overreact—"

"Shut up and say what you came to say."

"Linda, I – I'm sorry. She means nothing to me – it just happened and, well, I was her solicitor and her English . . . She's Senegalese—"

"I don't care if she's from Mars. Did you have the sex before or after the English lesson?"

"Linda, stop—"

"No, I won't, Tom. Before or after?"

"You're only upsetting yourself more."

Linda lets out a loud, neighing laugh. "You must be joking. Im-fucking-possible. Nope. It's the pregnancy announcement that actually hurts the most. Oh, and the fact that she's nine-teen years old. A little older than Fiona."

"Linda, it was nothing, honestly."

"Honestly? Please don't use that word. 'Honestly'? You wouldn't know 'honestly' if it jumped up and bit you in your well-ridden arse. So, Tom, tell me the scenario, how it should have worked if Miss Senegal hadn't come calling tonight."

I look at Tom, willing him not to answer. Doesn't he know by now that his replies are making her angrier? What a useless solicitor he must be. He should stick to giving English classes. I almost laugh when this thought comes prancing into my head.

Tom obviously can't read my mind because he launches into explanation mode again. "I'm sorry, Linda. I love you, I swear I do."

Linda leans back against the wall and eyes him up and down. He takes this as a sign that his pleas are working so he ups the ante.

"Please give me another chance, Linda. We'll all go on holiday tomorrow – a new beginning . . ."

Linda folds her arms across her chest, her head tilted to the side. If I was Tom I wouldn't go on about the new-leaf holiday.

"And I won't work as many hours, I promise—" Tom breaks off and tears stream down his face. "I'm sorry – it's just all the work . . . the stress I'm under. You have no idea how stressful my job is. She means nothing to me."

"What about the baby?"

"What?" He looks confused.

"The baby that Miss Senegal will produce in about seven months' time. Our children's half-brother or -sister. What about the baby, Tom?"

Again, I'm willing Tom to quit while he's ahead. I can hear the deadly calm in Linda's voice. The deadly calm before the storm.

"We'll sort that out."

"How? Oh, I know! We'll have it put down – the vet that put down Tiger will do it for us. You bastard. You dirty fucking cunt, you aren't fit to—" Then Linda launches herself at Tom, screaming, hissing, biting, scratching.

As the fight spills out into the hallway I worry that the two little boys upstairs will hear. And another thing bothers me. Linda. Perfectly groomed, perfectly married Linda. She has a bit of scumbag in her too. I don't even try to pull her off him.

The front door opens and Mam arrives home, all happy and wined up. Her face changes like in a cartoon as she sees Linda beating up Tom in her hallway. She can hardly blame me for this row. I watch Linda trying to tear out clumps of his hair and pieces of his face – she hasn't a bit of scumbag in her, she's got a whole team.

Eleven

"It's a volcano. We're going on our holidays to a volcano."

Mark yawns. "Please, Maevis Ravis, no geography lessons. We're on our holidays."

"Lanzarote is the easternmost island of the Canary Islands and has volcanic origin. It was born out of fiery eruptions and has solidified lava streams as well as extravagant rock formations—" Mark tries to clamp his hand over my mouth but I pull away from him. "The greatest recorded eruptions occurred between 1730 and 1736 . . ."

Mark does another exaggerated yawn and lays his head on my lap, pretending to fall asleep. The weight of his head feels lovely, and I stroke his hair lightly. He grins, eyes still shut. He reminds me of a cat. I look across at Cian in the aisle seat and roll my eyes. Mark snuggles deeper into me. His breathing is regular and I actually think he's asleep. He's a bloody cat.

"Is Linda still crying?"

Cian leans out and looks along the aisle. "Yep. Mam fell asleep after a few bottles of vino and now Linda's telling the flight attendant about her rat husband."

"No!"

"I swear. I passed a few minutes ago and she was describing to the poor young fellow in graphic detail how she was going to fleece him and chop him up in small parts that are easily carried."

"Stop, Cian."

He grins at me. "Not that bad. I feel sorry for the boys, though. I've never seen them so quiet. I thought the tsunami would have the plane dismantled by now."

"I can't believe she came, though, can you?"

Cian shrugs. "The boys would have been devastated if they didn't go and, anyway, what would she do in the house? Only fight with him. I mean, look what she did to him last night."

"I don't know what would have happened if you hadn't come home when you did." I'm still playing with Mark's hair and I look down at his perfect profile. The high cheekbones, the blond-highlighted hair. The long legs, all akimbo with nowhere to go, clad in the tightest skinny jeans. His mouth is perfect too, a pinkish rosebud. He could be a model, I think, as I examine him. I can feel Cian's eyes on me and I look across at him. But his eyes aren't on me; they're on the sleeping Mark.

He looks at me then and grins. "He's like a cat."

"I was thinking the same thing myself."

Fiona passes with Harvey in her arms and other passengers ooh and aah over him as she stops to talk to us. "I can't wait to lie on a beach and roast myself. I don't care if it's bad for me – I just want sun on my body." Fiona smiles at us.

Harvey kicks frantically and beams at the rows of people, almost like he's flirting with them. His cheeks look delicious, so fat and kissable. He's wearing one of his new holiday outfits – a gorgeous pair of miniature Levis and a Tommy Hilfiger sweatshirt. Eight weeks old and dressed to kill.

*

When we land I actually think the pilot made a mistake and flew us back to Shannon instead of a sun-drenched Canarian island. It's not just raining, it's absolutely bucketing down, and we're all soaked as we dash to a waiting taxi minibus. Fiona has a face like thunder as we drive to the outskirts of Puerto del Carmen. We pull up outside a neat villa in a cul-de-sac of neat villas all exactly the same. There's a horseshoe pool in the centre of the development, surrounded by lush wet foliage.

We dash from the taxi into the house, leaving a trail of rainwater on the marble-effect floors. It's quite big inside. A huge open-plan living area leads out onto a deck with a small private pool, and beautiful plants and trees. It's really quite pretty, even in the torrential rain. The bedrooms are lovely too, and some open onto the pool area. Fiona and I share one of those and it has a crib set up already for Harvey.

"This is so cool," says Fiona, as she bounces on her bed. "Pity about the stupid weather. I mean, you come all the way here, like, five minutes from Africa, and we might as well have gone to Kilkee."

"It might be sunny tomorrow." I sit down at the desk, thinking it would be grand to get in a bit of studying, maybe even drivel-writing. I'm glad now I brought my laptop, even though it was hell getting it on the Ryanair flight as hand luggage.

Fiona jumps up from the bed and checks her face in the mirror on the wall above the desk. "Jesus, look at the state of me – throw me over that bag there on the floor, will you?"

I hand her the large flower-patterned tote and she spills the contents out on the desk I'd been claiming for my laptop. There are pots of makeup, a selection of brushes that Van Gogh would have given his other ear for, wands of mascara, tubes of concealer. She's standing behind me now, making her emergency repairs to her face. I relinquish the chair to her and lie on the bed as she fixes her makeup.

"Mam said she'll babysit tonight," she says, opening her eyes wide to put on more eyeliner.

I can hear the others in the kitchen. The boys running around, Mam and Linda talking. "Are you hitting the town?" I ask, my eyes closed now. How can you be tired from flying? You're sitting on your arse for five hours straight. Go figure.

"Well . . . I was wondering . . . I was thinking maybe we'd go out – you and me and Mark and Cian?"

"Mm," I say, half-dozing now.

"We could have a laugh and forget about the rain and . . . you know . . ."

I don't answer. A night out on the town in Lanzarote with Fiona is not lighting any fires under me. She'll drink too much, get loud and inevitably meet up with scumbags.

"I mean, if we stick around here you know what'll happen."

"What?" I mumble, from my cosy nest.

"Linda will cry once the boys are in bed. She'll cry all night and Mam'll hit the wine."

I sit bolt upright. "You are so right. Let's leave now."

Fiona bursts out laughing and I join in and suddenly I'm back in the past, and Fiona and I are two little girls in shorts and halters and it's those first delicious hours of our annual holidays in Lahinch. We're dashing around the ancient, damp-smelling house, our bellies bursting with excitement and anticipation. We can hear the sea outside, fiercely crashing against the wall, and if we open the long windows we can hear the seagulls screeching and smell the air thick with salt. The memory is so strong that I want to keep it and follow it, but it shatters into tiny half-remembered fragments.

"What's up?" Fiona's looking at me strangely, her newly decorated eyes fringed with curly dark lashes.

"Nothing. What happened to your eyes? They have curtains on them."

She gives me a withering look and throws a hairbrush at me. I catch it deftly and grin at her.

So we hit downtown Puerto del Carmen. We meet up with Mark and Cian in Ralph's, a small tapas bar near the beach that Mark's uncle owns. They're sitting at a corner table, their heads close together, deep in conversation. Mark stands up when we come in and a tall man with curly blond hair crosses the pub floor to us, smiling broadly. "Hey, folks," he says, beaming a mouthful of too-even teeth at us. He's tanned and weathered and looks exactly like Mark, except an older, surf version.

"You're Mark's uncle, aren't you?" I say.

He grins. "And you're Maeve, I bet. I just know you are. I've heard loads about you."

I mock-glare at Mark.

He puts his hands into the air. "All good, all good, I swear, Maevis Ravis, I swear."

"You're the genius, aren't you?" Mark's nameless uncle continues.

"Hardly," I say, blood creeping up my face. I glare properly at Mark now and he ignores me.

"Am . . . Brendan . . . this is Maeve's sister, Fiona." Mark sends me a kind of forgive-me grin.

"Hi, how are you? Apologies for the weather. It's been a

scorcher until today. Now, what can I get you lot to drink?"

"A double vodka and Coke," says Fiona.

"Am . . . am . . . am . . ." I say. I actually don't want any alcohol but I know if I ask for water I'll be the night's wet blanket. And, hell, it's damp enough already.

Brendan smiles at us. "I have an idea. I'll bring you a selection of our cocktails. How about that?"

When he's gone back to the bar, Fiona says, "He's hot."

I sigh as I sit down at the small round table. There's a long red candle in the centre and a tiny bunch of flowers in a blue vase. Cian's sipping a bottle of Miller. "He's ancient," I say.

Fiona puts her beaded black bag on the table. "He's hot, Maeve. I mean, what age is Brad Pitt?"

"Forty, I guess."

"Yeah, well, that guy is in his thirties. He's a hottie."

Mark laughs. "He's thirty-five, my dad's youngest brother – the black sheep, really. He never made millions – just a couple."

We all laugh at this.

"Anyway, he might be hot but he's taken. His wife's Shauna, she's American."

"God, Mark, you say that like it's a disease – she's American. Get with the programme – it's OK to be American now. It's the Obama factor." I smile at him. His eyes dance in the candlelight and I think how romantic this is, all of us sitting around, chatting, laughing. Is this what they call a holiday mood? And maybe it'll be good. For all of us. Maybe Cian's right. He smiles at me like he knows what I'm thinking. Like he's saying, I told you so.

Brendan arrives back with the cocktails. The colours are so luminous and weird that I wonder if it's safe to drink them. I have a Tequila Sunrise and it's absolutely delicious. I've never ever had a drink as nice in my life. Think your favourite sweets multiplied by a hundred. And there are tiny umbrellas that you can play with in all our glasses. They really are like kids' drinks.

When Brendan joins us, he and Fiona seem to really hit it off. I try not to listen in on their conversation but there's definitely flirting going on. I'm thrilled when Mark suggests we go to another pub.

Outside, the rain has stopped and we walk through the narrow, cobbled streets of the old town. There's an Irish bar on the corner, Paddy's Irish Karaoke Bar, and Mark insists we go in for the laugh. Fiona lights a cigarette outside and I wait with her as she smokes it, shivering in the cool night air.

"Hope it's sunny tomorrow," she says, peering at the dark sky. Somebody in the bar is singing "With or Without You" badly. "Brendan says it will be. He checked the weather on the net for me."

She takes a long drag of her fag.

"Was he hitting on you? He's like way too old."

Fiona laughs. "Nope. I was hitting on him. We have a competition at school and— Shit, why am I telling you this?"

"Go on."

"Well, there's extra points if you – if you land an older one."

"No way. That's disgusting."

"Chill, Maeve, it's just a laugh. I mean, you wouldn't go out with them or anything. It's just for fun."

"But it's not fun."

She grins at me. "Some of us think it is. A lot of us, in fact. And you'd be very surprised at the guys some of us have landed."

"Like who?"

Her eyes narrow. "No one – just messing, that's all. And I was hitting on him – you know – just to see if I can still do it . . . I mean, after Harvey. You change and stuff."

"How do you mean?"

She steps on the butt of her cigarette. Then she fiddles with her hair. "I can't explain it. It's like before you have a baby you're you – but after, you're you and the baby and you worry all the time." She looks down at her sparkly black pumps.

I see it in her. The thing she's trying to explain. It's like she's still a seventeen-year-old girl but somehow parts of her are much older. Her eyes sometimes, or even the way she walks or holds herself. Part teenager. Part mother. I reach out and touch her arm. She smiles at me. The backing music for "Dancing Queen" comes on.

"Hey, my song from the rainy summer last year – come on, Maeve, let's sing." She drags me into the bar and straight over to the karaoke machine. There's a tiny stage next to it and she whips two mics from the DJ and launches into "Dancing Queen". I'm surprised at how good her voice sounds. She nudges me to sing and I can hear people shouting in the dark interior of the bar. I spot Mark and Cian grinning at the back of the crowded room. I try to sing along, mortified by the whole affair and just wishing the song would end. It seems like hours. I finally manage to run off the stage, just before Fiona launches into Rihanna's "Umbrella".

Mark's in stitches laughing at me, shaking his head and banging the counter top.

"Bastard," I yell but he can't hear with all the noise.

*

It's been a really good night. Mark and Cian force me to admit it as we walk home. It's two o'clock in the morning and I'm absolutely exhausted. Fiona's pissed and singing to herself as she wanders barefoot up the hill towards our house. The sky has cleared, I can see stars twinkling and I'm beginning to look forward to the sunshine tomorrow, to the holidays and sun and the laughs we'll have. Mark's linking me and Cian's linking him. We're staggering along, trying to walk three in a row. The boys are drunk. I stopped after two drinks – I'd had enough. The cocktails became too sweet, almost like Buckfast wine, the horrible Calpoly stuff I drank the night of the Results.

"Goodnight my friends, this is where I bid adieu to all of you . . . Jesus, that rhymed – I'm a poet." Mark laughs and has to hold on to the wall to steady himself. "See you all tomorrow. I'm just around the corner here." He waves at us and heads off down the road, whistling to himself.

"Will he be OK?" I ask Cian. Fiona's smoking again and doing a kind of dance thing up the street.

"He's fine. Brendan's place is two minutes away. And at least he doesn't have to climb this giant hill."

"You were right."

"About what, Maevis?"

That's the first time Cian's called me by that name. Only Mark uses it. "About the holiday. I feel good about it."

"My God, Maeve being positive?" He stares up at the sky. "Just looking for a blue moon."

"Shut up, you. Anyway, it's fun. So far."

"Ah, the old qualifying trick."

"What do you mean?" My breath is laboured now as the hill steepens. Fiona doesn't even seem to notice. She's still dancing and singing her way up Everest.

"'So far' – so if things get shit you can still say I told you so!"

I try to summon a laugh but I'm too busy gasping for breath. "I'm taking up smoking – look at her."

Things get a bit complicated once we reach the top. Every turn in the road is a cul-de-sac of identical white villas with blue doors. Exactly like ours. At the third I sit down on a low wall. There's a children's playground behind me and Fiona has grabbed herself a swing. She's swinging away, faster and faster, kicking up sand as she flies through the air.

Cian has gone looking for the right identikit villa and finally he peeks out from the fifth one down and gives me the thumbs-up.

"Come on, Fifi," I say, keeping my voice low so I don't wake people up.

"*Nooo* way! *Tooo* much fun!" she screams.

I end up climbing onto the swing beside her. And it's rhythmic once I start. Both of us swinging and swinging, a comfortable silence between us. It's a long time since I felt this good.

I wake with a start. For a second I think I'm at home in Limerick but then I sit up. Harvey's crying in his crib so I creep out of bed and go to him. He gives me a huge grin, even though he's probably starving and dirty. I pick him up, holding his wriggling body close to me. I walk to the patio door and pull back the heavy black-out curtains. I can't believe how pretty it is outside. I slide open the door and walk out into the warm morning sun. Everything is so bright, a kind of shiny bright you never see in Ireland. The luminous blue sky, the white-walled garden, the turquoise swimming pool. Even the green plants are a different shade of green, almost lime in the sunlight. I understand now why artists always liked to paint in places like this. I remember reading a book called *The Yellow House* about Van Gogh and his ill-fated stay in the south of France. The time he sliced off his ear. And the thing I remember most about the book was the constant search for the right light. And there was another artist with him . . . What was his name?

Harvey gurgles up at me, his huge brown eyes wide open. "What was the other guy's name, Harvey?" I ask him earnestly.

He gurgles again.

"Not good enough, Harvey. That's not the correct answer."

He starts to cry.

"I'm sorry, baby, you're hungry, aren't you?" I go inside, passing the snoring heap that's Fiona. Linda's in the kitchen, sitting at the table. There's an ashtray full of cigarette butts beside her, and a couple of empty wine bottles are lined up near the sink. "You're up early," I say, as I start to make Harvey's bottle. I know better than to put him in his chair when he's hungry so I keep him hoisted on my hip.

She doesn't answer me. Just sits there staring at her mobile phone, like it's going to jump up and bite her.

I take the heated bottle and sit opposite Linda. Harvey gulps his feed, catching my finger in the process. It's my favourite feeling in the world – that tight grip, those big eyes watching while he sucks. My heart does its usual little flip.

"Don't ever trust men," says Linda.

I keep eye-wrestling with Harvey.

"They're wankers, that's all they are. Wankers who will use you and spit you out." Then she starts crying. Big fat tears run down her face. Her eyes are glassy, like she's looking right through me. The crying gets worse, huge sobs shaking her body. I know I should do something, say something, but my mind has gone completely blank.

"Almost . . . almost eleven years . . ." She struggles to speak through the tears.

Harvey's staring up at me as if I'm the most important and beautiful person in the world. I stroke his cheek as he sucks away, still struggling to think of something to say. "I know," is all I come up with.

Linda takes a deep breath, her face wet, and reaches for the cigarette pack. She taps out a fag and lights it.

"Am . . . Linda . . . am . . ."

"I can't survive this."

"Am . . . Linda, the cigarette?"

"I want to curl up and die."

"Linda, the smoke? The baby . . ."

She glares at me and grinds the cigarette into the over-flowing ashtray. Fiona arrives into the room, rubbing her eyes.

Linda bursts into tears again and Fiona puts her arms around her tightly and lets her cry, like she's a small child. "It'll be OK, Linda, it'll be grand," says Fiona, as she strokes her hair. They stay like that for ages, Fiona stroking, Linda crying. I sit Harvey up and begin to wind him. He's all floppy and sleepy now, his belly full of milk.

"Come on, Linda, bed," says Fiona then, and leads her by the hand out of the kitchen.

Harvey does a huge burp. "Well done, Harvey! Well done!" I hold him out in front of me, legs wriggling, a smile on his face. "Nothing like a good burp, is there, Harv? Now your favourite auntie is going to give you – am – let's see – Life Lesson

Number Three. Burping. You'll be praised for doing it until you're about two – and then you'll be killed."

Harvey kicks his legs wildly, like he knows what I'm saying.

Fiona comes back into the kitchen and snaps on the kettle without checking the water level. "She's gone to bed. She fell asleep the minute her head hit the pillow. Poor Linda."

I look at my sister, in her Little Miss Perfect PJs, her hair tied up in a messy knot, her face scrubbed clean of the usual slap. She looks about twelve. "How did you know what to do?"

She stirs sugar into her instant coffee and throws me a puzzled look. "When?"

"Just now. With Linda. How did you know what to do?"

She kisses the top of Harvey's dark head and sits down at the table. "Dunno. Didn't think about it, really."

"Well, I hadn't a clue – I was completely speechless."

"Go away, Maeve, you always know what to say."

"No, I don't."

Fiona sips her coffee. "Please! You're the talker in the family – ever since you were small. God, I remember you always yapping. And you and Dad together were unbelievable. Nobody could get a word in."

"But that's not the same. That . . . I don't know . . . that's a different kind of talking."

Fiona gives me a look I know well from our years as siblings. She hasn't a clue what I'm talking about. "Let's go for a swim, Maeve. The sun's splitting the rocks."

"OK. We'll put this guy to bed first."

So Fiona and I take over the swimming pool. It's quite small and every one of the identikit villas has one the same, and the same garden furniture. But it's great fun. I feel like I'm six again and the day will never end. We'll just swim and eat and play all day long. And I'd forgotten how funny Fiona can be in a goofy kind of way. I watch her now, dozing on the sunbed in a snow-white bikini. She's rake thin – all the baby fat has just melted away – and beautifully proportioned. Unlike me with my gangly legs, no bum and short neck that gives me a double chin in photos.

The sun is hot on my back and I start to doze. Loud screams make me jump up on the sunbed and suddenly Fiona and I are drenched as Oisin and Andrew dive-bomb into the water, whooping and shouting. Fiona glares at them, water running down her flat belly. She dives into the pool and chases the boys, making them scream even more. I laugh and join in, the water cool on my toasted skin. Andrew, the tsunami, gets me in an iron grip and tries to drown me, climbing on my back and pushing my head under the water. I splutter to the surface and the boys laugh.

After lunch Fiona badgers me into a shopping trip. Mam and Linda are relaxing by the pool, a bottle of wine half-finished on the table. The boys are still in the water, floating on lilos, the scorching afternoon heat sucking the energy from them. Harvey's asleep in his crib, stripped down to his nappy, his skin a shade darker already even though he hasn't really been in the sun at all.

"Where's Cian?" I ask Fiona, as we stroll down the hill towards the town. The sea is aquamarine but the sand is very strange, a dark browny black that looks all wrong. Nothing like the golden sand in Lahinch.

"He's gone scuba-diving with Mark, or water-skiing – dunno. Something way too active for me anyway," she says, laughing. Her hair is in pigtails and she's wearing a tiny little ruffled lilac skirt and her white bikini top. She looks lovely, no makeup, no knacker wardrobe, no huge earrings.

"Black sand is so wrong," I say, nodding at the beach beside us.

"Yeah, how do they let it get so dirty?" She's dead serious but then starts laughing. "Gotcha! I'm not that dumb, Maeve. I know it has something to do with the volcano. Hey, there's a lovely little shop over there." She's gone before I have time to turn around, like she has a little homing device inside her for shopping.

The inside of the shop is deliciously air-conditioned and I watch Fiona, rooting through racks of clothes like a pro, selecting things and slinging them over her arm. Both of us squeeze into the tiny dressing room, giggling as we strip. Fiona tries on a gorgeous black halter-neck dress. She's stunning in it. My dress is exactly the same but longer. We stand in front of the long mirror in our bare feet, faces sombre. And then the giggling starts again.

I check the price tag. Fifty euro. Fiona tries on another dress, pink and backless this time. I shake my head at her. Not a good look.

"I love this one," she says, smoothing down the already skin-tight dress.

"Slutty," I say.

She grins. "Yeah, that's the look I'm going for."

"The black one is way nicer."

"Yeah – if you're going to a funeral."

We change back into our clothes and Fiona gathers the dresses and brings them to the counter.

"All of them? Fiona, that's like – that's loads of money."

"So? My book came through and Big gives me an allowance."

"What book?" I whisper, as the shop assistant adds up the purchases.

"Lone parents. Come on, let's get a drink somewhere."

We find a lovely little bar, right on the beach. The sun is setting and the sky is burnt orange, luminous and streaky against the huge blue expanse of sea. There's a slight breeze and we sit at a table outside, watching people stroll along in the evening sunshine.

We've just ordered two Tequila Sunrises and Fiona is in the middle of telling me a long, giggly story about her friend Carrie's mishap with self-tanning lotion when I spot him. He's standing at the top of the street, smiling at me. He's wearing sunglasses and doesn't have the Uniform on – he's swapped it for the Lanzarote version of same: a white wife-beater T-shirt and Nike calf-length tracksuit bottoms. I stare at him, and Fiona glances behind her. But he's melted into a doorway or a street. He's gone.

I blink and wonder if I imagined he was there. Dreamed him up because things are so nice and fun and the way they used to be and I'm obliged to prove myself right about the holiday. But my gut tells me that Big is here. Standing at the corner, showing himself to me, even smiling at me. Like somebody with a giant needle waiting for the perfect moment to burst my bubble.

Twelve

For the first time in my life I actually have a tan. Or the beginnings of one, at least. And I know now why I've never really bothered before. It's just such hard work – lying there roasting yourself and turning constantly, like a pig on a spit. But Fiona's militant about it, and after a while I'm enjoying the whole thing. We spend the day in a giggly, sleepy haze of sun and food and children playing around the pool. And now I have the tan lines to prove I put in all the hard work. Fiona and I are in our bedroom. Harvey's lying on the bed next to me, admiring his fists.

"Do you think we'll get anything to eat?" Fiona asks, as she slips into her new slutty pink dress. It fits her like a second skin.

"It's looking dodgy. They're on the second bottle of wine – Jesus, Linda can sure put it away. She's even better than Mam." Harvey's still staring at his fists, not realising they're actually part of his body.

"So much for Cian's birthday dinner. Hey – it's Hallowe'en. I nearly forgot." Fiona climbs into impossibly high stilettos and turns towards me. "So, what do you think?"

"I think pole dancing."

"Bitch – you're just jealous." She grins at me and sticks out her tongue.

"Cian doesn't care – he's too obsessed with this diving lark. Hey, Fifi, why don't we go tomorrow? Mark said it's brilliant and really, like, addictive."

Fiona has her magic brushes and paints out and is studying her face in the mirror before she begins layering it on. "Me at the bottom of the sea? Don't think so. How about we go to see that volcano yoke? Mam wants to go and the boys'll love it."

"OK – it's a date."

She begins putting on makeup. Harvey's found something else to watch – the curtain blowing in the warm evening air. Outside I can hear Oisin and Andrew, playing with a Lego set that Linda bought them earlier. Out of the corner of my eye I see my laptop on the floor – still in its case. I feel guilty suddenly – like I've deserted an old friend. Reams of work that I haven't looked at since we arrived. I'd planned to do at least a couple of hours every day but this tanning thing kind of took over. I'll start tomorrow. I'll get up early and work my butt off until we leave for the volcano.

"What are you wearing?" Fiona asks, as she smooths foundation into her skin.

"Well, you took the pole-dancing costume so I'll have to dress up as a witch."

"Very funny, Maeve. Anyway, Linda forgot the costumes."

"I'm not surprised. They weren't her main concern when she left her husband. Do I smell food?"

Mam decides to come out with us. She's well on it when Fiona puts the idea into her head and Linda encourages her. So, we're walking into town, down the huge hill and along the seafront, and there's Mam and Fiona linking each other and laughing and stumbling in their high heels. I feel like an outsider, like I'm the mammy who's tagged along for the evening.

We meet Cian and Mark in the stupid karaoke bar. Cian's in great form – a miracle for him. I can hear him laughing before I even see him. They're sitting at a table near the window, a stack of empty glasses already in front of them.

"Hey – sit down, sit down. I'll get in the drinks – cocktails all round?" says my brother, and goes to the bar before anyone can answer.

I sit down next to Mark. "You smell like a barrel of Heineken."

He grins at me, his eyes glassy. "Carlsberg actually – and it's been that kind of a day. A Carlsberg day, Maevis Ravis – did you ever have one of those?"

His face is a fraction from mine, and he's swaying a little and I'm annoyed that I think his drunkenness is cute. "The problem with alcohol, Mark, is that it alters reality for you so you may think you're having a great time but ultimately you can't tell because you're effectively in an altered state."

"Fuck – I thought we left Miriam O'Callaghan at home talking politics and having babies."

I laugh. "So, how's the diving going? Find any lost treasure?"

"Lots – you'd be surprised what turns up when you know where to look."

He's watching me as he says this, his face serious. A shiver runs down my spine and deep into my pelvis. I hate hormones.

Cian arrives back with a tray of drinks, all luminous colours and umbrellas. Mam and Fiona choose theirs and pass a lime green one to me. "God, it looks like snot," I say.

Mark laughs and takes a sip. "It's nice. Kinda limey."

"Think I'll go and get a Coke."

"Good girl, Maeve. Get into the party spirit. Have a Coke. Have two, even."

"Shut up, you drunk fool."

He catches my hand and holds it tight. "I missed you."

I look at him, his face serious, his hair flopping over his forehead. I don't know if he's just drunk and bullshitting me, but that shiver thing is happening again and I want to kiss him hard on the mouth. Cian squeezes in beside us, shaking the table.

Mark laughs. "Hey, Cian, Maeve thinks I'm a drunk fool."

"She thinks I'm one too, even when I'm sober." Cian laughs and Mark joins in, like it's the funniest thing he's heard.

I turn my attention to Mam and Fiona, who're deep in conversation. Fiona's showing Mam something on her phone. "So, what's up?" I ask, smiling at them.

The conversation stops and Fiona slips her phone back into her bag. Mam gulps her orange drink, forgetting to use the straw.

Fiona picks up the song sheet on the table and examines it carefully.

I shrug and head up to the bar for a Coke. Just as I'm ordering a crowd of guys come into the bar, their accents distinctly English, probably Liverpool. There must be ten of them altogether, all wearing blue T-shirts with the red *A Team* logo and the legend *Tommo's Stag* below that. They're your cliché stag gang, loud, drunk and tattooed.

I ignore them as they wink and nudge each other. As I leave with my Coke I hear them talking.

"Wow, look at her, she's seriously hot."

"And up for it too, mate – nice arse."

I turn to scowl at them but realise they're talking about Fiona, who's standing up now, chatting to Cian. I head back to our table. "Can we go somewhere else?" I ask, as I sit down next to Mark.

"No way – the music's just starting up and Fiona wants to sing a birthday song for Ciany," says Mam, her voice high and screechy.

I watch as Fiona makes her way to the tiny stage, taking the heckling from the stag party in her stride. The bar has filled up now, and as Fiona begins to sing, quietly at first and then belting out Amy Winehouse's "Valerie" , the crowd claps along with her, cat-calling and shouting. Fiona loves it. Loves every minute of the attention. The stag guys scream for more and she flirts openly with them, asking them to choose a song. They're like schoolboys now, all competing for her attention. Fiona launches into "Mamma Mia" and the crowd goes wild.

"We should make her enter *The X Factor* – she's brilliant," says Mam, her face shiny with pride. Or alcohol. Take your pick.

"Look at those guys – they're like a pack of wolves," I say.

"Fiona isn't exactly discouraging them, is she?" says Mark.

"What do you mean? All she's doing is singing."

He gives me an enquiring look. Like he doesn't believe me.

"OK, she's a bit . . . flirty, I'll admit that."

"So – is it a family trait?"

"What? The singing? Nope. I can't sing a note and Cian is worse – except he thinks he can."

Mark grins. "No. I meant the flirting. Family trait?"

"I don't flirt. Flirting is . . . dunno . . . dumb . . ."

"Flirting isn't dumb, Maeve. We all like a good flirt. Look at your mother – throwing eyes at Manuel the barman."

"Stop, Mark! He's half her age."

"So? It's big business now, Maevis – all these Irish women getting themselves foreign toy-boys."

I watch him as he sips his drink, the snot-green one that should have been mine. He winks at me and smiles. "Stop flirting with me, Mark."

"Oh, fuck." Mark is staring at the door, like he's seen a ghost. I know it's Big. I can almost feel his presence. I turn, and he's standing there, leaning against the wall, arms folded, watching Fiona singing. His mother, Vonnie, and his sister, Nicole, are walking towards the bar.

Big just stays where he is, eyes glued on Fiona. She hasn't seen him yet and I watch her as she sings to the stag party. I want to go up there and stop her. And then she spots him. Her voice falters and she finishes the song minus the last verse. She walks towards him. He hasn't moved a muscle. Still leaning against the wall, staring at her with laser eyes, as she makes her way through the crowd. My heart begins to pump in my chest. Mark is a ball of tension beside me too.

"Fuck," I whisper.

"Fuck is right," he says.

I look around but Cian is over talking to some girl. Mam's chatting to Manuel. She hasn't noticed a thing. Vonnie's at the bar, ordering drinks. I look back towards the door but they are both gone. "Be back in a minute," I say.

Mark grabs me by the arm. "Don't be stupid, Maeve. It's not your business."

"Yes, it is. He'll hit her – he saw her singing to the guys and he'll kill her."

"Maeve, it's not your business."

"Yes, it fucking well is," I say, pushing his hand away and marching over to the door. I'm fuming with Mark, not because of what he's said but the words he chose to say it. Big's words. Big's words written in shit on a wall in Mark's house. I can nearly hear Katya's sobs in my head. I'm not afraid of him, I tell myself, as I step out into the dark street. But my heart is pumping like mad now, so loud that the sound fills my ears, fills my whole head.

There's no sign of them outside. The street is busy and I walk to the corner but they're nowhere to be seen. I walk in the other direction and turn into a narrow cobbled street. I hear something ahead and stop dead in my tracks trying to figure out where the noise is coming from. It's a deep moan and I know instinctively that it's my sister. Adrenalin floods my veins as I creep up the street. There's a tiny opening into an alleyway and the sound is louder there. I glue myself against the wall and chance a peep down. Another loud moan makes me jump and as my eyes get accustomed to the dark I see them.

He's up against the wall, sort of leaning back, and Fiona's facing him, almost sitting on his lap but standing up. He's pushing himself into her, hard and fast. Her head is thrown back and she moans again as he keeps pushing into her. Her legs are splayed around him and he's pressing her bare arse down on him. Her knickers are on the ground. I know I shouldn't look but the scene transfixes me. And I know, watching it, that this is exactly like beating her. He's claiming her, making her his, marking his territory the way a dog would. And she's loving it. Just then he opens his eyes and seems to look straight at me. That laser look again. I freeze and my legs turn to jelly. He smiles then. A lazy smile like it's almost not worth the effort.

I lean back against the wall. Tears sting my eyes and I don't know why I'm crying.

I make my way slowly back to the pub. A group of people in vampire costumes run past me, screaming at each other. Someone in the pub is singing a terrible version of Take That's "Patience". I wipe my eyes, take a deep breath and go back inside.

The pub seems to be even more crowded. Vonnie and her daughter have ensconced themselves at our table, in my seat to be precise. Vonnie's wearing a leopard-print T-shirt so tight you can see her nipples protruding, and too-tight white jeans. There's no sign of Mark so I slink into his seat. The little girl watches me intently, a bag of peanuts in her hand. Vonnie whispers something to Mam and both of them laugh. Nicole keeps staring at me, almost like she's trying to read my mind.

"That's a good one, Vonnie, that's a great laugh," says Mam, picking up her drink and slugging it back.

"I know. It's hilarious, isn't it? Are you all right, Nicole, jew want another Coke?"

She shakes her head. She has a full glass in front of her and a fine muffin top of fat hanging over her short denim skirt. As I'm thinking this, Nicole looks down at her skirt, then back at me. I shiver and she even notices that. I can see it in her eyes. Weird.

"Anyway, I was telling you, the little pup has my heart broke and the last straw was the other day – he comes in with two horses, in through the house, and ties them up in the back garden."

"Horses?" says Mam, struggling to keep up.

"A mare and a foal – the foal was the cutest thing you ever saw, wasn't he, Nicole?"

Nicole nods, but she's still staring at me.

"So there I was, crying at the kitchen table, and my Big arrives in with his new laptop and just like that he'd booked me this holiday, didn't he, Nicole?"

Nicole nods again.

"So here we are, just the three of us. I couldn't bring the rest of them, sure then 'twould be no holiday, more like an endurance test." She laughs, her gold pendant shaking between her pushed-up Wonderbra breasts. Mam laughs too but I think she's lost the plot completely now. I scan the pub for Mark or Cian. No sign. And no sign of Fiona and Big either.

"So – who's minding the children at home?" I don't realise I'm speaking out loud until I see the look on Vonnie's face. Chin stuck out straight away like Fiona's when she's being a knacker. Nicole has folded her arms across her chest, like she's watching an episode of *EastEnders*.

"What jew mean?"

There's a moment of stillness in the noisy bar. Like everything stopped for a nano-second so that Vonnie's voice can be heard.

"What happened, Vonnie, with the horses? You never told us," says Mam, still struggling to keep up with the conversation.

Vonnie joins her daughter in staring at me. "We kept them. Big found a field for them. He sorted it."

I want to get out of here. The laser look must run in the family. I spot Mark and Cian coming in from the beer garden at the rear of the pub. I wave at them. A come-over-and-rescue-me wave but they don't get the message because they're men. They need it spelled out.

And suddenly Fiona and Big are back and I'm almost glad to see them so that the mother and daughter staring act will end. It's only when I notice Fiona holding out her hand to Mam and Big beaming from ear to ear that I realise what's happening. Like a bad twist in the *EastEnders* episode that is this night.

"Well, what ja think?" says Fiona, reclaiming the knacker accent already.

"Oh, Fiona, it's beautiful," says Mam.

"Are ye giving us a day out?" says Vonnie, holding Fiona's hand and admiring the glinting diamond on her finger. "It's fuckin' beautiful, Fiona, fab'lous. Ye'll make a lovely couple."

Fiona won't meet my eye as she allows Mam and Vonnie to fawn over her ring.

"So when's the big day?" Vonnie says to Big.

He grins. "You'll have to ask herself dat."

Fiona laughs. "We're just engaged, that's all. We're not planning to get married – sure we're not, Big."

For once in my life I manage to swallow what's on the tip of my tongue. That getting engaged is planning to get married. That Fiona seems to get really dumb the minute Big shows up. And what's with the knacker accent? Instead I get up and walk to the bar, not even acknowledging Fiona and her stupid ring.

Mark and Cian have disappeared again. I wonder to myself if Cian has taken to smoking. They seem to be constantly going outside. I order another Coke and have to shout over the noise and the bad singing to make myself heard.

"Well, Cunt."

I jump at the sound of his voice.

181

"Nothin' to be scared of." Big signals to the barman.

"I'm not scared of you." I hold his eyes.

He laughs. "You'll be a lovely bridesmaid, Cunt. We'll pick a nice colour for ya."

"Fuck off."

"Dat's terrible language to be using to your brother-in-law. Hey, can I have three double vodkas and Red Bull, and a Coke?"

The barman looks at him as if he's speaking Chinese. "*Qué?*"

"Three. Double. Vodkas. And. Red. Bull. And. A. Coke." Big almost shouts every word, pushing his face close to the barman, who turns quickly to get the drinks.

"Fucking thicko foreigner. Spanish cunt. Place is full of them."

"Maybe that's because we're on a Spanish island?" I take my drink and walk away.

"See you, Cunt," he says. I walk out to the beer garden, just to get away from everybody. But half the stag are outside smoking and they wolf-whistle as I walk by. They must have their beer goggles on, I think, as I find a space behind a giant palm. I lean against its spindly bark and blink back stupid tears.

Thirteen

The more the night goes on the stranger and more surreal it gets. This is no episode of *EastEnders*, it's a whole bloody movie with no director to shout, "Cut." Everybody's pissed and declaring undying love for each other. I'm sitting at the edge of the group nursing my fifth Diet Coke, squeezed in beside the only other non-drinker among us – Nicole. She observes everything that's going on around her, the laser eyes moving from face to face, like tiny cameras. Cian and Mark are huddled in the corner, laughing at me every time I beg them with my eyes to rescue me.

"Jew want another Coke, love?" Vonnie says to Nicole.

If Nicole has any more to eat or drink she'll be able to roll home.

"See her, Marie? She's a star, her. I'd be lost without her. She does all the housework, the washing and all, don't ya, love?"

My mother smiles, glassy-eyed, almost unaware of what Vonnie's saying to her, figuring a smile just about covers everything.

"Jew know somethin'? She should have been a boy. I had a

scan and they could see a little willy – pointed it out and all to me."

Mam smiles again, swaying slightly this time.

"And we'd his name picked out and all – Niall, after 'There is an Isle . . .'"

I guffaw at this and Vonnie stops and stares at me. As do Big and Nicole.

"It's an Isle – not Niall . . . not 'there is a Niall' . . ." My voice trails off. Vonnie glares at me.

"Don't mind her, she's a terrible know-all – you should hear her at home. It's like living with a professor," says Mam, slurring a little.

They all laugh, and I smile even though I can feel the pinprick tears again. Faces swim in front of me like I'm drunk. I glance at Mark, but he's being plied with a tray of shots by Big. He takes a drink and, smiling at me, downs it in one go. Big claps him on the shoulder and offers him another.

"Are you tired?" I ask Nicole.

"No. This is fun," she says.

"Wouldn't you rather be home watching a movie or something?"

She looks at me. "By myself?"

I shrug. She has a point. Suddenly Mam wobbles to her feet, knocking a glass to the floor. She tries to do her usual look-how-sober-I-am walk, the one that's so slow and deliberate you know she's langers.

I grab her by the arm, then march her out of the door and across the road. She vomits, managing to aim it over the sea wall. I hold back her hair as she empties her stomach.

"Is she OK, Maeve?" Cian asks, from behind me.

"Nope. We'll have to take her home. Round up Fiona and we'll get a cab."

"Am . . . well, look, let's put her in a cab. She'll be fine, won't you, Mam?"

As if in answer Mam begins another round of vomiting.

"Look, we'd planned to go to a club. There's this brilliant place called the Paradiso."

Mam's vomiting seems never-ending. At least I inherited something from her. "I see. So we'll dump her in a cab and we'll all go off dancing?"

"Maeve, chill. It's no big deal."

"Off you go. Have a great night. Same to Fiona," I say, my voice icy.

"Spare me your fucking disapproval, Maeve. I'm not in the mood for it."

"Fuck off," I say, as Mam lifts her head. I wipe drool from her mouth.

"Can you walk, Mam?"

She smiles and nods vigorously and begins to stagger down the footpath. Cian throws his arms into the air and marches back into the pub. I link my mother and walk to the end of the street where I can see a taxi sign. "I love you, Fiona," Mam says, as she skitters along in her high heels.

"That's lovely but I'm Maeve."

"That's what I said. Maeve. My clever one, you are."

I will a taxi to come so that this drunken bonhomie will end.

"I love you. I love all of you, but I love you the most, Fiona."

"Great," I say, as I hail an oncoming cab.

*

Back at the villa Linda fusses over Mam, making her black coffee laced with brandy, which seems a complete contradiction to me. I point this out to Linda, then sneak into my room, listening to Harvey's soft, rhythmic breathing. I lift him gently out of his cot and into my bed. I doze off, snuggled against his tiny warm body, thinking about puke and laser eyes.

When I wake up the kitchen is buzzing with activity. I can hear Oisin and Andrew running up and down the hallway and Mam and Linda bustling about. Harvey's gone and I presume that Fiona's taken him to feed him. But there's no Fiona in the kitchen. Harvey's asleep in his buggy by the open patio door. Mam and Linda are packing a cool box with what looks like the entire contents of the fridge.

"There you are, Maeve. I thought you'd never wake up," says Mam. She's as bright as a button after her night of drinking and puking. "Get dressed quickly. The bus is coming in half an hour."

"The bus to where?" I ask, as I push bread into the toaster.

"The volcano, of course. Don't you remember?" She laughs as if I'm the one who was drinking all night.

"Where's Cian?" I ask, pouring tea into a cup.

"He's not coming. He didn't get in until all hours."

"Fiona?"

"Speak of the devil," says Mam, as Fiona comes in through the patio doors. Her face is made up already, hoop earrings and all.

"I'm taking Harvey to the beach," she says, busying herself packing his bag.

"By yourself? What about the volcano?" I ask, as I butter my toast.

186

She doesn't answer me. Doesn't even look at me. I stand at the patio door and there's Big, leaning on the low white wall in front of the villa. He smiles at me and winks. Fucker.

"See you later," says Fiona, as she manoeuvres the pram out of the door. "I'll be late. We're going shopping and Vonnie's taking us out for something to eat."

Cian appears in the kitchen just as the happy couple stroll off into the bright sunny day, Fiona pushing the buggy, Big's hand resting on her bum. "My head," he says.

"Self-inflicted," I tell him.

But my head is aching too, like the worst hangover you could imagine. I gulp down two paracetamol as the bus honks outside. We all go out and climb in, the boys in high spirits. As the bus rolls down the hill towards the old town my stomach begins to feel odd and my head pounds despite the painkillers. We crawl through the town, the heat on the bus adding to my sickness. Just as we're pulling onto the main road I jump up. "I can't go," I say. "I feel sick."

The bus driver smiles knowingly at me as he opens the door. I get off, my legs shaky. Mam and Linda wave at me and the bus pulls away just as I vomit into a large bush with bright yellow flowers. A couple walking a small white dog tut at me as they pass. Finally the vomiting stops and I feel better almost immediately. I gulp in huge breaths of sweet morning air and stroll back towards town, glad now that I'm not sitting in a hot bus all day, listening to kids fighting and Mam and Linda motor-mouthing.

I get a takeaway coffee in a small deli and sit on the prom for a while, watching as people settle down on the beach for a hard day sunbathing. Most of the older people have that dark leathery skin of too many sun holidays. There's one man in a thong, his wrinkled little belly hanging over it like a deflated balloon. There's another woman with bare breasts so round and perfect they must be fake – she stretches out beside me on a straw mat. The stag guys from last night have resurfaced and boldly ogle the girl as they push and jostle each other on the black-brown sand. The sun is warm on my back and neck. A small child, Spanish, I know because he's chatting away to himself, digs a tunnel in the sand, working steadily, like he has an exact plan in his head of what he's building. I finish my coffee and realise I'm starving. I pass Brendan's pub and notice they're doing food.

Inside it's cool and dark, and I order a panini with iced water. Brendan arrives in just as my sandwich appears. "Hello, Maeve, how are you this lovely day?"

"Great. Is Mark around?"

"Mark amazes me. Out half the night and then up with the lark. He was gone before I even got up. No idea where he is – unless he's gone off diving again."

"I'll text him, no problem."

Brendan goes off, cleaning tables, and I text Mark. I sit there waiting for my phone to chirp a reply. No answer. I leave, calling goodbye to Brendan on my way out, and start the big climb uphill. I'm in two minds about what to do. Either study or hook up with Mark and do something mad for the day. Maybe take a boat trip out to Fuerteventura. And I'd love a swim. I check my phone again and decide to ring him quickly even though it'll seriously eat into my credit. No answer. Strange.

The villa is cool inside and so quiet I can hear birds singing in the garden. Cian must have left – his room door is thrown open

188

and his bed is empty. I'm just about to go into my room when I hear a long, low moan, almost like a whispered one. It's coming from Mam's room. My legs start shaking and my stomach does a little somersault as my imagination runs riot. Before I lose my nerve I push open the door and walk in, stopping almost immediately when I see them. He's straddling somebody, from behind, his bum facing me. They don't know I'm there because the low, deep moaning is the soundtrack, that and the constant motion of the bum in the air, pushing and pushing and quivering and pushing. I can't make sense of it all, it's a tangle of bodies – arms and legs and arses and that awful low moan. Why doesn't it stop?

And then the images slot into their rightful places and the arses separate and one is Cian's – the one I'm looking at – and the one under is Mark's. The moaning is louder now, urgent, almost a shout, and then I'm moaning too and looking into Mark's eyes. He's on his belly on the bed, Cian behind him, and he's turned his head and I know it's my moaning that's made him look . . .

"Maeve . . ." There's a scramble of bodies, some pushing, Cian hiding his huge erect penis and someone is laughing and I realise it's me but there are huge wet tears on my face. I can feel them running down my cheeks. Mark sits up straight. Says it again. Says it like it'll help. "Maeve."

I shake my head at him. Not believing, wanting him to tell me it's a joke. A weird elaborate joke. Hallowe'en. That's it. A Hallowe'en joke for my benefit. My stomach flips again and then I'm gone, tripping over shoes and racing down the hallway and out through the patio doors.

I'm flying down the hill, my legs at full sprint, my lungs fit to burst. I can't stop, even if I want to. I can't stop because of the momentum. And because of the ugly pictures in my head of tangled arses and penises and Mark's eyes.

I end up in the port, sweat and tears blinding me as I sit on a low wall and gulp air into my constricted lungs. My whole body shakes uncontrollably and I can feel the panini in my stomach churning around, threatening to come up. The tears won't stop. People stare at me but I don't care. I cry my heart out, head down, shoulders shaking. There's a ball of black anger inside me and I want to kick something or someone until it goes away. Kick and spit and rip and tear until it's all gone.

I know he's beside me without even looking up. I can feel him there, next to me, almost touching me, but I'm afraid to look at him in case I thump him. Eventually he speaks. "Maeve."

I hold my breath, waiting for the tears to stop.

"Maeve."

I still don't look at him, still don't trust myself, but the shuddering has eased and the tears are almost spent. The sun beats down on my back and neck and I can feel it burning into me, seeking out pale Irish skin to zone in on and toast relentlessly.

"This is hard," he says.

I don't answer him. Don't make it easy for him.

"I don't know what to say to you."

I look at him then, straight into his eyes. I see guilt there. And shame.

"You're a fucking bastard. A sneaky little bastard."

Mark blinks, like I've slapped him.

"Why didn't you tell me? Why did you lead me on, kissing me, getting close to me . . .?" My voice is a whisper and it falters now as the stupid tears start again. "Why didn't you fucking tell me, Mark? Why didn't you tell me that you're gay? That you and my . . . my brother are . . . Jesus Christ . . ."

He puts an arm around me and I push him away. "Don't touch me," I scream, and he jumps away from me. "I hate you and I hate Cian. I hate my drunken mother and my dumb sister. I hate the whole fucking lot of you. Selfish bastards, all of you, stupid, silly, selfish fuckers . . ."

"Maeve . . ."

"Stop saying that. Stop saying my name like it's an answer. You're a fucking creep and I hate you – and now a lot of things are clicking into place. My brother sneaking off to meet you behind my back – behind my fucking back, if you don't mind. I fucking hate you, you fucking gay boy."

"So that's what's wrong, is it, Maeve? You're a secret homophobe despite your well-documented higher intelligence. That's what you resort to instead of reasonable discussion? Name-calling? Gay-bashing?"

"You betrayed me. You betrayed our friendship – the one person I confide in, the one person I'm totally honest with." I grab his arm. "Look at me, Mark."

He blinks back tears and meets my eyes.

"Why didn't you tell me? Why didn't you say something?"

He shakes his head.

"Answer me. Why didn't you trust me?"

"Because I didn't know."

"What kind of a stupid answer is that? You didn't know?"

He takes out a cigarette and lights it. I notice that his hands are shaking. "I didn't know. I still don't know."

"I never heard anything as dumb as that."

He takes a long pull from the cigarette. "It's the truth. I

191

don't know if I'm gay or straight or bi or any of the other names we have for our sexual orientation."

"So you were doing a little experimenting with my brother. That's nice and cosy. Keep it in the family. And if the brother doesn't work out you can always move on to the sister. Nice plan, Mark."

"Don't be smart."

I hug myself, shivering despite the heat of the midday sun. "Well, you have your answer now, Mark. You seemed dead happy back there in my mother's bedroom. It would have made a nice little gay-porn movie, soundtrack and all."

"Stop it, Maeve."

"OK. We'll pretend it never happened, that I never saw it, and we'll all go out on the town tonight and have a great time. We'll get drunk – how about that for a change? We'll all get langers."

"You're sad."

"I'm sad? Spare me your pity. You're disgusting. You and my brother."

He flicks his cigarette away and shrugs. "Be like that, Maeve. Be like all the other cretins."

"And actually, now that I think of it, it's illegal. You're under age. Does Cian know that? Does my brother know he's fucking a minor? That he's breaking the law?"

Mark stands up, brushing ash from his T-shirt. "I won't listen to this. When you feel like talking, like really talking, you know where to reach me."

"You won't listen to it because it's the truth. The hard, ugly truth."

Both of us are standing now, facing each other, and the way he looks at me, those eyes seeing into me, makes me want to hug him to me so tight. Instead I strike him hard across the face and I'm more surprised than him.

He rubs his cheek. "The hard ugly truth is that minors have sex all the time. How many girls in our year are virgins? How many guys? How many in the year below us? Fourteen-year-olds give blow-jobs behind the bike sheds in our school. You know that, Maeve."

He walks away then, just turns and walks away. The black ball of anger inside me explodes. I can feel its adrenalin pumping through my veins. The little scumbag anger ball busting to get out. "I hate you, you fucking bastard. I hate you and you can tell Cian I hate him too. Bastards – cowardly, lying bastards." I'm screaming this and kicking the wall repeatedly. Mark doesn't look back. Not even once. I stop kicking the wall when I notice the blood on my sandal-clad feet.

Fourteen

Maeve didn't want to go to the Harrison Summer School for Gifted Children. She didn't want to go because Daddy was sicker now and she'd be gone to Dublin for a whole week, and what if the thing in his brain exploded while she was gone? And everybody was laughing at her, saying she was going to Nerd School.

But Daddy wanted her to go. It was all his idea and he got her a scholarship at his work, and before she knew it she was on a train with Mam and then at the school. It was the middle of summer and she had to go to school. And she hated it. Every minute of it. She hated the other children with their posh accents, all of them trying to be cleverer than one another and talking about college. They weren't even teenagers yet and they talked about college and points and Trinity and even Oxford.

And then there was Rodger Taylor. Rod – that's what everybody called him – was thirteen, two years older than her and the oldest boy in the school so everyone liked him. Maeve often wondered about this. How if you're the prettiest or the oldest or the funniest everyone likes you. But that it wasn't true if you were the cleverest. Rod was clever as well as old, but she knew she was smarter except she refused to play the Who's-the-Cleverest game like the rest. She wouldn't do her best at the aptitude tests or participate in class discussions. She hated it all and just wanted the week to end.

And she would have managed it except for Rod. He told her he liked her. They were walking in the grounds of the school. Lovely gardens with giant oak trees and tons of flowerbeds. He told her he liked her. That she was the prettiest girl. That she was funny and made him laugh. Maeve questioned this in her head but she so wanted to believe it too. She let him kiss her on the mouth. And then he took her hand and put it over his crotch and said that if she liked him she had to rub him there. He smiled when he said it and for a minute she wanted to just do it so he'd still like her. It was easy to do – like rubbing Puffin, her cat. But she couldn't do it because it seemed so silly. And it made her feel dirty. So she said, "No, but you can kiss me if you like," and Rod laughed at her and called her a silly ugly little kid and ran off.

So she decided to get him back. She dreamed up elaborate plots in the classroom while he giggled and whispered with the others. They all knew. He'd told them lies and they all knew she'd rubbed his willy – even if it was, like, only for a nano-second.

But she did a simple thing in the end. Rod was sitting on a bench by himself, reading a book, his glasses perched on his beaky nose. She found a rock, a nice flat one, and crept up behind him and dropped it on his head. It was so easy she didn't believe she'd done it until she saw the blood pouring down his neck and his glasses on the gravel.

They sent her home. Her mother came to collect her and she could hear the master talking with her in his office. Asking her mother if she'd ever had Maeve assessed. That she didn't mix with other children. If she'd ever considered Asperger's Syndrome. Considered *it like it was an option in a multiple-choice question.*

Maeve was sorry that her mother was angry. Sorry when she heard how disappointed Daddy was in her. Sorry that she'd caused a huge fuss. But she wasn't a bit sorry about the rock. Not one bit.

And Daddy was disappointed. She could see it in his eyes. He didn't say anything about it to her but she could see it there all the same. He didn't have to say a thing. And then the next day Mam went to take a nap and Fifi was in charge of the house, bossing her around and telling her to be quiet all the time cos Daddy was asleep. She crept into the living room where Daddy slept now and sat beside his bed, reading a book about butterflies. When he woke up he stared at her for a minute like he didn't know who she was. Then he got out of bed, slowly, like an old person and she said, "Daddy, what's Asperger's Syndrome?" and he sat on the edge of the bed, so still, and she wanted to take it back. Take the words back.

And then he toppled over and began jerking, a horrible jerking, with his tongue lolling in his mouth and she froze watching him jerk, just stood over him frozen to the spot, and she tried to scream but nothing came out except a tiny croak. He tried to talk but he croaked too and stretched his hand up to her, like he wanted her to help him get up off the floor, and still she stood watching and croaking.

It felt like ages since she'd said the words. Hours and hours ago. And then the jerking stopped as suddenly as it had started and then she heard her screams, so loud they made her ears buzz, and then Fifi was in the room, shouting at her and ringing an ambulance and leaning over Daddy trying to make him breathe.

Mammy came in and screamed at Maeve too, why didn't she call her and what happened, and Maeve ran away. Ran away up to her bedroom.

She never cried. Not once during all the fuss afterwards. The ambulance and the priest and Auntie Linda. Mammy crying all the time. Cian and Fifi white-faced and tear-streaked. She never cried because she knew she'd killed him. She didn't drop a brick on his head like she did on Rodger Taylor's but she might as well have. She killed him with disappointment. With not being good enough. With not being the cleverest.

There's a knock at the door. I try to ignore it and turn back to the computer screen, wiping tears from my eyes. I'm cold even though the heat from the day is still in the room. It's night-time and I'm in my new black dress, the one Fiona made me buy yesterday – was it only yesterday? Yesterday, before this holiday turned into something horrible and lonely.

The knock comes again and I ignore it. The door is locked. Shut tight against the world. I can't bear to read what I've just written and I know now that nobody ever will. There will be no short story, no competition, no pages for Mr Hynes to mull over. Because now that it's written the job is done. Complete. Finished. Over. Now that it's done I can go back to the very start and delete it all. I scroll right back to the very beginning and select all the text and then press the delete button. Like magic it's gone from the screen. Blank white pages fill the file now. Then I empty the recycle bin just to be doubly sure it's all gone.

"Maeve, open the door, please. I want to talk to you."

Cian's voice is plaintive, almost begging.

"Maeve, please."

Now it's a whine. I stand up straight, faltering a little in Fiona's borrowed high heels. I've used her makeup too and barely recognise myself in the mirror. I look so much older. A woman. I walk to the door and Cian comes in, but I don't look at him. Instead I sit down in front of the mirror and pick up some of Fiona's nail polish. I begin to apply it, the acrid smell filling the room.

"Can we talk?" He's sitting on the bed, right behind me, hands in his lap, head down.

My hand shakes so much as I paint my thumbnail that the polish goes everywhere.

"I'm sorry you walked in like that today. I know it must have been horrible for you."

"Fuck." I swear at my nails, which look like they're bleeding.

"I'm gay. I've known for a while but tried not to be." He laughs at this.

"I'm sorry you walked in."

I search the dressing-table for nail-polish remover but there doesn't seem to be any. Fuck it, I'll just have to go out with nails that look like they're bleeding.

"Please talk to me, Maeve."

I turn around and smile at him, waving my nails in the air to dry them quickly.

"Please excuse me. I'm going out on the town to get fucked in every possible way you can imagine." I grab my handbag and walk out of the room and through the kitchen where Mam and Linda are sharing a bottle of wine.

"Have a great night, Maeve. You look lovely," says Mam.

I smile sweetly at her. "Thanks. See you later."

I don't go to any of the obvious bars because I don't want to bump into Fiona or Cian. And definitely not Mark. So I find little places in the back streets and start drinking cocktails.

And I flirt with every guy I see, waiting for the right candidate to come along. A nice scumbag, a bit of rough like my sister's. In the fifth bar I strike lucky. There's the stag party from the night before, the *A Team* T-shirts looking a little grubby now. But they have tattoos to die for. I'm sure Fiona'd approve. And then one of them starts sending over drinks. I smile appreciatively at him. A big blond guy with a Liver bird tattooed on his neck. He comes over, followed by the others, and suddenly I'm the centre of attention. We head off to the next bar in a big gang, and I'm all giggly and happy and thinking, This is fucking great. Like being a different person for a night. Like stepping into someone else's life.

Tony – that's his name, my blond Liverpudlian chosen one – is very funny, or else I'm drunk and just imagine he is, but who cares as long as we're having a good time? We're sitting at the bar, our legs pressed together, me smiling up at him as he tells some long-winded story about losing his luggage. I sneak my hand onto his lap, just resting it on his crotch. He stutters on with his story but I can feel his hard erection as I rub the inside of his thigh with the bare tips of my fingers. "Let's fuck," I whisper into his ear.

He smiles at me, gulps down his beer and we leave. The rest of the stag jeer and wolf-whistle as the bar door closes behind us. I stumble in the street and Tony steadies me. We link as we walk to his apartment complex. He fumbles with the key of the door and I'm busting to pee. I push in the door and stumble again, spilling the contents of my handbag all over the hallway. I race into the toilet, never so glad to see one in my whole life and make the longest pee ever. As I'm sitting there on the loo, the wall in front of me begins to move and I laugh, thinking it's some kind of clever trick wall, but when I stand up the floor moves too. So weird.

In the living room, Tony's sitting on the couch, the contents of my handbag strewn beside him. He has my passport in hand and he's flipping it like you would a beer mat. I straddle him and start kissing him, pushing my tongue into his mouth. But he's like a statue underneath me. I stop and look at him, trying to focus on his face as it seems to move around of its own accord every few seconds.

"I'll call you a cab." His accent is thick Scouse.

"What's wrong?" I don't wait for an answer. I stand up and begin pulling my dress over my head.

He stands up too and pulls the dress back down my body. "This isn't going to happen, Maeve. Get your stuff together and I'll ring a cab."

"What's wrong with you? I thought we were going to . . ." The whole room sways now in front of me and I want to die. Curl up in a ball and die in a corner.

"You're sixteen, love, and you're really drunk, so nothing's going to happen, OK?"

I start crying like a baby, and Tony gets up and puts his arms around me. I close my eyes to stop the room swirling around.

I wake up in a strange bed. I can hear snoring in another room and I groggily climb out, wondering where I am. Bits of last night come back to me in fast, furious flashes. The bars, drinks, Tony. God, Tony – and me being a total slut. I notice that I'm still wearing my dress and somebody's put my shoes and bag on the floor beside the bed. I steal out of the sleeping house and walk down towards the port – at least I'll know my bearings from there.

I walk up the great hill to our house as sunbathers pass me, ready to take their place on the black sand for another day's roasting. I pass a collection of apartment complexes that seem to run into each other in their sameness. Low white stucco buildings, horseshoe pool, lush foliage. Airport buses have arrived already, dispensing new holidaymakers to their chosen accommodation. They're all high-spirited and full of holiday hope. I stop and sit on a wall, watching them roll suitcases into Reception, all laughing and cheerful. Then the empty buses pull off, back to the airport, no doubt, to collect the next batch. Delivery and collection – the conveyor-belt to a modern, sunny concentration camp.

I continue my climb up the hill and pause at the top to look back down at Puerto del Carmen below me. Legoland with sun. Shiny white buildings, blue sky, happy holidaymakers. I realise with absolute clarity that I fucking hate Lanzarote. I hate it for its mockness. Its unreality. Its picture-postcard lie of fun and relaxation. I want to go home.

Fifteen

Fiona has a new smile. It's a kind of enigmatic, cat-got-the-cream one, and she does it mostly when she's talking about or is being asked about the New House. And it's permanently plastered on her face today because she finally has the keys.

"Are you excited, hon?" says Mam, for about the millionth time.

It's a cold Saturday morning in November and I'm heading to the city library to study for the day.

Fiona does her smile thing, Harvey perched on her hip in a Man United Babygro. "I can't wait. It's fabulous and Social Welfare gave us a cheque for brand-new appliances and furniture. Only right too – I'd hate to be using someone else's stuff."

I'm making sandwiches to bring with me and biting my tongue at the same time. I know I have to be extra nice to Fiona now she's moving out – otherwise how do I get to see Harvey? I keep buttering bread, just saying in my head what I've bitten back. So you get a brand-new house – rent paid – and cheques for shiny new stuff and a lone-parents book even though we all know Big will be living there with you. You get all this stuff so you and your scumbag boyfriend can play house. Mark would love this turn of events. Pity I'm not talking to him.

"Guineys is great for bed linen. We'll pop in there in the afternoon when I'm finished my shift," says Mam.

Fiona does her smile thing again. Jesus, it's so fucking annoying, that smile. It's a look-at-me-I've-a-baby-and-a-house-and-sex-any-night-I-want smile.

"So, Maeve, what are you up to today?" Mam says, and I know she's trying to include me.

"I'm off to town with Ciara and Sophie, doing some shopping," I say breezily.

Mam eyes my freshly made sandwich and knows I'm lying. "That's nice. Call into Fiona's house – oh, my God, Fiona has a house – on your way home for a look."

"I'd love to," I say, and now Fiona stares at me suspiciously. Harvey gurgles and I shake his legs until he's chuckling out loud.

The library is packed but I find a seat in the corner next to a man with a stack of physics books in front of him. My study goes badly. Mark keeps popping into my head, his eyes searching me out in class, wanting me to forgive him or understand him or maybe just acknowledge he exists. And Cian. My big brother. Pretending to Mam that's he's loving his course, loving UCC, when all the time he's fucking my ex-friend in the North Circular Road. Oh, God, how stupid was I not to know what was going on? Their little movie nights, Cian so familiar with Mark's house, the third-wheel dates we went on. Bastards. They probably had a great laugh at my expense.

I watch the man devouring knowledge beside me, like it's water in a drought, and accept that today I'm not in the zone.

Not in that lovely place where I forget absolutely everything except study and the precise task in hand. A theorem to be learned, picked apart, understood. A tract of history to be devoured, a scientific experiment to be written up.

But today I doodle odd-shaped hearts in my notebook, and clock-watch my time away and allow my mind to wander around the circumstances of my life post-Lanzarote. And the decisions that I made on the plane home. Two decisions. Two promises to myself. The first is an easy one: popping my cherry. Trust me to meet a decent scumbag in Lanzarote: St Tony of Liverpool. Anyway, I've picked a new cherry popper: Colin Ryan. He doesn't know it yet but Colin is going to have some fun, possibly even tonight. And my second promise: get Big and get him good. I still don't know exactly how I'm going to do this but I know for the time being that I have to be in Fiona's life – even when she moves out I have to be there, indispensable, believable, innocent.

Already Big suspects I'm up to something. I think it was my offer of computer lessons last week when I saw him struggling with his new high-powered Apple MacBook. An Apple MacBook, for fuck sake! The drug trade must surely pay well. But he took the lessons out of sheer frustration with the sophisticated machine and next week I'm going to teach him Word and Excel. Why he needs Excel is anyone's guess – maybe drug-dealers have to do tax returns now, and profit and loss spreadsheets. Who knows? But one thing I do know about Big: he's very clever, he has no problem with concepts and if he'd gone to school he'd be a straight-A maths student. I watch him sometimes when Fiona's prattling on about some silly rom-com movie or what Danni Minogue wore on *The X Factor* and

I know he's just as bored with the prattling as I am, but I suppose he's getting the ride and that helps.

At last it's time to go and the industrious student beside me looks distraught that he's being disturbed from his work. I know that feeling well. Outside, in the rainy street, I text Ciara to see whether they're going out tonight. I haven't been out with them in weeks and I know she doesn't really know what to make of me. But needs must. Colin is in their group and I have plans for him. The little darling.

Number 2 Fuchsia Park is a brand-new terraced house in an estate of identical houses just around the corner from our street. Fiona hasn't moved far. I learned from Mam that the city council has bought a number of houses in the area. Not rows of them, just one or two here and there so there would be a good mix of people. A good idea in theory, but now as I walk up the newly cobbled footpath I can see a young woman leaning on a spade in the garden next door. She's looking at me suspiciously. I know several people are in the house already. Big's souped-up Honda Civic is in the drive and two cars are parked on the road. A silver Jeep and Mam's little Corolla. I check my phone before I go in. No reply from Ciara. Bitch. And the last time we were out I stopped her stripping for the jocks and ending up on YouTube. And I saved her from explaining to her mother how she was blotto for the night.

I ring the doorbell and Big answers.

"Come in and have a look. It's fuckin' beautiful," he says, and I follow him into the pristine hallway, the smell of new paint permeating the air. He's stopped calling me "Cunt" since the computer lessons began.

Fiona and Mam are in the kitchen, an open-plan affair, equipped with brand-new stainless-steel appliances and fitted out with high-gloss cream presses and shiny cream floor tiles. There are double doors leading to a sitting room, the only piece of furniture is a giant plasma TV resting on the floor. Fiona's friend Carrie – Blondie from the hospital – and her child-boyfriend Jay are in there admiring the room. Carrie's holding a beautiful blonde baby girl, decked out in a bright pink furry coat. I spy Harvey's buggy in the corner and walk over to say hello to him.

He's admiring his fists again, examining them and cooing at them, and when he sees my face bending down towards him he breaks into a huge toothless grin, a melt-your-heart one, saucer brown eyes delighted to see me. Big's in the kitchen popping a bottle of champagne and drinking it from the neck, like winning racing drivers do. Mam and Fiona are engrossed in the shiny new oven, almost climbing into it to admire it. I feel like an intruder – a stranger who was passing by and decided to take a peek into somebody's house. Big looks at me, champagne dripping from his chin, and I smile at him. He doesn't smile back, just laser-eyes me. A shiver runs down my spine and I feel the urge to run far away from these people who will end up in a bad place. Big keeps staring and I get the impression that he's warning me. In some strange way he's warning me not to touch anything in his life. That he can take care of it all. I go bright red and only then does he return my smile.

Jay comes into the kitchen and Big hands him the champagne bottle.

"Partay!" says Big, arm around his friend.

Jay takes a huge slug and straight away spits it into the brand-new circular stainless-steel sink. "Fuckin' poison, man, what the fuck is dat?"

"Fuckin' champagne, you eejit," says Big, and takes back the bottle for another huge slug. Essence of elegance.

"Well?" says Mam. "What do you think of the new abode?"

"Lovely," I say. "Absolutely perfect."

"We're moving in fully tomorrow, Big's friend has a van and we're going to bring all our stuff in. Did you see Harvey's room? Come on and I'll show you."

I follow my sister upstairs and into a bright yellow room. There's a sky blue carpet on the floor and tiny crooked red boats are painted in a row across one wall. "Big did the mural – isn't it lovely? He loves boats," says Fiona.

She walks out and I follow her.

"This is our room, an en-suite and all," she says, as she flings open the door to reveal a minuscule bathroom.

"Lovely," I say. My favourite word of the day.

We walk into another room, painted pale pink and furnished with an already elaborately dressed bed. "Your room." She smiles at me. Not the new smile but the old one that sometimes reminds me of Dad.

"My room?"

"There's always a room here for you, Maeve. I know you're making a huge effort with Big and I'm delighted, like. All I want is a happy family. That's all. And you're my favourite sister." She laughs at this and I join in. but as I follow her downstairs I'm strangely touched by her gesture. And there's a tiny wedge of guilt growing inside me about my decision to get Big out of our lives.

They're all about to order Chinese and someone's put on a CD with a thumping bass underscore. Big has thrown a slab of cans onto the worktop and more people have started to arrive.

People I've never seen before in my life. Mam is packing Harvey up to take him home and "let the young people at it" – her words not mine.

"Maeve, why don't you stay? We're having a house-warming," says Fiona, her face eager like a child's.

"I . . . I—"

She shoves a can into my hand, the ring pull already popped. "Let's party," she shouts, and Big shimmies up behind her, pushing his groin against her bum.

I want to get out and I can't believe it when my phone suddenly starts ringing. A miracle. My phone never rings. It's Ciara, all breathy, saying we just have to go out tonight, there's a party in Jamie's.

I step into the hall to hear her and we agree to meet in the little park near the shopping centre and go on to Jamie's from there. I go back in to tell Fiona I have to leave, that I'm meeting someone later. She winks at me, like I have a boyfriend or something. I wink back. Sisters in cahoots.

I shout my goodbyes over the music and the noise and as I leave I notice the woman still digging her square patch of garden next door. "Hi," I say, as I pass. She nods at me quickly and returns to her gardening. But not so quick that I don't notice the fear in her eyes. She's worried about her new neighbours. Part of me wants to tell her she has nothing to worry about. That Fiona's a lovely girl and just wants to make a home for her baby. But I know that's not really true. And the noise from the house gives weight to it as a lie.

I keep on walking, trying to work out what I'll wear for the deflowerment. I laugh out loud when this word pops into my head. Deflowerment. A word borrowed from another era. Cherry popping seems more apt.

*

I wear my skin-tight black dress that Fiona bought me in Lanzarote. My cherry-popping dress. Ciara, Sophie and I walk the short distance to Jamie Burke's, a large period house on the Ennis Road.

Jamie answers the door. "Well, look what the cat dragged in," he says, as a form of greeting.

He has that drunken glassy-eyed look that reminds me of the horrible night of the Results and I have a mad urge to thump him in his big dumb rugby face. Instead I smile sweetly at him. "Some nice birds – what a clever cat," I say, as I enter the hallway.

Jamie actually laughs at my raw attempt at flirting. So fucking dumb, this guy.

"You look . . . that dress . . . Girls, is this really the Robot? The Computer Brain?"

Sophie and Ciara giggle at Jamie's incredible wit.

We go into the huge living room, and it's like the whole school has turned out for Jamie's birthday party. A girl with pink streaks in her hair hands us bottles of Miller. I survey the crowd, looking for Colin. Instead I see Mark, sitting on a couch at the far end of the room, talking animatedly to a small blonde girl from sixth year. He half-waves when he sees me. I turn my back on him and take a long slug of Miller. It tastes disgusting but I need it for courage.

Three bottles later the walls are moving slightly and somebody has produced glasses. We're all downing shots in the kitchen when Colin walks in, holding hands with his ex – the one with the made-up name I can never remember. A small knot of fury burns inside me. I walk up to Colin and notice that he drops the girl's hand immediately. "Hey," I say, smiling at him.

"Hi, Maeve. You look . . . nice."

"Thanks. So do you." I lean in close to him, and touch his arm. "How have you been? I haven't seen you in ages."

"Oh, you know . . . I'm training and . . ."

"Here, have a beer," I say, and hand him a can from the worktop. I ignore the girl completely. "So . . . what's your favourite Coen Brothers movie?"

His face lights up. "That's easy. *Fargo* – no competition."

The girl fidgets beside us, bored by the conversation. She eventually moves away, while Colin and I rehash every Coen Brothers movie on celluloid. Now it's time to move in for the kill. "Come outside, I need to talk to you," I whisper into his ear, giving it a tiny lick and pulling him by the arm through the crowds to the French windows and into the garden. Then I pull him towards the side of the house, push him against the wall and kiss him hard on the mouth. He puts his arms around me, pulling me in tight to him, his hands travelling all over my back and then my bum. I can feel him hard against me and my heart is thumping. I drop my hands and try to open his fly.

He groans out loud. "Oh, God . . . Maeve . . . oh, God."

The feeling of power is incredible. I open his fly and slip my hand in.

Suddenly he pushes me away with both hands. "No . . . can't do it . . . not like this . . ."

"What's wrong?" I ask.

He pulls up the zipper in his trousers and looks at the ground as he speaks. "Not like this . . . not with you like this . . ."

I lean against the rough plaster wall, my heart still

thumping. "What I mean is . . . I like you, Maeve . . . and . . . just not like this . . ."

"So, Colin, let me get this straight in my head. You like me so you can't fuck me. That makes loads of sense. It's all crystal clear now."

He touches my bare arm. "That's not what I—"

"That's exactly what you meant. Now be a good boy and go back into your little dumb blonde." I leave, my heels clicking loudly on the path. Mark's standing by himself near the door. "Maeve . . ."

"Well, if it isn't Mr Gay Pride himself. How are you? Are you still fucking my brother and, if so, how's that going?"

"Maeve . . ."

"Maeve, Maeve, Maeve. Can you say anything else to me except my name?"

"Yes, I can. You're pissed out of your head and you should go home."

I guffaw at this, my laugh loud and disconnected, like a laugh I'd just borrowed to try out. I grab a drink from the worktop, somebody else's drink in a long glass, and slug it all back in one go, almost gagging. Vodka. Disgusting. "There's a taste of more from that," I say to Mark, as I put the empty glass down. "Now, let's see, what would I like to drink? Something nice and strong – Jamie, hey, Jamie, what would you suggest?"

Jamie lopes over and puts an arm around me. "You look stunning tonight. I have a great suggestion," he says, eyeing me up and down.

"So what is it?" I say, smiling at him. Mark is still standing there, glaring at me.

Jamie whispers in my ear, "Come upstairs, and I'll tell you."

I laugh, that weird stranger's laugh. "Lead the way."

Jamie takes my hand, and tunnels through the crowd, grabbing a bottle from a table on his way. Like an eejit, Mark follows us out to the hallway and even tries to follow us upstairs. "Maeve."

"Maeve." I imitate him in a high-pitched voice.

Jamie laughs. Mark stands on the bottom stair, watching us. I give him a wave and a grin as we disappear. Jamie barges open a door into a huge bedroom with a king-size bed.

"Mammy's room?" I ask, giggling.

He takes a long drink from the bottle and hands it to me.

We sit side by side on the bed and I take a huge drink too. I don't know what it is but it's really strong. Jamie's running his hands up and down my back. Then he takes the bottle from me and puts it on the floor. Suddenly I'm nervous. I think it's the smell of him near me, reminding me of the horrible night last September. He takes my face in his hands and kisses me slowly. The room starts to spin.

Sixteen

"Go fuck yourself." I try to pronounce the words properly but they jumble up the minute they leave my mouth. But Mark understands the meaning. He's leaning over me, pulling me up by my arms. Jamie's standing over me too. My head swims again, off down a lovely lazy river, winding down and down.

"She looks green. Man, don't let her be sick in Mam's bed – Jesus, man, get her up."

I smile at Jamie, as both he and Mark try to lift me from the bed. They stand me up and half-walk, half-drag me towards the door. I hiccup suddenly and burst out laughing.

"Ah, man, she's gonna be sick, I know she is," says Jamie.

"Pink," I say, laughing again.

"Come on, Maeve, let's go home," says Mark.

"Pink vomit's right, Jamie?" I say, but again it's a complete jumble. They walk me down the stairs, Jamie in front, looking back worriedly all the time. "'S OK, Jamie, I won't vomit on your lovely hair," I say, and it actually sounds like a sentence. I'm very proud of myself for that.

And then somehow, like magic, I'm in a cab and Mark's in the front seat and the rain is lashing the windows, trickling down in a river. My eyes begin to close and I nod off, my head falling to the side. I find a soft, comfortable place to rest it except it seems to be pushing me away. I straighten up and realise that the little blonde one Mark was talking to all night is sitting beside me. She knows I'm staring at her but looks ahead, her face tiny in profile. Like a little girl's.

My stomach is churning now, a washing-machine full of alcohol, swilling around, looking for a way out.

We pull up at Mark's house just in time. I jump out and puke behind an ornamental fern near the front steps. I can hear Mark paying the cab driver and the crunch of wheels on the driveway. I wipe my mouth with my sleeve. My whole body's shaking and Mark puts his coat around my shoulders. "I love you," I tell him.

"Yeah, I know. Sure. Now let's get you to bed."

I link him and it isn't until we are going into the hallway that I notice the little child-woman, holding his other hand.

"So, where's the booze? The fizzy champagne will do nicely," I say, as we go into the kitchen.

Mark laughs and fills the kettle with water. "Tea and then bed."

I manage to perch on a stool without falling. "So, who are you?" I ask the child.

She looks at me coolly.

"Thought you knew each other. "This is Sarah. Sarah – Maeve," says Mark.

She gives a tiny nod, like it pains her to move her head.

The phone next to me rings suddenly and I almost topple from my perch. Mark answers it, walking into the living room with it.

I jump down from my stool and begin bustling around the kitchen, making tea, finding cups, even biscuits. Letting Sarah know I have the run of the place.

"So. Mark. You know, don't you?" I pour tea into small white cups.

Stony silence from her.

I spoon sugar into my tea and sip the hot sweet liquid. My head is suddenly very clear. "You know he's gay is what I mean."

More stony silence but I can see a little flicker in her eyes. Curiosity. Annoyance.

I smile at her. "Yeah. What a waste." I take another sip of tea while she lets hers go cold in front of her. She's fixing her short blonde hair behind her ears so much I want to grab it all and toss it until it's standing on her tiny pea head.

"You're an incredibly rude little girl, do you know that?"

"Why? Because I have difficulty taking silly drunk people seriously?" She says it in a small, tight voice, exactly like her body.

I laugh. "You'll need a few drinks yourself tonight if you're planning to . . . am . . . how will we put it? Planning to fuck my brother-in-law."

She's rattled now. I can see it in her face, and in the constant hair-grabbing thing – Jesus, that'd drive a saint mad.

"Yep. Brother-in-law. Mark and my brother, Cian. Ask him. They're as tight as – let's see, what analogy could I use? Tight as Victoria Beckham's arse. Now that's a good one cos she's like a gay icon so . . ." I realise that Mark is standing in the doorway, listening.

"Maeve, I think it's time you went to bed. You can sleep in

the guest room, top of the stairs, first door. And you can apologise to both me and Sarah in the morning. Goodnight."

He walks over to Sarah, takes her face in his hands and kisses her hard on the mouth right there in front of me. Her small hands pull his face into hers like he's badly needed oxygen.

I bang my way out of the kitchen and up the stairs, burning with anger. And shame. I march into the bedroom and collapse on the bed. Tears come, hot and fast. I thump the pillow while I cry, wishing it was my own face. My own mean, disgusting face that I barely recognise any more.

Something wakes me. I sit up in bed trying to work out exactly where I am. For a second I think I'm still in Jamie Burke's house, in Jamie Burke's mother's bed. Did I have sex with him? I flick on a bedside light and realise I'm at Mark's. Little bits of the night prick my conscience. The drunkenness. Mark banging on Jamie's mother's bedroom door. A cab ride and a small blonde girl who looks like a child. I stagger out of bed and check the time on my phone. Two o'clock. It feels much later than that. I creep out to find the bathroom. There are rows of doors along the large hallway. Mark must be able to sleep in a different bedroom every night of the week. I see a small light towards the end of the hall and head for that, my bladder bursting from all the stupid alcohol.

And then I hear it again. The noise that woke me in the first place. A low moan. Strange but familiar at the same time. I stand riveted outside the door where the noise is coming from. There are two moans now – a his and hers – and my face burns bright red. I want to throw the door open and scream at Mark. Scream at him and his disgusting habit of having sex in front

216

of or within earshot of me. And having sex with anyone. Boy, girl, it makes no difference. Fucking bastard. I want to kill him. Instead I pee and as quietly as I can I find my shoes and leave the house, accidentally setting off the alarm as I close the front door.

I walk home, my shoes in my hand. I realise I've left my bag in Mark's with my house keys in it. There's no way I'm going back now. I'll have to wake Mam. I tap lightly on the door, waiting for a light to flick on. Nothing happens. I knock next time, the noise loud in the quiet night street. No answer. I ring the doorbell next, keeping my finger pressed down. Still no answer. The book club must have been particularly lively tonight, Mam in a deep Chardonnay sleep. Coma.

I head for Fiona's. The lights blaze in every window. I tap at the door and Big opens it. He doesn't even say hello, just goes back in, leaving the door open for me. I walk in, feeling like an eejit. There's a small crowd in the living room. Fiona's asleep on the couch, Big and Jay are leaning over a table, snorting lines of coke with tightly rolled-up notes. Big's eyes are hard, narrowed to slits.

Jay's girlfriend rouses herself from a deck-chair in the corner and kneels down to snort a line too.

"Babe, want some?" Big says, as he shakes Fiona awake. She sits up and they all crack up laughing.

"What?" she says. "What's so funny?"

They get into fits of laughing at this and when she faces me I can see why. Somebody's shaved off her eyebrows while she was asleep.

"Maeve? Why are you here?" she asks.

More laughter. Big's slapping his thigh, tears squeezing out of his slitty eyes.

"What's so funny?" Fiona says again, standing up to look in the freshly hung mirror over the fireplace. She doesn't say anything. Just stares at her eyebrowless face. She keeps staring and the laughing dies away until there's silence. Then she cries. Keeps staring at her nude face, tears silently flowing down her cheeks. I walk over to her and put my hand lightly on her arm. She buries her head in my shoulder, sobbing quietly.

Big jumps up, knocking the table over with the last line of coke. "Babe, 'twas only a joke like. Come on, babe . . ." He tries to lift her head from my shoulder but she's glued to me.

"Leave her alone, you thick bastard," I say. Jay and Carrie watch us from the couch, faces dead serious.

"Shut up, Cunt. Listen, babe, we were only havin' a laugh, like – they'll grow back in no time. Remember when ye did it to me in Pa's and we had a great laugh . . ." He puts his hand on her shoulder. She shrugs him off.

"Come on, Fiona, let's go to bed," I say. She nods into my shoulder and we leave. She never raises her head at all. Just lets me lead her upstairs. We climb into bed together, the two of us in our knickers and bras. She puts her arm around me in the dark room, Harvey snuffling in his sleep.

"You OK?" I whisper into the dark.

"Yeah," she whispers back.

"We'll fix those eyebrows in the morning. We can draw them on like Mrs Mooney does."

She giggles at this. We spent many hours as children expounding on the artistic endeavours our neighbour went through every morning so she'd have eyebrows for the day. I'm delighted I've managed to cheer her up. But I feel her silent sobs as I drift off to sleep.

Seventeen

"So, Ms Hogan. Where's your entry?" Mr Hynes smiles at me. He's leaning against his desk, arms folded. Modern-day Mr Darcy.

I wonder if he has sex on a regular basis. I shake the thought out of my head before it reaches my tongue. "Entry? To what? *The X Factor*? Thought I'd give it a miss this year."

He cocks an eyebrow at me. "You promised me."

I drop my eyes and shrug at the floor.

"Deadline's tomorrow."

Another shrug.

"OK, Maeve. Look at me."

I raise my eyes but my face is starting to burn bright red.

"What's going on?"

"Nothing."

"Come on, Maeve. I know there's something going on with you."

This makes me mad so for the first time I look straight into his eyes. "How? How do you know there's something going on? Are you a mind reader? A mystic? How do you know?"

"Hey – take it easy. I just wondered if—"

"Is there something wrong with my work?"

"No, your work is excellent . . . too good in fact, too much effort."

"If you have no problem with my work except that it's too good then I'd like to go home now."

He studies my face, saying nothing. The silence makes me blush all over again. "Look, if you ever want to chat, you know – off the record, just between you and me – I'm your year head and that's what I'm here for."

"OK. I have to go."

"Are you sure you won't enter the competition? You can just hand me the entry in a brown envelope – I won't even look at it."

I haven't the heart to tell him that my drivel-writing is now cluttering cyber-space. Gone for ever. "No. I'm not interested."

"That's fine, Maeve."

"Bye," I say, and walk out of the stuffy classroom, glad to be away from his gaze. I bump straight into Colin Ryan as I walk out of the school gates.

"Maeve."

"Colin." I keep walking, my shoes clacking on the footpath.

He runs to catch up with me. "Maeve."

I keep walking, thinking about all the things I need to do before heading to Fiona's to babysit. It's Big's birthday and she's planned a night out. They're going for a meal in the new restaurant on O'Connell Street. French. Would love to be a fly on that wall when Big is presented with the menu.

"Maeve."

"What?" I shout, stopping to face Colin.

He goes bright red and then I start the red-face thing too.

"I . . . Look . . . about that night . . ."

"Forget it. I was pissed . . . Forget it."

"No . . . I just wanted to say that I . . ." He stops and looks at me like he's waiting for me to finish the sentence.

"Am . . . I . . ."

"Forget it. It was a dare. That's all."

His face is crimson, so red I can feel heat from it.

"Oh."

I smile at him. "See ya." I start walking again.

"Maeve."

"Colin, forget it. I have."

"Will you . . . go . . . Will you meet me?"

"For what?" I'm still walking and he's trying to keep up with me.

"You know – a date."

I stop and he bangs into me. "A date?"

He nods.

"When?"

He smiles, encouraged. "Tonight . . . we could go to the cinema."

The cinema. Such originality. "No can do. Babysitting for my sister."

"Oh. Well, maybe I could call over. I have the new Tarantino movie on DVD – it's a pirate but good quality."

I consider this in my head. A date. I'd actually never been on a date. And I'd love to see the movie. Spare me having to watch the wooden puppet that is Pat Kenny. And it'd be nice to do a normal thing, like watch a movie with a guy, someone who isn't your brother or your gay/bisexual friend. Or your Chardonnay-filled mother. "OK."

"OK?"

"Yeah. OK. It's number two Fuchsia Park. The new houses – do you know them?"

He grins and nods. "Fuchsia Park. New houses."

"Around nine. Bye." I walk away, leaving Colin standing there smiling.

They leave bang on time. Fiona's all dressed up in a cobalt blue minidress. Big's effort consists of a shirt, instead of a tracksuit top, over denim jeans. I take a picture of them with Big's new state-of-the-art digital camera he's bought as a present to himself.

Harvey's wide awake and I'm delighted. I haven't seen him for three whole days and I drink him in now. All the tiny little changes in him, the fleck of gold in his dark brown eyes that I'd never noticed before. The new cooing sound he makes when you talk to him.

And he's still up when the doorbell rings and Colin is standing there in front of me, a huge tub of popcorn in his hand.

"In here," I say, hoisting Harvey onto my hip. Colin follows me into the living room and sits beside me on the couch.

"So," I say, taking Harvey's bottle from the coffee-table and sticking the teat into his mouth. He greedily latches on, kicking his feet with pleasure and wrapping his hand tightly around mine. It's a new habit of his and every time he does it I get a jolt in my heart, almost like a physical pain.

Colin sits there tongue-tied and I resent his presence. Resent him intruding on my Harvey time and even on my Kenny time when I watch five minutes, then switch it off and pick up a textbook. Colin is hard work.

Harvey's eyes start to droop and his body becomes heavy in my arms. I take him up to bed, laying him down in his cot. I stand there in the quiet room looking at him, his face visible in the soft glow from the nightlight. I sit on the bed and watch him through the bars of the cot, his face turned towards me, his breathing rhythmic and soothing. I lie down on the bed, still gazing at him, listening to his soft baby breathing. I've missed it so much since Fiona moved.

There's a soft tap on the door and Harvey stirs in his cot. I jump up – I'd dozed off. Then I remember Colin.

"Ssh – you'll wake him," I whisper, as I pad out of the room. I follow Colin downstairs.

"Couldn't settle him," I say, glancing at my watch. Half ten. I'd been asleep a full hour. Jesus.

"No problem. Who owns the camera?" He's flicking through the memory on Big's new toy.

"That's Big's and I wouldn't break it if I were you."

"Jesus." His eyes are wide as he stares at the screen. "Oh, fuck, I'm sorry . . . I . . ." He's gone that pinky red colour for the second time today.

"What's up? Show me." I grab the camera and look at the picture. It's Fiona, smiling seductively at the camera, in a porn version of a school uniform. I flick to the next image. Fiona naked, smiling at the camera, holding her boobs like those silly girls in men's porn magazines. I'm disgusted but fascinated all at the same time. The next image is a graphic close-up of Fiona's bum. I almost drop the camera. "Fuck."

"We shouldn't look – it's their private stuff. We shouldn't look."

I slip the camera back into its case. "You're right. Let's watch the movie."

But I can't concentrate on the film. I'm thinking all the time about those pictures of Fiona. Weird pictures, really. Slut pictures to please that fool. I'm watching the clock, too, because I want Colin well gone before Fiona and Big get home.

So I'm shocked when I feel his hand snake up my back and rest lightly on my shoulder, like it hopes I won't notice. The movie is a blur, my concentration zero. Colin presses his leg closer to mine. I fight the urge to move away, and an inexplicable desire to laugh. Why do I find it so funny? This is supposed to be normal. This is what I want, isn't it? He turns me to face him and I almost burst out laughing when I see his expression. Adoration is the only way I can describe it. He leans towards me and kisses me on the lips, gently, like he's kissing something precious. I sit back a little and look at him and then he does it again, his lips so soft yet so urgent. My insides melt and my heart thumps and this time I kiss him back, my body doing and feeling things that I never knew it could. And somehow then we're lying on the couch, and he's pulling at my clothes, at my sweatshirt and then my bra and then he's kissing my nipples, again like they're the most precious things he's ever touched. My breathing is ragged, matching his, and I want him not to stop, to just keep doing it, making me feel like this, so wanted.

"What de fuck?"

Big is standing in front of us. I can see his short butty legs from my position on my back on his couch.

Colin jumps up and starts pulling on his jumper. I sit up, covering my breasts with my hand, trying to maintain some dignity. And then I see Fiona behind him, her face tear-streaked. "What's wrong?" I ask, trying to pull on my clothes.

She ignores me. "Fucking bastard, that's all you are. On

your phone talking to those scumbags all night . . ." Fiona comes really close to him and her voice is hysterical.

"Shut up and help me, you gowl," Big says. He's running around now, like he's looking for something, tossing cushions, almost pushing me out of the way. Then he's flying up the stairs, Fiona following.

Colin is sitting on the couch, looking puzzled. I go out to the hallway, wondering what's going on. I can hear Fiona crying in the bathroom and Big still doing his manic search. The doorbell rings. I answer it.

"We have a warrant to search these premises," a guard says, waving a piece of paper in my face. He pushes past me, followed by three others and a woman officer.

When I follow them into the living room they have poor Colin up against the wall, searching him. I have a terrible urge to pee. Next thing Big is in the room, followed by Fiona.

"What de fuck do ye want, ye shower of cunts? Fuckin' nothin' better to do than harass people? Go out and catch the real scumbags, fuckin' waste of space."

A guard grabs Big and pushes him up against the wall too. Fiona's crying and I am as well. Hot tears of fear and shame. The woman asks Fiona and me to step into the kitchen. "I have to search you," she says, and begins to pat down my body. I want to die of shame.

"Take your hands off my sister, she's only sixteen," says Fiona, her chin out, head high. The tears have vanished.

"What age are you?" asks the guard.

"Sixteen – I was the oldest in my class but I skipped transition year so I'm not any more." I don't know why I'm motor-mouthing but I can't help it. "I don't have any drugs on me and neither does my sister," I continue. Fiona gives me a shut-up glare.

The woman ignores me and starts to pat down Fiona. "Are there any other persons in the house besides you all?"

"My baby is asleep upstairs. Do you want to search him as well?"

"Actually, yes. Lead the way, please."

Fiona gives the woman a venomous look as she marches out of the kitchen and up the stairs. I follow the guard, still not believing that she's going to search a baby. A small, sleeping, innocent baby.

Fiona lifts Harvey from his cot and he rubs his eyes with his balled fists as the light blinds him. She lays him on the bed, talking softly to him all the time. I hear a sob and realise it's coming from me. The woman bends over him, smiling at him as she examines his clothes. "You'll have to open the nappy for me."

Tears well in Fiona's eyes but she does as she's told.

"I'm sorry," says the cop, "we have to do it." She turns her attention to the cot, which she searches methodically. Harvey's wide awake now and gives me a big gummy smile.

"I have to search the room," says the woman. Her walkie-talkie crackles in her belt as she begins rifling through Fiona's underwear drawer. Fiona walks out with Harvey and I follow her downstairs. The cops have moved to the kitchen and they have every cupboard open, contents dumped on any surface available. Big is standing by the open back door, smoking a fag.

He winks at Fiona. "You OK, babe? Don't mind dose cunts, only lookin' for something to do on a Friday night. Fuckin' *Late Late* that borin', is it, that ye have to call here to us?"

The two cops on their knees in front of the dishwasher laugh and roll their eyes. One of them, a young guy with a smooth, hairless face, catches my eye and looks me up and down, then turns back to his task of rooting through dirty dishes. I know the look. It's the *Pramface* look. The disapproving, disgusted look. I watch his head as he opens another cupboard. I want to jump on his back and thump him and tell him I'm not the person he thinks I am. I'm not a druggie scumbag, I'm an A student with an exceptionally high IQ – much higher than his.

Instead I go in search of Colin, who's sitting on the couch, watching the credits roll on the movie we never saw. "I'm sorry, Colin." I burst out crying.

"Hey, Maeve, it's OK. It's nothing. I know one of the guards – he works with my dad and I told him you're cool. It's grand, honestly." He pulls me into him and holds me really tight, stroking my hair and kissing the top of my head. And it's a lovely feeling of being minded, like when you're small and your daddy has the answer to everything and as soon as he holds you everything's going to be grand. My crying turns into dry sobs and we stay like that for what seems like ages. And then finally they're gone. I can hear the door closing and the car doors opening and the engines revving.

"Let's go," Colin says. "I'll walk you home."

"OK," I say, even though I'd planned to stay the night so that I could steal Harvey in the morning while Big and Fiona slept off their hangovers.

Fiona and Big are fighting again. I can hear them upstairs, angry mean voices, and poor Harvey having to listen.

He kisses me again outside my house. Another delicious

one, like a tiny bite of your favourite chocolate. "I'll ring you," he says, dropping his head to give me one last kiss.

My head is swimming as I open my front door. Guards and drug searches and kisses. Especially kisses. Who would ever have thought that Colin Ryan – who can't string a sentence together – would be so good at kissing?

Eighteen

I want him to get in touch. This surprises me and I actually waste precious time in the library the next day waiting for my phone to ring. I have it on silent but can't take my eyes off it as it sits there next to my construction notes. The physics guy is sitting opposite me again and he's really pissing me off. He's working so hard that he's hardly conscious of what's going on around him. But every now and again he throws a glance my way when he hears me fidgeting with the phone.

Finally it glows. A message. My heart thumps and I read it as surreptitiously as I can. Mark. He's in town. Can we meet for a coffee and a chat? Fuck off, Mark. I go back to my construction and can't believe it when the library begins its closing-up routine.

He's leaning against a car, right in front of the library door making it impossible for me to ignore him. "I knew you'd be here."

"Genius." I keep walking and he falls into step beside me.

"Fancy a coffee? I'll buy." Mark grins at me like old times.

"Nothing better to do."

We go to Café on the Row and I order a grande cappuccino

seeing as Mark is paying. The café is Saturday busy, full of young people.

"So, Maeve, you're headline news today," Mark says.

"What do you mean?"

"The Big Raid. Everyone's talking about it."

I go scarlet, letting this bit of information sink in. "That wasn't anything to do with me. I was just in the house."

Mark laughs. "I know that. But you know how some people are. They hear something and suddenly it has wings and it's a whole other story by the time it boomerangs back to you."

Our coffees arrive and Mark thanks the blonde Russian-looking waitress. She doesn't crack a smile. "What happened? I trust this involves Big in some way."

"You tell me what you heard first."

He sips his coffee. "OK. Here's the most up-to-date Bebo version. You and Colin Ryan were caught with a load of coke in your sister's house last night."

I laugh but there's a slightly hysterical note to it. "Not true. I was babysitting and the guards raided Fiona's while I was there and they found nothing so they left. End of story."

"So, no coke and no Colin?"

I feel myself reddening straight away. Mark smiles knowingly at me. "There was popcorn and Tarantino."

He laughs at this and for a second it really is like old times. Like the stuff with Cian never happened.

"Colin's sister is involved in the rumour – she's friends with Sarah."

"Why would Colin tell his sister anything?" I say it without realising that I'm admitting he was there. Not that I care if Mark knows or not – I just don't want to treat him like before. Like a real friend.

"Colin isn't the source. Colin's daddy is. He's a detective in Henry Street."

My stomach tightens and my hand shakes. Some coffee spills on the white tablecloth. I mop it up with a serviette, trying to keep my face blank. I can feel tears stinging my eyes and I can see the face of the young cop last night, that look of judgement and disgust. "Yeah, well, nothing happened. So, how are you? How's the romance with the child-woman? Or are you back in the boys' camp again?" I laugh the hysterical stranger's laugh. The couple at the next table look over at me.

"Get it, Mark? Camp – play on words? That was a total accident but it was rather clever, you'll have to admit."

Mark blinks and I know I've hurt him and I know it's a cheap shot but I don't care. He broke up our friendship – not me.

"I miss you Maeve."

This takes me completely by surprise. Again the tears prick my eyes.

"I miss you and I want us to be friends again."

The tears come. Silent. Soundless. Falling on the white tablecloth, making big round blotches.

He reaches out and holds my hand tight. "I love you."

More tears and I finally raise my head and look at him. "No."

"No? No what?"

"No. You can't fuck my brother and have me walk in on it and then pretend it never happened." I try to keep my voice down but I know it's loud by the stares our table is receiving.

"Maeve, I love you and we can move on from this and—"

I snatch my hand away from his, knocking the coffee cup. A brown stain spreads across the table. I wipe my eyes with another serviette, then snatch my bag and coat from the chair, rocking the table as I stand up to leave. "You were *my* friend, Mark." I run out of the door, almost crashing into a woman with a young child, then run down Henry Street and out the Dock Road. I run until my lungs feel like they're going to burst. Fucking cheek of him with his moving-on crap. Fucking girl. As gay as Christmas. I march home getting madder and madder with every step. But it's not him I'm mad at. It's myself.

And the last person I want to speak to is Cian and, sure enough, he wants a love-in with me as well. "Can we talk?" he asks, when I'm barely in the door.

"What's this – a concerted effort cooked up between you and your boyfriend? To answer your question – can we talk? Yes, we can. Fuck off," I say, and run upstairs, banging the door so hard the house shakes. I throw myself on my bed and check my phone again. Nothing. Colin won't be in touch now. Not with his daddy in the picture.

There's a knock on my door.

"Go away, Cian, I'm tired."

"It's Mam. Can I come in?"

I don't answer and she takes that as a yes. Her hair is wrapped in a towel and she's wearing her old dressing-gown, once white, now a kind of blue grey.

She sits down beside me and strokes my hair. I pull away from her. She does it again, just keeps stroking my hair, and the tears start all over again. She never says a word. Keeps stroking and stroking until eventually the tears stop. "It'll be fine," she says, her voice almost a whisper. And then she leaves.

It's a whole week before I hear from Colin. I'm in Fiona's babysitting and Harvey's in bed. Pat Kenny is on TV, prattling on with some guest who's peddling her autobiography. My head hurts from studying and I'm tired – but a nice tired when you know you've worked really hard. The physics guy in the library would be proud of me. And then my phone beeps and it's a text from him. I haven't seen him all week in school and I'm presuming he's avoiding me because Daddy doesn't like me. But the text is all friendly, apologising for not texting, a mixture of no credit and a really bad flu. Sure, I think, as I delete the text. I also delete his number from my contacts.

I'm just thinking about going to bed when Fiona arrives home. There's a couple with her, people I've never seen before. And no sign of Big. "Hey, you're early."

She hiccups and the couple laugh, a girl and a guy, older than Fiona, in their early twenties. "Big had to go off on business and the pub was, like, so boring that Gerry and Kim said we'd have a laugh back here. Who wants something to drink? What do ye think of the house? Rapid, isn't it?" Fiona does a shaky twirl in the middle of the sitting room, then collapses on the couch, laughing.

I go to bed.

The noise of the TV wakes me. It's a music channel, MTV or something, and just as I creep downstairs I hear Big's car pulling up. I'd know that souped-up sound anywhere.

I get a drink of water in the kitchen and peep through the glass-panelled door into the living room. Big comes into the kitchen and drops his keys on the worktop. In the living room they all look like they're asleep, Gerry and Kim on one couch, heads touching, and Fiona on the other, her head lolling forward. Big fills the kettle behind me.

"Fuckin' telly is very loud – is she deaf or what?"

"They're asleep," I say, and leave with my glass of water.

The scream makes me drop the glass on the hall tiles. Big's scream, urgent and dangerous. I try to open the living-room door from the hallway, forgetting that the couch is blocking it, so I run through the kitchen and into the living room. Fiona's exactly where I saw her a minute ago but now I see what Big is screaming about. There's a tight band around her arm, bright red – a tie, I think – and a syringe on the Winnie the Pooh cushion beside her. Big is paralysed in the middle of the floor, running his hands through his hair and screaming.

"Fuck, fuck! Do something – fuck it, she's done for! She's done for . . ." He runs out of the room and comes straight back in, dancing now, his legs moving almost involuntarily. The couple on the couch stand up and rub their eyes, watching the scene before them.

"Do something, fucking cunts – what did ye do? Fuckin' never touch the product. Golden fuckin' rule in this business, never fuckin' touch it. I told her, man, I told her . . ."

I shake her. I know she's breathing because I can see her chest rising and falling. "Fiona, come on, Fiona, get up, you have to stand up." I try to lift her but she feels so heavy. Big is crying now, tears and snot mixing together, running down his nose. "We have to get her up – help me," I say, but he doesn't even hear me. He's wringing his hands and mumbling and doing the dancing thing with his feet. I look for the couple but they're not in the room.

"Big, listen, help me get her up. Now! Help me get her up, for fuck sake." I'm shouting so loud that my own ears are ringing, and for a second I actually think it's working. There's a spark in his eyes, a spark of reason and sanity. He comes over, still crying, and hoists Fiona under her other arm. We have her between us then, like a limp dead body. We struggle with her weight, trying to force her to walk. Suddenly her body starts jerking. Big screams again and runs to the door. Fiona slides to the floor, her whole body rigid in spasm. Big is silent now, frozen, eyes fixed on Fiona.

I pull her into the recovery position and clear her airways so she can breathe.

"Ring an ambulance!" I shout at Big, but I might as well be talking to myself. He's rigid, like a statue, and when I look down at Fiona I see Daddy. I blink and try to contain myself. Daddy's face merges into Fiona's, her lips blue, her eyelids veined and transparent.

"Ring a fucking ambulance or she'll die!" I scream. He jumps, and looks at me glassy-eyed, but he goes into the kitchen, dials and speaks. I lean over Fiona, stroking her hair, whispering a mantra over and over – *not like this, Fifi, not like this, please, not like this, not now* . . .

I can hear my voice outside myself, murmuring and murmuring, and Big crying, walking in and out of the room, then the lovely sound of an ambulance screeching closer and closer. They burst into the house, taking control, barking orders. I surrender myself to them, glad to hand over the responsibility. They put her on a stretcher and rush her out of the door. I follow them and climb into the ambulance after the stretcher. Big tries to get in too.

"Get the fuck back into the house." My voice is icy cold.

He's pleading with me, "I'm coming, like, I love her, you know—"

"I'll stay with her. You stay with the baby. Remember him? Harvey? Your son?"

Big stands there, staring at me, his face childlike in the blue flashing light. And then the doors slam and the siren blares and I wipe away my own snot and tears and watch the paramedics try to keep my sister alive.

Nineteen

Fiona is in a coma. The word comes from the Greek and means "deep sleep". A profound state of unconsciousness. A comatose person cannot be awakened, fails to respond normally to pain or light, does not have sleep–wake cycles and does not take voluntary actions. The underlying cause of coma is bilateral damage to the reticular formation of the mid-brain, which is important in regulating sleep. I can see the page in my head quite clearly. An abandoned medical book in the library one rainy Saturday a few months ago. I'd devoured it. Something to learn that wasn't on the syllabus. That I'd never seen before.

And in this dark room with its soundtrack of beeps and the soft thump of the ventilator, these words give me comfort. Like knowing your enemy. Knowing as much as you can so you can beat it. Fiona is a child in the bed, wired and intubated and impassive. Her face is white, pinched, dark splotches underneath her eyes. They've told us to talk to her. Mam and Linda spent hours doing it earlier. Talking and talking. Going outside to cry. Big came. He cried and did the little dance thing. What's with him and that little dance? Like a puppet on a string. Like Michael Flatley on crack cocaine. I told him to get out. Unless he could hold himself together, talk to her, soothe her, then he could just fuck off. He cried some more and left.

Cian's no better. Hovering around like a lost boy. Scrunching up his face trying not to cry. Great fucking help. And Mark – why would he even bother turning up? No help whatsoever. I'm glad I turfed them all out. Vonnie in her pyjamas, seeming to enjoy the drama of it all, whispering to the nurses, whispering things about my sister. Fucking cheek when it was her useless scumbag son put Fiona in here.

I want to tell them all that I was right and they were wrong. All of them, including Mam. I warned them that something bad would happen. That any intelligent person knew it'd be one great train wreck. But I don't need to tell them. I don't need to say the words. All I need to do is look at Fiona and then at them. And they know. Fuck them. Afraid to upset the apple cart. Wait until it has run its course. Wait until Fiona has a couple more babies, is a full-fledged addict, an alcoholic, a victim. Wait and watch her ruin her life. Throw it away on a waster.

And Harvey. I don't even want to think about Harvey. About what lies in store for him. People are so stupid. So thick it makes me want to hurt them. Beat them until they get brains. Thickness is the worst affliction in the world. I'd rather be blind, deaf, paraplegic – anything but have a thick, dumb, meaningless life. Like an animal but worse, because animals fulfil their potential by being what they are.

The sound of the ventilator is rhythmic. Soothing. Making me sleepy. But I can't sleep. I mustn't. It's my turn to stay with her. I reach out and hold her small lifeless hand, careful not to pull out the cannula taped onto it.

"Harvey's looking for you, Fifi. He's smiling and happy but I know he's looking for you. There's just something about him – like he's not quite settled. So you'll have to wake for Harvey. Don't mind anyone else. Think of Harvey. Fiona, if you don't wake up, Big's family get Harvey and . . ." I stop whispering to my sister, realising the truth of this. They'll take him if she dies. They'll take him and in a few years he'll be like Big. He'll be just like Big's kid brothers. They'll be heroes to him. I see it all as clear as day. Even if she doesn't die, Harvey will see them as heroes. He'll think it's OK to constantly be in trouble with the law. OK not to go to school. I won't let it happen.

"I won't let it happen, Fifi, I swear on my life I won't let it happen. I swear on Daddy's grave . . ." I lean over her whispering into her ear. "We'll go away somewhere, Fifi. Just you and me. It'll be like when we used to go on holidays when we were small. Remember? We'd be awake all night, unable to sleep from excitement, and then the morning, packing the car, sneaking in our favourite teddies, whole gangs of them, so Daddy wouldn't see cos he said we could only bring one—"

"I want to stay with her."

I jump up, hitting my head on a heart monitor. Big is standing behind me, his eyes, like lasers, staring at me.

"You did this. You did this to her," I whisper.

He puts his face right up to mine, so close I can see the pores on his nose. "Listen, Cunt, I know you want to blame me for this but I wasn't even fuckin' there and if I was, Cunt, it'd never have happened. You fuckin' know it wouldn't, so shut up and fuck off out and leave me alone with my woman."

He bends down and kisses Fiona on the forehead. Then he sits on my chair. I leave, wondering how much of my conversation he overheard. And I realise I don't care. I hope he heard it all.

The waiting room is crowded but it has the atmosphere of a morgue. Mam, Linda and Cian look expectantly at me. Like I'm the doctor come to tell them she's grand. That she's awake and everything's grand. I shake my head at them and slump into a seat next to Cian. He puts his arm around me. I don't shrug him off even though I want to.

So we all play the waiting game together. The faces change every so often. Vonnie and Nicole. Mark. Mam and Linda. People bring coffee in paper cups. Somebody brings in salad sandwiches wrapped in tinfoil. Somehow night becomes day and the procession of people constantly changes. I feel drugged from lack of sleep, eyes watering, stomach grumbling. But food just won't go down my throat.

And then I'm back with her again. Whispering to her as twilight falls outside. I must have slept because Big shakes me awake and resumes vigil at the bedside. And I'm back in the waiting room again. Mam is crying. Cian is patting her on the shoulder, and asking if she wants coffee. Everyone is offering coffee like it's some kind of panacea for the pain. And I'm asleep again and dreaming that Fiona and I are in Paris, standing under the Eiffel Tower and we can't believe how small it really is. Like a pylon. And so rusty. And then Big bursts into the room.

"She's awake, man, she's awake and she's flying it and she wants to see Harvey – man, this is fucking rapid this."

And he's gone and I'm wondering did I dream it and then we're all in the room and the doctor's there and Fiona gives us a weak smile. Mam's bawling her eyes out and the doctor's trying to shoo us away but I hear Fiona's little tiny whisper: "I'm sorry."

"Don't be. It'll be fine," I say, kissing her head. She gives me another little smile, a smile of reassurance. But it doesn't reassure me at all. It's like somebody sucked all the teenager out of her and left us this shell in her place.

Mark's in the corridor when we come out. "Well? Is she OK?"

I nod, and tears come finally. He takes me to his house. I'm like a zombie being led around by him. Katya's there, fussing over me, cooking something for me in a big silver pot. Seeing her makes me cry more. I try to eat the food, just to please her, but only manage a couple of spoonfuls. Then Mark is leading me again, this time upstairs, into his bedroom. I lie down on the bed and he does too, stroking my hair and murmuring things to me. Things I can barely hear. But none of it matters.

I'm so tired I don't care what he's saying as long as his lovely soothing voice keeps talking, and his hands keep stroking. And then I sleep again and when I wake he's leaning over me, kissing my forehead, my nose, my mouth. I kiss him back, seeking out his tongue, wrapping my legs tight around him. And then somehow we're naked and he's inside me, and it's delicious and uncomfortable and strange and familiar all at the same time. He pushes harder and I arch my back willing him on, and then I have the most incredible sensation, like tension building and building until it explodes deep inside me. An orgasm, surely. Whatever it is I don't want it to end. He rolls off me, his breathing ragged, his body slick with sweat.

"Jesus." He sits up, rooting for his cigarettes in the dark.

"So that's sex?" I sit up too, feeling wide awake for the first time in days.

Mark laughs. "Typical Maevis Ravis. Matter-of-fact. Another to-do thing off your list."

"I liked it. Now I see the attraction . . . I don't mean with you, I mean with it."

He laughs again. "Don't kill me with flattery whatever you do. Anyway, I don't know how it happened but it did. I hope you're OK about it."

I run my hand through his hair. "It's no surprise. I read an article once about how – in times of crisis – people have loads of sex. Take funerals, for example . . ."

Mark takes a pillow and pretends to suffocate me.

I go back to the hospital the next day and it's like a whole different world. Fiona's surrounded by people – Carrie and Jay, Big and various members of his family. And loads of balloons tied on to her bed. Just like when she had Harvey. And the party atmosphere's the same too, voices high and loud, Big back to his scumbag best, swagger reinstated. I can see it in his eyes when he looks at me now. When Fiona was in the coma I was in charge. She was my Fiona. Now he's challenging me again, letting me know he has the power back. He knows this and I know it. Big is very clever.

I hang back, watching them all, and then Vonnie arrives in with Harvey. He's all dressed up in a new outfit, a sky blue Adidas tracksuit and tiny Nike Air runners even though he can't crawl, let alone walk. Big's cock of the walk, dangling Harvey, talking louder than anyone. He puts Harvey on the bed beside Fiona, her face paler now next to Harvey's sallow skin. Big takes out his new camera and starts snapping away, making her pose and smile and tilt her face for the camera. I want to thump him.

There's a little tornado of hate inside me and I know that I'm actually quite capable of killing him. Of sticking a knife

241

into his heart, plunging it in as deep as possible until he gurgles his way to death. The camera clicking and whirring is making me madder and madder. And then it comes to me. In my altered state of anger and hatred it comes to me like a little nugget of gold, first covered with earth and then slowly revealing itself. I smile as it grows in my head. The camera whirs and clicks. And now I think it's a lovely sound. A lovely simple plan. Easy to achieve. Big turns around. "Jew want to go into a photo with her?" he says.

I smile at him. "Of course I do. I'd love to."

Twenty

It's very hard to do it for the first time. It's trying to find the time and the space. The privacy. And the camera. It's a Saturday night. Fiona's going out with Big – her first night out since her overdose. She's still very pale and he's stuck to her side like Super Glue. Minding her, watching her. Pity he wasn't doing that all along. But I'm sweetness and light to him. I have to be for the plan to work. I know that now. No fighting or name-calling. No disapproving looks. Especially the last because Big can read my face like he's watching television.

Harvey's in bed, sound asleep. And Big, the little gentleman, has left his camera right there on the new Argos bookshelf. It's a lovely Nikon – retailing at four hundred euro. I have my research done inside out and upside down. I know everything there is to know about this little piece of equipment, thanks to the internet and a very helpful guy in Ferguson's Pharmacy on O'Connell Street.

I take the camera and my overnight bag from the hall and go upstairs. On the landing I can't make up my mind which bedroom to use. Which would be the best? Their bedroom, and a dirty, evil thought comes into my head but it's not workable tonight, while Harvey's in it. I'll have to file it away until the room is empty. So it'll have to be my little guest room.

I throw the camera and the bag on the bed, then turn on the light and the two bedside lamps. I open the bag and take out my school uniform, a little crumpled and worse for wear. Then I take out some tiny lace knickers and thongs in four different colours. Then there's a corset yoke that I can hardly make sense of, complete with suspenders and sexy black stockings. All courtesy of Penneys, the whole lot for twenty-five euro. There are also some flimsy see-through nighties, scrunchies and hairbands. I strip off my jeans and sweatshirt, my bra and panties, and stand there naked in the room, shivering in the cold December night. I choose the suspender thing and stumble into it, no longer cold with the effort of getting into it. I end up in a knot of string and lace and have to yank the whole thing off and start again, this time trying to apply logic to the exercise.

And it works. It's an all-in-one suity thing, sheer black with built-in thong and suspenders. There's a push-up bra incorporated into it and it actually works. My breasts look like breasts for once, not two little mini-cupcakes. I look at myself in the mirror and burst out laughing. I'm like a horsier, lankier version of Britney Spears in her heyday when Fiona thought she was the best thing since hot chocolate. Exactly the image I want. Hit me, baby, one more time. I hum this tune now as I break open the package containing the stockings. I roll one up my leg, feeling it snag on the hairs on my calves. Then I clip the suspenders into place, surprised at how easy this part is. I ladder the second stocking as I roll it up but decide this will make it more authentic.

Next is the hair. A simple ponytail, high on my head, is

perfect. Then I slip on my uniform over the slut underwear. I check myself again in the mirror. Definitely not working. My school skirt reaches the floor, hiding what I want to display. That won't do at all. I sneak into Fiona's room, careful not to wake Harvey, and root around in her wardrobe in the dark until I find what I'm looking for. A short black miniskirt. This works brilliantly.

Then I set up the camera. I've already worked out the height and distance it needs to be to operate effectively on a self-timer. I screw the tripod together – my most expensive purchase but absolutely necessary, according to the camera guy in Ferguson's. Now the hard work, the posing. The trying to be sexy and childish all at once. The whole ridiculous nature of it. I bite the inside of my mouth to stop myself laughing, then set the camera and jump on the bed. The first shots are terrible. I'm way too happy-looking, a little grin playing at the corners of my mouth. I delete these and start again. Posing like the pictures I'd studied on the Internet on Big's laptop. There was one that really grabbed my attention and this is what I try to emulate now. Innocent face, innocent school uniform, not so innocent underwear on display.

These turn out really well so I go a step further and take off the skirt altogether. I also pull the tie down and open the shirt buttons to my waist. Again the pose, but this time I try to look scared as well. Like I don't want to be there, doing this. The shots are excellent and I'm actually quite proud of myself. A noise downstairs makes me freeze. I listen carefully, my heart pounding in my chest. But it's just the fridge kicking in. This fright tells me it's time to call it a night so I hurriedly strip, climb back into my jeans and sweatshirt and pack up my little bag of tricks.

Downstairs I boot up Big's laptop. Top-of-the-range Apple MacBook. My dream machine. I know its mechanics inside out. I log on and upload the pictures into a file. The next job is to make the date of that file be any date I want – which is easy when you've had a tutorial with a Japanese cyber-genius on Skype – and then hide the file and all traces of the picture download in case Big comes across it. I security enable the file. For my eyes only. For the time being anyway.

Then I delete the pictures from Big's camera until the memory card is blank. I helped him to upload pictures on Wednesday and he has a whole gallery of them. Including the naked ones of Fiona in a little file by themselves. Big is a fast learner – show him how to do something once and he has it nailed. I'm glad now I had the excruciatingly long conversation with the Japanese boy who knows far too much about computers for it to be healthy. Big might be clever but not as clever as me.

We have a day off on Tuesday. I head to my favourite spot in the library but there's nowhere to sit. Stupid Leaving Certs are starting to panic and cram. Fools. If they want points they should have put in a couple of years' work, not a couple of months. I head into town instead and bump into Mark in Tesco. I consider hiding but it's too late.

He's in the queue in front of me, buying cigarettes with his fake ID. A state-of-the-art one, of course. It would have to be for Mark. Everybody else's looks like it was made by their kid brother in playschool. Mark's would pass any test. I observe him for a minute as he chats with the cashier. Hair perfectly coiffed, clothes immaculate, trendy, even daring. He has something – presence, command of the world. I can't put my finger on it exactly but he has it in abundance. I stand my ground. I won't run away. Fuck him. He didn't text like he said he would. He didn't ring to see if I was OK. Didn't have any urge to see me. Exactly the same as Colin Ryan. Only worse because we slept together.

His face lights up as he comes towards me. The Mark-aged-four grin that's like a beacon. "Maeve – been meaning to text you."

I'm bright red but I smile at him and try to act casual. "No problem. I've been so busy myself. You know, Fiona out of hospital, school work . . ."

He examines my face and I feel myself reddening even more.

"I've got to go. I'm going home to study – can you believe the library's full?"

"Hey, I'm heading your way. Come on."

Outside on the pavement Mark lights a cigarette and takes a long drag. "So – how are you?"

"Grand – like I said, busy, busy, busy."

He stops in the middle of the footpath, bends down and kisses me hard on the mouth. I can taste tobacco and coffee. A whore's breakfast, as Mam would say. I can feel myself responding and will myself to stop. To be ice inside. It's all just hormonal. That's all. The feelings, the wanting him to get in touch. The whole stupid idea of attraction. Just hormones buzzing about in my body.

We stand in the middle of the path, forcing shoppers and buggy-pushers to circumvent us. Then he pulls me into him, into his soft wool coat, and does the stroking thing with his hands. This time my insides melt and I want to turn my face up to his, feel his lips on me while he strokes my hair. The stroking thing is my weakness. I push him away. "Stop, you fool – the whole street is looking at us."

"So what? I don't care." He puts his arm around my waist and I stagger a little, bumping into an elderly man passing by.

"Sorry," I say, giggling, as Mark moves his hand down to my butt.

"Ashamed of yourself you should be," the man says crossly.

"Slut," says Mark, grabbing my hand and swinging it in his.

"Shut up, you. You're the slut. Any sex. Any religion."

"Yeah. That's me – a twenty-first-century boy. Fancy going to the movies some night?" He says it casually. Friends. Like before.

"Sure. Throw me a text."

We're walking over the bridge, towards the cathedral. It's a beautiful winter day, blue sky and a crisp chill in the air. The streets are busy with early Christmas shoppers.

"Well, I was thinking maybe Saturday night and we could grab a bite to eat afterwards?"

My stupid heart flutters as the hormones have a party in there. "Yeah, sure." I keep my voice as casual as possible.

"Great. I'll ask a couple of the others as well. We can make a night of it."

And then the let-down. The hormones running off to hide. I nod and smile and keep up my casual bravado. "Hey, is that Fiona over there?"

I follow Mark's gaze, over to the City Courthouse, a beautiful old building right on the riverfront. The area is swarming with activity. There's a huge garda presence, with parents and children milling about on the steps of both the Courthouse and City Hall. Fiona's standing next to Big, one hand on the buggy, the other holding a cigarette. Vonnie's there too, dressed in a bright pink coat and what looks like pyjamas underneath. Big's younger brother Joey is beside her, his face sullen as he surveys the action around him. Lawyers, some in wigs, wander in and out of the building, laughing and cajoling with each other.

"What the fuck is happening?" I say, walking towards Fiona.

"Children's court. First Tuesday of the month," Mark tells me.

"What's that?"

"Exactly what it says on the tin. My uncle's a judge."

"Really? I didn't know that."

Mark grins. "Yeah. He tells me great stories about the children's court. Some of it's hilarious."

"Like what?" We're approaching Fiona now but she hasn't even seen us yet. She's in deep conversation with Big, gesticulating.

"Last month there was a twelve-year-old girl up in court for robbing a police car while the guards were doing a raid. Imagine the nerve of that – you have to admire her for sheer brazenness."

"I don't think it's hilarious."

Fiona spots us then and I can see that she's surprised. Her face is pale and the caked-on makeup and black eyeliner only make her look paler.

Vonnie's the first to speak. Her makeup and hair are done too. From the waist up, she looks dressed for the day. From the waist down she looks like she's ready for bed. "Little pup there is in trouble – went off and broke into the house down the road. A retired guard's house. Hadn't the sense to go somewhere else. Don't ever shit on your own doorstep is what I say – that right, Big?"

Big looks at us, the laser eyes sharper than ever. He examines Mark first, up and down, smirking at him. Then it's my turn. I smile at him and bend down to talk to Harvey. He's sound asleep.

"Why aren't you at school?" says Fiona, her Attract-a-Knack accent in full flow.

I almost start laughing at this. Why isn't she at school, where all her classmates are? "Day off."

"Can you take him home? We're goin' to be here for the day. Joey's free legal aid didn't show up yet."

Suddenly there's a scuffle right beside us. Two young girls, twelve or thirteen, are tearing at each other, pulling hair, scratching. A guard standing on the steps nearby spots them and leisurely picks his way through the people to them. By the time he reaches them, one has torn an earring out of the other's ear. We stand there watching, paralysed by the quick violence of the fight.

"Do something, stop it," I say, to no one in particular.

"Yeah, and they'll slap a huge claim on you," says Vonnie, arms folded watching the fight.

The guard separates them but they're still fighting, screaming incoherent insults at each other. The smallest one, a tiny thing in a belly top and leggings, spits at the other girl, the gob landing on the guard's shoulder.

"Fuckin' scumbags," says Big. "Pure waste of space."

I take the handles of the buggy and say goodbye as fast as I can, Mark scurrying to keep up with me.

"That was some laugh," says Mark, still trying to catch up, as I pound along the pavement.

"Fuck off, Mark. Why don't you fuck off home to the North Circular Road?"

"Hey, Maeve, what did I do?"

"You're just an arsehole, do you know that?"

"Maeve, for fuck sake what have I done?"

"Mark, if you don't know what you've done then you're way dumber than I thought." I stop dead, gripping the handles of the buggy to calm myself.

"That's unfair. Maeve, all I said was that it was funny."

"Funny? *Funny?* How was it funny? You tell me how two girls – nope, two kids – ripping pieces out of each other outside a courthouse for children is funny. You explain the humour in that." I only grasp that I'm shouting when passers-by stare at us.

"What's got into you lately, Maeve? What's happened to you?"

"It's called growing up. Something you know fuck-all about." I'm trying to control my voice but the end bit is another shout. A woman with a small terrier tuts as she passes us.

"Have you a problem?" I yell after her. She hurries away, the little dog trotting after her.

"I think, Maeve, you're the person with the growing up to do."

I laugh at this, my stranger's laugh that I thought had deserted me. "'I'm gay. I'm not gay. I like her brother. No, no, I like his sister. No, I like the little child-woman. Candy in a sweet shop. I'm from the North Circular Road so I'll have it all . . .'" I say this in a high-pitched petulant voice.

Mark's eyes darken. "Is this because of the other night? Maeve, look, I'm sorry about that. We were stressed, you said it yourself – remember? You said the thing about funerals and

I just thought . . . It was one of those things that just . . . happened . . ."

"That's right. It happened. Let's forget about it."

Mark shakes his head. "You're mad at me."

"No, I'm not. Forget it. Good luck." I take the handles of the buggy and go. He follows me and I walk faster, wanting to be out of his sight.

He grabs a buggy handle to slow me down. "Hey, listen, I'm sorry if I hurt you. It shouldn't have happened at all . . ."

"You're such a fool, Mark. Why don't you go home and find a nice boy to play with?"

That finds home like a kick in the face. His eyes blaze. "That's a great idea. Hell of a lot better than hanging out with a psycho."

Tears sting my eyes but I won't let them out. "You're a bastard. A spoilt snobby little shit."

He laughs at this. "Snobby? Me? You're the snob, Maeve, the worst kind of snob. The fucking smarter-than-all-of-us snob." He turns and walks back towards town.

I gulp in air and blink back tears. I watch him as he fades into the crowded street. I have a physical pain in my chest exactly where my heart is. I wipe at a runaway tear with the sleeve of my coat. There's a tiny thought in the back of my head but I'm afraid to let it surface. I push it away, deep down, as far as it will go. And I push back the tears too because the tears and the tiny thought are related and if I let one in then the other will have to come too. Only then do I realise that Harvey's roaring his little heart out. So I carry him in one arm and push the empty buggy with the other. By the time I get home my anger has simmered to a slow burn inside me.

My aunt Linda opens the door. "What do you think?" she

says, twirling for me to see. She's dressed in a navy Aldi uniform, with a little name tag clipped to her breast.

"Hardly Gucci," I say, leaving the buggy in the porch and walking past her into the house. Mam's in the kitchen, a stack of ironing in front of her. A collection of miniskirts and baby clothes.

"Hello, Harvey, you found your auntie in town, did you? Aren't you clever?"

"No, actually. I found him outside the children's court." I hand him to Mam and root in his nappy bag for his bottle. "Fiona's ironing?" I smirk, not even waiting for an answer.

"She's still a bit weak so I said . . ."

I leave the bottle on the table and walk out while Mam is still in mid-sentence. In my bedroom, I sit at my laptop and boot it up, listening to its soft whirring as it comes to life. I won't cry – *I won't cry. It's all such bullshit. I won't cry. I won't.* But the tiny thought arrives all by itself, floating in my head so that I can't see the screen of theorems in front of me.

I want Mark. I want him to like me. I want him to tell me that the sex was special, not a little accident, like we bumped into each other by mistake in bed. I want him to think that I'm special. Beautiful. Sexy. That I'm all he needs. But he doesn't want me. Simple as that. He wants what he wants in the moment.

It's a magic wand. Thinking things out. Once it's done, it makes the anger melt. And the tears.

Twenty-one

"'Love is any number of emotions and experiences related to a sense of strong affection and attachment. The word "love" can refer to a variety of different feelings, states and attitudes, ranging from generic pleasure ("I loved that meal") to intense interpersonal attraction ("I love my boyfriend"). This diversity of uses and meanings, combined with the complexity of the feelings involved, makes love unusually difficult to consistently define, even compared to other emotional states. As an abstract concept, love usually refers to a deep, ineffable feeling of tenderly caring for another person.'"

Mr Hynes pauses in his reading and glances at me. I'm Friday-afternoon slumped in my chair, doodling on the cover of my copy of *Wuthering Heights*. My classmates are similarly slumped, one or two actually asleep. I smirk at Mr Hynes, eye-challenging him to continue.

"'Even this limited conception of love, however, encompasses a wealth of different feelings, from the passionate desire and intimacy of romantic love to the non-sexual emotional closeness of familial and platonic love to the profound oneness or devotion of religious love. Love in its various forms acts as the major facilitator of interpersonal relationships and, owing to its central psychological importance, is one of the most common themes in the creative arts . . .'"

He stops altogether, putting the pages of my essay down on his desk. "Maeve, this is not the assignment. You can do it again over the weekend. I'm very disappointed in this." He lifts another essay from his pile on the desk and clears his throat before he begins to read it.

I shoot my hand up in the air. "Excuse me, sir?"

"Yes, Maeve?"

"The title of the assignment was 'Love. Discuss'. I think I did exactly that so I won't be rewriting anything at the weekend."

Mr Hynes looks at me for a very long few seconds. I can hear some of the others straightening up, waiting for a little excitement before the last bell of the week. "Don't be smart."

"I'm not being smart. I'm just stating facts. I took the word 'love' and I discussed – very well actually. And if you'd read on you would have come to the good bit – where I simultaneously prove that neither God nor love exists. It's quite brilliant even though I say so myself."

The others laugh and someone says, "Abouy, Maeve, give it to him." Another claps.

I hold Mr Hynes's eyes with mine, grinning widely now. There's a flash of anger in his.

"First, the assignment was part of our ongoing exploration of the theme of love in *Wuthering Heights*. Second, if I'd wanted an immature smartarse definition of the term 'love' then I'm quite capable of Googling Wikipedia all by myself to achieve same." He picks up my essay, scrunches it into a ball, then slams it into the wastepaper bin. "Rubbish. I'd like you to do the exercise properly. And I'd like to see you after class."

He begins to read another essay. One that hits all the *Wuthering Heights* notes, robbed from a *Less Stress More Success* handbook on the novel. I know because I can see the pages of the book in my head. I can remember whole paragraphs of it, boring, standard textbook drivel.

The bell finally goes and I gather my books and walk out. I can hear Mr Hynes calling my name but I pretend I don't. I walk home with Ciara and Sophie, who're full of excitement about a gig tomorrow night in Dolan's.

"Oops! *Problemo*!" says Ciara, as we walk in the rain. "I've no ID. My mother found it when I came home pissed last Saturday night. She ripped it up, the bitch."

"You can have mine," I say, rooting in the front pocket of my bag.

"But aren't you coming? You can't miss the Prophets – Colin Ryan is the new lead singer. They're fucking brilliant."

The Prophets are like any other angst-ridden, self-indulgent teenage band with bad lyrics and bad vocals. The addition of Colin Ryan can only make them worse – a tongue-tied lead singer, for fuck sake.

"Babysitting. My sister is going to see Beyoncé in the Point – staying the night." I hand Ciara my ID. "Here it is. Both of us have dark hair, that's enough to get you in."

The three of us laugh because it's true.

"Lousy you can't go. You'll miss a great night."

"I know," I lie.

They turn off at the shopping centre and I stroll on, keeping a subconscious eye out for Mark so that I can duck him. But it's not Mark I meet, it's Colin Ryan. "Maeve."

I don't even turn around when I hear his voice, don't even acknowledge his existence.

"Maeve . . . wait. Listen . . . I've been trying to get in touch. I haven't been in school . . ."

I keep walking. Eyes down.

"And I tried to text you but I couldn't. Is your phone broken or something?"

I stop, dropping my heavy schoolbag at my feet. "Colin, listen to me. Daddy won't allow you to talk to me because my sister has a dodgy boyfriend so let's stop this bullshit. It's fine." I pick up my bag and walk away.

"Maeve, please . . ."

"Colin, do me a favour and go fuck yourself."

He grabs my hand, forcing me to stop walking. "My dad has nothing to do with this. Look, I explained . . . am . . . everything to him and he was grand about it. He trusts me. Am . . . I didn't text for the first three days because . . ." He looks away, embarrassed. I can't imagine him overcoming his shyness in Dolan's tomorrow night. "Well, because of the Three-day Rule. That's why." He shrugs.

"The what rule?"

"The Three-day Rule. Don't contact them for at least three days or they'll run a mile." He's mortified now, face shiny red.

I burst out laughing, dropping my bag on the ground. I laugh so hard tears come out of my eyes. Colin joins in, just grinning at first, then laughing with me.

"Anyway, are you going to the gig tomorrow night?" We start walking again, even though he's going in the wrong direction for his house.

"No. I'm babysitting."

257

"Oh, right."

We're almost at my house.

"So, see you around, Colin," I say, as I swing the gate open with my knee.

"Am . . . OK. Am . . . I'll text you, right?"

"OK."

I go up the path and he turns back the way he came. There will be no texts. I have his number blocked on my phone. That way no hormones can run riot inside me to make me say and do stupid things. Exactly like being drunk.

So, it's me and Big alone together at last. Fiona's gone off on the train with Carrie, both of them with naggins of vodka in their handbags. I've spent most of the day with Harvey, playing with him, walking him, bathing him. He's so funny now, always smiling, exactly like Fiona when she was younger. Always laughing. Big seems to be ultra-busy today. There are cars and people coming and going and he's in and out all day like a yo-yo.

At around seven I put on a pizza and some garlic bread while Big puts Harvey to bed.

He comes back down, takes a can of Bavaria from the fridge and goes into the living room to watch the football. I bring in a tray of food and offer him a plate. He looks at me suspiciously at first. "Go on, have some – I put on enough for both of us."

"I'm pure starving. Ta," he says, taking the plate and putting it on his lap. We both eat as he watches the football, shouting and swearing at the television every now and again.

"I bet they're having a great time. Where did you pick up the tickets? That was sold out weeks ago."

He answers me while keeping his eyes riveted on the TV. "Bloke owed me a favour, like. Didn't pay his debts, if you get my meaning. Fuck sake, ref! That was a fuckin' blatant penalty, you blind cunt."

I wait until the football is over before I execute my plan. "You should go out. Meet up with your friends."

He gives me the narrow-eyed suspicious look again. Like a rat.

"You haven't gone out since . . . Well, you know. I'll babysit. It's pointless both of us missing out on Saturday night."

He doesn't answer. Just watches *The X Factor*. I say no more, letting our silence and the screechy noise of the show do the talking for me.

"I might so. Might go down the road and have a few beers. Haven't been on the lash in weeks." He gets up, all business suddenly, and goes upstairs for a shower. There's one thing about Big – he's the cleanest person I know: five showers a day. And he can clean a kitchen better than my mother.

He comes down wearing his best tracksuit – a sky blue one like Harvey's miniature version.

"You look great."

He gives me the rat look again. "See you later." He walks out to the kitchen, then comes back in again. "Maeve, t'anks, like."

He leaves then and I have a little wobble of doubt about the Plan. I know that this is my chance, that the Beyoncé tickets and an overnight stay were a stroke of luck that might not come around again. And I'd known it'd be easy to talk him into going out. It doesn't take a genius to grasp that a night in with me and Simon Cowell is not exactly Big's cup of tea. But the wobble is the name. He used my name for the first time ever.

Fuck him. He's just a scumbag. He's bad for my sister and for Harvey. He'll drag her down with him. And all the running around he does. Selling fucking drugs. Fucking up lives. No. I have to be strong. I go to the kitchen and check for alcohol. I know what's there already but I double-check and then take out a bottle of schnapps, 60 per cent proof. That'll do nicely. Then a couple of shot glasses. I leave them on the worktop so he'll see them when he comes in.

Next is the hard bit. The camera. This problem has been doing circles in my head ever since I came up with the Plan. The tripod has served me well but won't work if everything pans out tonight. I set the self-timer on the camera and place it on the bookcase, then sit on the couch opposite. The camera clicks. Bingo. I go to check the memory. A great photo of my forehead. I delete it, reset the timer and place the camera on a lower shelf. This time it's perfect. I know generally where we must be sitting.

Next my outfit. I run upstairs and take a quick peep at Harvey before I go into the spare room. My holdall is already on the bed. I take out the slutty outfit, the one with the suspenders, strip off and climb awkwardly into it. Then the stockings, now a little worse for wear. I debate about the uniform. If I put it on now he'll be suspicious. No. I'll wait until he comes home, then nip back upstairs at the right time. I pull on my jeans and sweatshirt over the slut suit. Tight but manageable.

Downstairs I make some tea and half-heartedly watch a movie about how to lose a guy in ten days. Really dumb film. Then I watch a programme about couples in America who adopt monkeys. This is interesting in a kind of freaky, morbid way. I have butterflies in my stomach but I try to keep watching TV, keep busy to steady my nerves.

There's the sound of a key in the front door. I almost scream. I take a deep breath. It's time.

Twenty-two

Jay is with him. Stupid, skinny Jay with his lapdog nature. Laughing at everything Big says, hanging on his every word. Apparently he's had a fight with Carrie and disappeared with Big. But at least the bottle of schnapps works. They're guzzling shots like it's going out of fashion. I check my watch. One o'clock in the morning. We're sitting in the living room, the TV on mute in the corner. Jay's put on some tunes as he calls them – 2 Pac, I think – and Big's pouring more shots. I'm pretending to drink mine, then flicking it into the rubber plant beside me while they regale each other with stories about how brave/smart/funny/mad they both are.

Big's eyes are glassy with alcohol, slightly unfocused, the pupils a pinprick. I know that if he wasn't drunk he'd wonder why I'm·bothering to stay up at all. But it's Jay who is my immediate problem. How do I get rid of him? I thought earlier that a skinny drink of water like him would be unconscious after a load of shots but no such luck. It's livelier he's getting as the night goes on. I think about ringing the guards to make an anonymous complaint about the noise. Not that it's noisy. But I know Big too well. The couple living next door have rung the guards many times about noise and Big just laughs at them. Sometimes he makes even more noise after the guards have gone just to antagonise his neighbours.

I go into the kitchen to make coffee. I need something to keep me awake. Jay's phone is sitting on the worktop like the answer to my prayers. I pick it up quickly and scroll for Carrie's number. I ring it, hoping she'll answer. And, of course, she does, screaming drunkenly down the phone, "Where the fuck are you, you bastard, leaving me in the Icon by myself? If you don't get home right now I'm fucking leaving you, mind." I hang up straight away and she rings back. I don't answer, just bring the phone in to Jay. Big is trying to stand up but he keeps falling back on the couch. Carrie screeches down the phone at Jay. Big makes another attempt at standing up, this time succeeding. He takes the phone from Jay.

"It's cool, Carrie, we're just, like, having a few drinks . . ." He hiccups and bursts out laughing.

The phone goes dead. Jay shrugs and Big cracks up again. But my plan works. It takes Carrie only fifteen minutes to arrive, banging on the door, screaming to be let in. I answer, and she pushes past me, a little tornado of fury in animal-print leggings and a silver bomber jacket. "Fuckin' cunt is all you are. The cab is waiting – you bastard, leaving me there on my birthday and all, fuckin' bastard."

She launches herself at Jay, who's as shaky on his feet as Big. She grabs him by the arm and pushes him out of the room. He's too drunk and too scared of her to protest. She bangs the front door as she leaves. Big has collapsed on the couch, head thrown back, mouth open. I run upstairs and look in on Harvey. Sound asleep. Then I go into the bedroom and change into my school uniform, complete with Fiona's miniskirt. My heart is pounding and I'm full of doubt. This'll never work. He'll wake up, he'll kill me.

I take a deep breath and close my eyes tight. Fiona's pinched coma face floats in front of my eyes. Then Harvey, but an older Harvey with his father's laser eyes and sullen face. Fuck it, I've nothing to lose. Big's so drunk he won't actually know what's real and what isn't. I creep downstairs, suddenly self-conscious in my slut get-up. Big's in a deep sleep now, snoring softly. An idea pops into my head. His phone! I'll take some pictures of myself with his phone. Before I lose my nerve I slip my hand into his tracksuit pockets searching for it. No luck. I then have to push him back to reach his pants pockets and as I do so, his eyes flick open for a second, piercing brown slit eyes. Like a reptile's. My hand freezes mid-search. His eyelids flutter closed.

I find the phone and sneak it out of his pocket. Then I arrange myself, legs splayed, face scared and click. Shit. A photo of my knee. This time I go all the way, pulling at the crotch of the slut suit. Click. A perfect shot but so ugly-looking. All that hair. Disgusting. I take another couple with my breasts exposed. Big stirs beside me. I slip the phone back into his pocket.

Now the hard work. I check the camera, set the self-timer. Then I arrange myself beside Big, pushing his head around so that he's facing me. I put his arm around me, pushing his head into my exposed chest. The camera whizzes. A sequence of shots. Big's so out of it that it makes me even bolder. I stroke his leg, just to see what'll happen. He seems to come to life, seeking my mouth with his, murmuring into my hair. "I love you, Fiona, I love you – jew know that?"

His voice is a hoarse whisper. His hands are all over me and

I want to throw up. His ferret eyes are still shut tight and I wonder if he's actually still asleep. I pull back from him and he starts hugging the cushion instead of me. I have a mad idea then. A crazy idea that might just work. Before I can change my mind I go over to the camera and set it to video. Then I sit down beside Big, extricating the cushion from his arms. I stroke his leg again and he climbs on top of me, trying to push me down on the couch. I panic. If we lie down on it we'll be out of view for the camera. I look at it, willing myself to appear distraught. Big pulls at my skirt, lifting my butt up to take it off. Then he tries to suck my breasts while pushing his fingers between my legs. Tears come to my eyes, real ones.

"No, please, no," I whisper, loud enough for the camera to pick up. But I mean it too. Suddenly I'm in way over my head.

Big's breathing is fast now and I can feel his erection pressing into me. More tears come and I try to push him off me. I can barely breathe with the weight of him and he finally manages to push me down on the couch. I'm crying now but I can't scream. I try to, but nothing comes out except a tiny croak.

"Fiona", he says, "Fiona."

He nuzzles my neck and tries to pull down his tracksuit bottoms with one hand. He sits up. My eyes are closed but I know his are open. Laser eyes on me.

"Fiona . . . what the fuck? What the fuck, man?" He jumps off me, staggering and falling over the coffee-table. There's an almighty crash as bottles and glasses spill onto the floor. I'm sick with terror but I make myself move. Make myself sit up, pick up my clothes and run before he has time to right himself. I fly upstairs and into my room, my heart pounding, adrenalin pumping through every blood vessel. Fuck fuck fuck. I sit on the bed, trying to control my shaking body. Fuck. What made me come up with such a stupid idea?

I hear noise downstairs and I freeze, waiting for his footsteps. Waiting for him to charge into my room and call my bluff. But the only sound is my heart racing. I make myself calm down, taking Hynes deep breaths. I strip off the slut outfit, ripping it in my haste. I'm just climbing into my pyjamas when I remember the camera. Oh, God, the camera. That's why he's so quiet. He's found the camera.

Twenty-three

I needn't have worried. Big is asleep on the floor exactly where he fell. The camera is still on the shelf winking its self-timer light at me. I step over the mess of bottles and glasses strewn everywhere and take it off the shelf. Big snores reassuringly behind me. My courage is topped up by this so I take his laptop from a side table and hurry upstairs.

It takes me a full hour to get it right. The video is excellent. All I have to do is edit out the bits where he thinks I'm Fiona. So easy. The photos are good too. I upload them into the dedicated file but it's the video that's the *pièce de résistance*. My tears and my terror are so real. Hardly a surprise because they were real at the time. My eyes are closing by the time I have everything done. Now all I have to do is put the camera and laptop back. I tiptoe down the stairs and into the living room. Big is still asleep on the floor. I put the camera back into its little case and place it high on the shelf where Big normally keeps it. I'm putting the laptop down on the side table when he frightens the life out of me.

"What are you doing?"

I actually scream and clamp a hand over my mouth to stop

myself. He's sitting up, rubbing his eyes with his hands. "Jesus, you scared me. I'm just tidying up a bit . . . Am . . . I heard a noise . . . You must have fallen . . ." I wave my hand in the direction of the mess on the floor.

He stands up, still rubbing his eyes, and I imagine what he's really doing is trying to rub the alcohol fog from them. I can see his eyes are narrowed – he's trying to decipher what exactly happened while he was drunk. Picking at the hazy images in his head, his brain whirring like a hard drive. I'm praying the images will stay nice and hazy.

I start to pick up glasses and bottles, chattering to distract him. "Hope Fiona enjoyed the concert – they showed a bit on the news earlier. God, it looked fantastic . . ."

He has his arms folded now, watching me.

"I'm going to heat up a bottle for Harvey – Fiona says he sometimes wakes at around five – oh, my God, it's almost six!" I rush out to the kitchen, putting the bottles in a crate near the back door. Big follows me, still not talking. Not saying one word. I heat up a bottle for Harvey in the microwave – the longest two minutes ever. I can't wait to escape his gaze. The puzzled air around him. He's on to me. I just know in my gut that he's on to me.

Finally the microwave pings and I snatch the bottle and walk out of the kitchen. But Big follows me once again, out through the hallway and upstairs. I check on Harvey, praying he's awake. No such luck.

"Something happen tonight?" Big says, as I make my way into the spare room.

I shake my head at him. "No. What do you mean?"

His gaze is so intense I'm forced to look away. I can feel

colour flood my neck and face, right up to the crown of my head.

"Somethin's up. I'm not a fuckin' eejit, you know." With that he walks away.

I creep into bed, sick with dread. My head is throbbing, unable to keep up with my thought processes. The what-ifs come hard and fast, stumbling over each other as they unfold in my head. The birds are singing outside. I can hear their thin offerings as they stir to life. I try to quiet the revolt in my head. Why did I ever think this was a good idea? That I could beat him with his clever X-ray eyes? I'll get up and sneak downstairs and wipe it all off the computer. Yes. I'll just wipe it all. Send it off to cyber-space to join my drivel-writing.

I get up, shivering in the cold morning air. The wooden floor is ice. The boards creak noisily as I creep across them. I open the door as softly as I can but it's like every noise is amplified by a hundred. Down the stairs slowly. Into the kitchen. I'm just opening the door to the living room when I see Big sitting on the couch, laptop powered up in front of him, his fingers flicking over the keys like he's been doing it all his life.

I retreat back upstairs. I'll just wait until an opportunity presents itself. I'll wait until he goes out. He'll have to go out at some stage. He went out about forty times yesterday when he was conducting his "business". And then something niggles at the back of my mind. Something – a detail I can't remember. It floats to the surface and I have to stick my hand in my mouth so I don't scream. His phone. The pictures on his phone. Oh, how stupid am I? Why did I do that? Panic engulfs me, swallows me, invading my brain. I can't think straight. His phone. Whatever about the laptop, his phone never leaves his sight. Never leaves his hand. I want to be sick. I want to go home and for none of this to be happening.

I get dressed slowly, wondering what to do. I can hear Harvey stirring in the bedroom and I'm just about to go in to him when I hear Big running up the stairs.

"Well, look at you, wide awake," Big says to Harvey, as he passes my door.

I sit for almost an hour trying to think of a way out. I can hear Big pottering about downstairs. Going out to the small shed in the garden. Coming back in. Moving something in the living room.

The doorbell rings. Voices. Big says something. Someone laughs. Finally I decide. I'll go downstairs. Play the innocent. Tell him I'll mind Harvey until Fiona gets back. I don't know what I'll do about his phone but maybe he won't look in his photos. Maybe I'll be able to get hold of it and delete them. Anyway, one problem at a time. The laptop. Once he leaves I can clear the laptop.

In the kitchen I lose my nerve again. I stand outside the door, watching Big bending over the coffee-table, engrossed in something. There's a fat young guy with bad skin sitting opposite him, nervously scratching his shaved head.

"You did de right t'ing, Paud, digging them up. Fuck, man, the shades are all over the place lately. Wouldn't ya t'ink they'd give us a fuckin' break for Christmas? My market'll be fucked from them."

Fat Guy laughs. I open the door. Big jumps up, stands in front of them. But he's too late. I've seen them. Three stubby little handguns on the Winnie the Pooh cushion. A dirt-smeared zip-lock bag beside them. Harvey's at the other end of the couch, gurgling and cooing at his fists.

The coffee-table is unrecognisable. There's a weighing scale and sachets of white powder piled neatly in rows. Blades and a little pile of powder not yet bagged.

"Get out, Cunt, we're busy," says Big.

I retreat backwards, unable to take my eyes from the guns.

"Hey," says Big, just as I'm about to close the door. "Mind your business, right?"

I'm shaking in the kitchen. Mam. I want Mam. I want her to stroke my hair and tell me it'll be fine. I want it all to go away. Especially the guns. I want the guns to go away more than anything else. And then he's in the kitchen, putting Harvey in his car seat, stuffing bags of drugs into his nappy bag. Fat Guy follows, carrying Big's laptop in its case. They leave with Harvey. And that's what pushes me over the edge. The sight of Harvey in his car seat, cooing up at his scumbag daddy.

Twenty-four

"Maeve, why didn't you tell someone? Why didn't you tell me?" Cian's holding me tight, the way Daddy used to, holding me so tight I can hear his heart beating in his chest. Mam's crying, head in her hands, tears streaming down her face.

"He said if I told he'd hurt Fiona. I believed him. Wouldn't you?" My voice is small and I'm choking back tears. I'm in it now, there's no going back. I feel like I'm outside my body, detached, observant, watching from the corner this other Maeve who looks and sounds exactly like me.

"We'll have to make a statement, Maeve, you know that, don't you? We'll go with you, Mam and myself, and you're not to worry, you're not to be scared of him – fucking dirty bastard. Fucking scumbag . . ."

"He'll do something to Fiona if I . . ."

"No, he won't. I promise you he won't, Maeve. Come on, sit down, Linda's coming over. She's bringing a friend of hers from the Rape Crisis Centre. Are you OK with that?"

Cian guides me to a kitchen chair opposite Mam. The second she looks into my eyes she starts crying again. "I wasn't . . . he didn't rape me, Cian. That's going overboard . . ."

"Maeve, you're a minor and he abused you. That's statutory rape. Linda rang Tom . . ."

I start crying, hard, painful tears.

"Jesus, Maeve, I'm sorry . . . Hey, it'll be OK." Cian takes a bunch of tissues from a box on the worktop and hands them to me. Then he paces up and down the kitchen. "I should have known – you were so withdrawn – and I thought it was me, what happened in Lanzarote. Jesus, he's some bastard – and he took videos and pictures of you. That's horrible."

"Poor Fiona – how is she going to cope with this?" says Mam, shaking her head.

This infuriates me. Typical Mam. I'm the one who's been abused, theoretically at least, and her sympathy still lies with Fiona. "I'm sure she'll manage," I say, my voice bitter.

The doorbell rings. Linda arrives in, her face grave. She hugs me, tears shining in her eyes. "Claire from the Crisis Centre is in the living room. Now you don't have to speak to her if you don't want to, Maeve," she says. She's wearing her Aldi uniform and a wave of guilt chokes me. I'm upsetting a lot of people, interrupting their day, causing them grief. I want to stop and tell them it's a pack of lies, but once the ball is rolling it takes on a whole momentum of its own. It's like I have no control now over any of it.

So Claire from the Rape Crisis Centre listens to my story, while Cian paces the room, fists clenched. I'm almost matter-of-fact now in the telling. It started a month ago. Just touching at first. Then pictures and dress-up. A video last night and an almost rape. He said he'd hurt Fiona if I told. He'd hurt Fiona and put a petrol bomb through our window and I'd never see Harvey again. He said I was to be a good girl and do what I was told. Linda, Mam and Claire exchange knowing looks at this last lie.

The ball gets bigger and faster. We're in the police station in a white room with a table and four chairs. The guard is so nice to me that I want to tell her the truth. My head pounds from tension and lack of sleep. And then there's a man sitting down opposite me. A man with a handsome, kind face. "Hi, Maeve. I'm Detective Ryan, you know my son Colin."

I have a terrible urge to pee.

"Please don't tell him," I whisper, my head bowed.

"Maeve, don't you even worry about that. Everything you say will stay within these four walls. I promise you. I shouldn't have mentioned . . . I'm sorry . . ."

"It's fine," I whisper, keeping my eyes on the table in front of me.

"They've arrested him, Maeve."

Now I really need to pee. Oh, God, what have I done?

"Where? What about Harvey?"

"They arrested him at the railway station. He'd just collected your sister . . . am . . . Fiona . . ."

I look into his eyes for the first time. Piercing blue like Colin's, but more searching, more probing. He's not going to believe me. And a part of me hopes he doesn't. Hopes he calls my bluff. "Where is he? Is he here?"

The detective raises his hand and pats my arm. "He's way down the corridor. You won't have to see him or speak to him. I promise." The piercing eyes never leave my face. But all they are seeing now is the truth. I'm scared to death. Scared to death because the ball I started to roll is now a planet spinning out of control.

"Your sister is very upset, as you can imagine. She was outside in Reception but your mother took her away."

"I'm scared."

"I know. But you've done the right thing. I know it's hard to come in here and talk to strangers about it but you did the right thing."

Claire is beside me, nodding. I can't meet the detective's eyes.

"I want to go home."

"Of course you do. We're almost finished. Garda Callaghan has your statement. She's just printing it off now for you to sign it."

"Did ye . . . did ye go to the house?"

"We conducted a search of the premises an hour ago. We have the laptop and the camera. Other items too."

"So you saw . . . you saw the stuff? The stuff he did?"

He steeples his fingers together in front of him. I look at these instead of his face. "They'll be examined in detail by Forensics but Garda Callaghan has seen some footage. We'll get him, Maeve. I promise you. We'll get him good." He stands up, scraping the chair along the floor.

Claire pats me on the back as the detective leaves the room. I'm getting sick of Claire with her big roundy concerned eyes and her back-patting and her textbook victim stance. I just want to be by myself. And for all of this to disappear.

Cian drives me home. His knuckles are white, tight on the steering-wheel. I can feel the anger radiating from him. He doesn't talk, just drives likes he's mad, like he has no patience for road safety or courtesy. I'm almost car sick by the time we reach our house.

Cian gets out but I don't move. Rain drizzles on the

windscreen, steaming it up until I can't see a thing. Cian comes back and sits into the car. "You OK?"

I nod.

"I know what it is Maeve. It's Fiona, isn't it?"

A tear escapes and runs down my cheek.

"Look, come on home. You didn't cause any of this and she'll just have to live with that."

I climb out of the car thinking how wrong Cian actually is. I've caused all of this and I'm the one who will have to live with it.

She doesn't look at me when I walk into the kitchen. She examines her nails like they're the most interesting thing she's ever seen.

"Are you hungry, Maeve? I've made soup. Here, I'll put some in a bowl for you. Linda's gone to work but she said she'll call back on her way home." Mam stops trying to fill the void and busies herself with the soup instead. Cian pulls out a chair and gestures for me to sit down. I have that out-of-body feeling again, like I'm watching Fiona and Maeve sitting down to an awkward, silence-filled meal.

Mam pours two bowls of soup and cuts thick slices of soda bread. Then she spreads butter generously on the bread and puts the plate in the middle of the table. Fiona raises her head as Mam places a bowl of steaming chicken soup in front of her. Her eyes are raw-red from crying, her face so pale it's translucent. A fist of guilt clenches my heart. I want to make it all right for her.

Mam shoos Cian out of the kitchen and we're left behind, the silent sisters with so much to say to each other.

I drink some soup, just for something to do, and take a slice of the bread. It tastes like cardboard in my mouth.

"If you say it happened, then I believe you." Fiona doesn't look at me as she speaks, just keeps stirring her soup with her spoon, round and round in circles.

"I'm stunned and I can't believe . . . I can't believe Big'd . . ." She stops as tears slip down her face. She wipes them away with the back of her hand. "It's just that you think you know someone – that's all. You think you know them and then something like this happens . . ." More tears and now I'm crying too. She gets up and puts her arms around me and hugs me tightly. And my tears take over then, like a flood, unstoppable.

"It's not even that. It's that I trusted him. When you trust someone with your heart and then he . . ." She mops her eyes with her sleeve. "I love you, Maeve," she says into my hair. This makes me bawl even more. And now I know I can't go back. I can't go back because if I do I'll lose my sister for ever.

Twenty-five

Princes who set little store by their word but have known how to over-reach men by their cunning have accomplished great things, and in the end got the better of those who trusted to honest dealing. The prince must be a lion, but he must also know how to play the fox. He who wishes to deceive will never fail to find willing dupes. The prince, in short, ought not to quit good courses if he can help it, but should know how to follow evil courses if he must.

From The Prince *by Niccolò Machiavelli*

I read the text on the computer screen, although it's already imprinted in my head from a previous reading. It's Monday. Mam made me take the day off school so I've spent it trying to justify myself to myself. Hence Machiavelli. The end justifies the means. I've discovered that this is a very bad translation from the Italian in Machiavelli's most famous treatise, *The Prince.* I've also discovered things I'd rather not know. Like how Machiavelli said that this philosophy – the end justifies the means – was OK for a prince but could not be applied to ordinary individuals as they conduct their life. I scroll down the page.

> *Morally wrong actions are sometimes necessary to achieve morally right outcomes; actions can only be considered morally right or wrong by virtue of the morality of the outcome. The end justifies the means.*

A noise downstairs makes me jump. There's shouting but it sounds muffled. And then someone bangs on the door so hard I think the glass is going to break. I run downstairs just as Mam opens it to Vonnie. I paste myself against the landing wall as Vonnie pushes her way into the hallway.

"Now, Vonnie. It's in the hands of the guards. We'll leave it at that . . ."

Vonnie's in a tight pink velour tracksuit, her hair tied up in a loose ponytail. Her face looks so old without makeup. "I've one thing to say. Just one thing to say to that daughter of yours. She's a lying, fucking bitch and she tricked him. He told me he knew something funny was goin' on and she tricked him . . ."

"Maeve's no liar. Now, please get out of my house."

Vonnie sticks her face right up to Mam's. "My Big'd never do a thing like that and the truth'll out, mark my words." She glares at Mam and then storms out of the door, slamming it after her.

Mam is gulping air, fanning herself with her hand.

"Are you OK, Mam?" I say, going down the stairs.

She nods. "These hot flushes, they'd drive you mad. I used to think they didn't exist, that menopausal women imagined them."

"They are actually a physical condition and it's got to do with the hormones or lack thereof that . . ."

Mam smiles at me and then hugs me close. "I love you, Maeve Hogan, even though you're a terrible know-all. I love you to bits." She pushes me away from her and studies my face. "You heard that?"

"Yes."

She smiles at me. "Don't worry. It'll be over soon and he'll be in jail where he belongs and we can all get back to normal. Now, I made a nice casserole. Fiona's gone to the baby clinic with Harvey and we'll have it as soon as she gets back. The poor pet."

School is hard. People know. They stand around in little knots at break-time whispering and as soon as I approach they fall silent. It's the hardest week of my life and I'm so glad it's Friday and I'm home safe in my bedroom. Stupid Ciara and Sophie are really annoying. Afraid to come out and ask about the gory details, waiting for me to fill in the blanks. Which, of course, I don't.

And Mr Hynes knows. So nice to me in English class. I can't stand people's kindness. Mr Higgins next door with his "How are you, Maeve? How are you coping?" Linda arriving with chocolates and a really expensive bottle of perfume that she'd have to work a half-day in Aldi to pay for. Fiona, her tight, pinched face full of love every time she sees me. Cian, finally the big brother I wanted, growing balls by the minute, ready to thump Big. And poor Mam – bending over backwards for me, killing me with kindness. But at least I haven't missed any of my Christmas exams. And I aced English, I just know it. If only it was true. If only Big had actually done it then everything would be perfect. It's been the hardest week of my life and I'm so glad it's Friday night and I'm home safe in my bedroom.

My head is alive with thoughts. There's a huge void to fill

now because the exams are finished. I have to think of something to do so my head is full up and there's no room for anything else. And there's Harvey. Back here where he belongs.

He's lying on my bed right now, kicking his legs with all his strength. I lie down beside him, nuzzling into his warm, fat little body. I can hear Pat Kenny downstairs droning on and on. Somebody finally switches the channel to Jonathan Ross. Not much of an improvement there. Same drivel, different accent. Harvey's eyes close and his body goes still. I love the way he does that, just falls asleep out of the blue. I lift him up carefully and put him into his cot in Fiona's room. I switch on the nightlight and the room is bathed in a soft glow.

The doorbell rings. Every time it does my heart jumps. I'm waiting for Big to somehow appear, screaming and roaring at me for what I did. There are low voices in the hallway and footsteps on the stairs. I dash into my room and close the door.

"Maeve, can I come in?"

It's Mark. I haven't seen him all week. Cian told me he'd gone over to his uncle in Lanzarote for a family wedding. I thought it was an excuse, that he didn't want to see me after our last little spat.

He opens the door. "Hey."

"Hey."

"How are you?"

"OK. How are you?"

He smiles and sits down beside me on the bed. "Sorry I wasn't around when it . . . when you . . . ."

"It's OK."

"Cian told me . . . he told me what happened."

"Cian's been great. So has Fiona."

"That's good. That's great . . . you know . . . your family . . ."

"Yeah."

"Look, I won't talk about it if you prefer not to . . ."

I nod. Long silence.

"So . . . want to do something? We could go to the cinema – Cian said he'd drive."

I look at him as if he's joking.

"I'm sorry. I don't know what to say."

I don't know what to say either. Mark's a stranger to me now. My best friend is gone and there's this other being in his place. He glances around the room like he's looking for something to talk about. "Who owns the tripod?"

My face floods with colour. The stupid tripod is on the floor next to my hold-all. "I do."

"That's for a Nikon 400 – like my camera. Did you get a new camera?"

Suddenly there's a siren screaming down our street, flashing its blue light into the bedroom.

"Fuck – what's that?" says Mark, going over to the window. "Jesus, the whole street is out, something's happened."

He runs out the door, with me following. Mam and Cian are already halfway up the footpath. "Go back inside, Maeve. It's Big's house. There's something up at Big's," he says, as he runs up the road. But something compels me to go, regardless of the danger of Big being there.

Somebody's put in all of Vonnie's windows and there's a smell of petrol in the air. Vonnie's in the driveway, talking to the guards, her voice hysterical. "Sittin' watchin' Pat Kenny and a rock comes in and misses my Nicole by inches and then

I smelt the petrol. They'd thrown a petrol bomb in my letterbox, the luck of God it didn't go off . . ."

I hide behind Mark, waves of nausea rising in my throat. I can feel it in the air. I can hear it. The ball rolling, getting bigger and bigger, crashing and banging and flattening anything in its wake. I throw up near Mr Higgins's wheelie-bin.

Twenty-six

"Shut the fuck up, Cunt, and do what you're told."

It's Sunday and I'm walking down to the shop to get Fiona and myself some chocolate and Pringles for a girls' night in. It happens in a flash, like he's invisible, and suddenly he's there behind me, pushing something into my back. A gun? A knife?

"I'll scream – let me go, you fucker," I say, rooting in my pocket for my phone. It's not there.

He grabs my hand so hard it hurts. "Move, Cunt, or I'll give you a reason to scream."

I do as I'm told, almost relieved. This is it. The thing I've been waiting for. The thing I've been dreading.

"Turn into the lane behind Danahers', keep walking, don't look up."

In the laneway he pushes me up against a wall and I'm amazed at just how strong he is for such a shrimp.

"You could've done fuckin' anything to me except that. Fuckin' anything except this fuckin' shit. Jew know what you've done to me, do ya, Cunt?"

His face is in mine. I can smell his breath – toothpaste and gum.

"You think you're clever? Think you're smart, do ya?"

He's leaning his whole body against me now. I'm pinned to the wall, his spit in my face. But I can't look at his eyes. He catches my face with one hand and swivels it so that our eyes lock. And then I almost wet myself. He's crazy. Drugged. Definitely.

He laughs, a manic, hysterical sound. "Scared now, aren't ya? Fuckin' clever, my hole. See I'm out on bail. Did you think this thing out at all? Did ya?" he shouts.

"Let me go – I'll ring the guards, I'll—"

"You'll do fuck-all while you're pinned up against this wall. Sweet fuck-all. You think the guards can mind you?" He laughs again, a chuckle this time, confident. I feel urine drip down my leg but I can't remember peeing. I can feel the cold dampness between my legs.

"So think it out now, Cunt. I go to jail. So what?"

I turn my face away from his. My arms hurt.

"So I'll get you anyway, you gowl. I'll get you from inside."

I'm crying, whimpering like a puppy, and my legs are jelly. He's right. Of course he can get me anyway. This is never going to be over. I've only made it all worse.

"Smart? You're as thick as a plank. Fuckin' cunt is all you are. I wouldn't touch ya, jew know that? If you were the last woman on the planet I'd sooner wank myself to death than touch you."

There's a noise in the laneway, a kid on a skateboard. Big lets me go and I almost slump to the ground. Then he's gone, hood pulled up over his head, flying down the lane into the night. The kid on the skateboard whizzes past me, barely giving me a second glance. I stand up, shaky at first, using the wall to steady myself. I wipe my face and walk slowly down the lane, into the bright, welcoming streetlight. The shop beckons, flashing its neon sign at me. Inside I manage to find the Pringles and chocolate. I even manage to pay. I walk home without running even though I really want to.

Finally I'm safe indoors. I run upstairs and lock myself in the bathroom. Only then do I absolutely fall to pieces, sitting with my wet bum on the cold tiled floor. Oh God oh God oh God, what have I done?

There's a tap on the door. "Are you OK?"

Fiona. I struggle to stand up and flush the toilet.

"I'm fine. Nearly finished. Will be out in a sec."

She retreats down the stairs and I run into my bedroom and change my jeans and underwear. Then I wipe my face again and go downstairs to the living room. Fiona's curled up on the couch flicking through a magazine.

"Hey, you flew up the stairs when you came in. I thought you were sick or something."

"No. Just needed to pee really badly. So what movie did you decide on?"

She roots through a heap of DVDs on the cushion beside her. "Here we go – *How to Lose a Guy in 10 Days*. It's, like, really good – Big brought . . . I'm sorry, Maeve, I wasn't thinking."

Her eyes are round in her pale worn-out face. I sit down beside her and hug her to me. "No worries, Fifi."

"Pringles. Chocolate," she says, into my hair. We both burst out laughing for no reason. We laugh and laugh like we used to do when we were small, holding onto each other, rolling around on the couch. Finally it winds down to giggles and I go and get the treats while Fiona slips the DVD on.

As the credits roll I wonder if I can sit through this movie once again. But Fiona's enthralled from the very start so I pretend I am too, stuffing myself with Pringles and chocolate out of sheer boredom. And then somehow I'm asleep and there are voices in my dream. Voices having a whispered fight. The movie. I open my eyes. The DVD is on pause, the characters frozen in mid-sentence. The voices are in the hallway. My heart starts thumping like it senses the danger before I see it. And then there's a scream. Fiona. He's in the hallway with Fiona.

Twenty-seven

"Calm down, Big. Let me go – let me go and I'll talk to you."
He has her up against the wall, exactly like he did to me. I'm
frozen to the floor, as if my feet have grown roots. He looks at
me and his face is barely recognisable. His eyes are insane now,
even worse than earlier, and his body is taut with tension.

Fiona glances at me. "It's OK, Maeve. He'll be gone in a
minute."

"I'm going to ring the guards."

"Don't, Maeve. I can handle it."

And then I see it. The gun. Glinting in his hand, pressed
hard into her side.

She smiles at me. "It's fine. He'd never hurt me."

"Fuck off, Cunt, we're talking." Big glares at me. I step
back a few paces.

"Come with me, Fiona. Get Harvey and come with me.
She's lying. You know she is. You fuckin' saw her helpin' me
with the laptop – you saw her with your own eyes . . ."

"Stop, Big, you're hurting me, stop it now."

"Don't pack nothing just come with me. I've twenty grand

288

in the car, you and me and Harvey. That's all I want. I fuckin' love you . . ."

"Stop it. Stop it, for fuck sake, Big. It's over – it's over, so just go home, please, just leave now . . ."

I'm holding my breath. I'm willing Mam or Cian to come through the door. Willing them to come with every pore of my body.

Big's crying, tears and snot running down his face. "I love you. We can make the last ferry if we go now. Please, babe. Please."

Fiona shakes her head. She's crying too.

"I love you." He whispers this into her ear. "I love you."

He drops the gun on the floor. It clatters across the tiles. Fiona reaches out, touches his face. "Go."

And he does. Unbelievably he does. Just leaves. Fiona sinks to the floor, crying her heart out. I can hear him revving his car outside, revving it so hard I think he's going to point it towards the house and drive it straight in at us. I go over to Fiona and slide down beside her. She leans into me, sobbing now, her whole body shaking. We sit there on the cold tiles just holding each other. Rain beats against the porch door. A siren screams somewhere outside. Mr Higgins's dog is barking his head off.

There's a key in the front door. I try to stand up but my legs are numb from sitting on the floor for so long. Mam comes in. I know straight away there's something wrong. No Chardonnay smile tonight. Her face is white. "There's been an accident. It's Big's car. I saw it on my way home, the taxi driver slowed down. Oh, God, Fiona, I think he's dead."

Fiona's on her feet immediately. "What? Where, Mam? Where?"

Mam leans against the door. "It was horrible. The fire

brigade . . . oh, Jesus . . . The car was wrapped around a pole, like he'd driven straight into it."

"For fuck sake, Mam, where is he?" Fiona screams.

"At the top of the road, near the Credit Union . . . Fiona, where are you going? You can't go up there – stop her, Maeve, don't let her . . ."

But Fiona's gone. Out through the door and up the road, running at a sprint, me in hot pursuit. We run and run, the rain lashing down on us. Fiona's ahead of me and I almost crash into her when she stops abruptly. There's a small crowd gathered on the corner. An ambulance and a fire engine, throwing out their flashing blue strobe lights, eerily illuminating the scene. Big's car is concertinaed to a pole at the corner where the road meets the main road. Guards are telling people to stay back. Fiona walks towards the car, pushing a young guard out of the way.

"You can't go any closer, Miss. You're hindering the rescue operation."

"No," says Fiona. "No no no no no." She collapses to her knees, beating the ground with her fists. "No. Not this way. Not like this."

I kneel down and put my arms around her. And then Vonnie's beside us. "My son, oh, God, my baby, let me in or I'll fuckin' kill you – let me see him, ye bastards, ye," she screams, as a guard holds onto her. Nicole is with her, tears and rain streaming down her face.

"Fiona, come on, we can't stay here," I say, but she doesn't even hear me. She's watching as they lift Big from the car. I follow her gaze, my heart thumping so fast I think it's going to burst. They lay him gently on a waiting stretcher.

Fiona calls out, "Big, Big, you'll be OK. There isn't a mark on you, you'll be OK, and we'll go away, like you said, and . . ."

But he's dead. Vonnie knows because I can hear her wailing beside us. And there's blood coming out of his ear. I can see it as they lift him into the ambulance. A trickle of blood running from his ear and pooling on his sky blue tracksuit top.

Someone grabs my arm. "Happy now?" says Vonnie. "Are you happy now?"

"No . . . I . . . it's terrible . . ."

"Don't you fuckin' dare open your mouth. You killed him. You killed my boy! I hope you can fuckin' live with that, you liar." She's screaming and suddenly Detective Ryan is there, ushering Vonnie and Nicole into the ambulance. Mam has arrived too and Fiona's sobbing in her arms. As they close the ambulance doors Nicole looks straight at me. Laser eyes. Knowing laser eyes. I stagger, punch drunk with guilt.

We're in the kitchen. Detective Ryan is drinking a mug of tea. Mam's in the living room with Fiona, holding her while she cries and cries. Her crying is heartbreaking to listen to. Like it comes from deep down inside her.

"Look, all I can say yet again is that you and your sister can't blame yourselves. He came to your house armed and doped up. These guys inevitably die the way they live."

I just want the detective to go. To leave me alone so that I can get used to living with the big rock-hard lump of guilt inside me.

"Anyway, I'm off. Tell your mam we'll have a chat tomorrow."

I nod, and jump up to open the kitchen door so that he won't change his mind about leaving. I walk him out to the front door and even open it for him. He goes out onto the path and I'm just closing the door when he calls me. "Maeve, did I tell you this? When we broke the code on his files, he refused to tell us the password, said he didn't know what we were talking about . . ."

My heart starts it's now familiar steady thump, quickening with each second.

". . . password-protected files. Said he didn't know what they were. The password was niccolomachiavelli. All one word."

He walks back towards me. "He said the only Nicole he knew was his sister. I thought it was the strangest thing. In my job you get this feeling when things don't fit. But he insisted he hadn't a clue what I was talking about."

His blue piercing eyes search me. Tears stream soundlessly down my face.

"Goodnight," he says, and finally leaves.

I close the door and beat my fists off the wall. "What have I done? What have I done at all?"

"Maeve?"

Mam walks towards me and my eyes blur with tears.

"I did a terrible thing. I did a terrible thing and I wish I was dead." She hugs me to her and I bury my face in her chest. "I did a terrible thing."

Twenty-eight

"So I set him up, Mam. I caused it all to happen." My throat is dry from talking and now it's all out in the open. "I'm sorry. I'm so sorry."

We're sitting in the kitchen. Fiona's asleep in the living room. I wanted to wake her. I wanted her to hear it too but Mam wouldn't let me.

"I'm going to tell her, Mam. I'm going to tell her first thing in the morning and . . ."

Mam shakes her head. "No, you're not, Maeve. You're not going to open your mouth to your sister."

"But she has a right to know. She—"

"What will it achieve? It won't bring Big back. It'll just cause more arguments and fights. No good'll come of it."

"I have to tell her. The guilt will kill me."

"You only want to tell her so that you don't feel guilty? You'll have to suck up the guilt. Live with it, Maeve. That's the price you pay."

She's right. I know she's right the minute she says it. I know that the hard knot of guilt inside me won't ever go away, no

293

matter how many people I tell. There's no point in telling Fiona.

"I'm sorry, Mam. I've let you down. You must be so ashamed of me."

Mam stands up and fills the kettle. "No, I'm not, Maeve. Never. You see, a little knowledge is a dangerous thing. Your father was like that. So clever he despised anyone with even average intelligence." She makes a pot of tea and brings it over to the table. Then she slices a swiss roll and puts the pieces on a plate. "Here, eat something."

I pick up some cake and put a tiny piece into my mouth. "Did you love him? Dad – did you love him?"

She stirs sugar into her tea. "At the start maybe but when I realised he couldn't stand talking to me – that's the truth. He thought I was stupid."

"No, he didn't, Mam. What makes you say that?"

"Where will I start? He had a very high opinion of himself. His intellect. He blamed me – no, he blamed all of us because we were real life. Mortgages, bills, children with dyslexia. We weighed him down. Forced him into a stupid job. He blamed us."

"I never thought of it like that."

"He loved you, though. You were his favourite, his big white hope. You almost made it worthwhile. If he couldn't have the great academic career then you would have it instead. I felt sorry for the other two."

"It wasn't my fault."

"Nobody's blaming you. I felt sorry for you too. Being gifted makes you different and that's hard when you're a kid." She smiles at me then. A smile full of love.

"I always thought you didn't like me. That I scared you."

"That's not true. How did you scare me?"

"Remember the time I told you God didn't exist? You were scared of me then."

"You were eight years old. Anybody would be scared if their daughter declared her atheism at such a young age." She pours another cup of tea. "I was going to leave him, you know."

I'm shocked at this. "What?"

She nods vigorously. "Yeah. And then God – the one you don't believe in – interfered. Your father got sick. He got sick and died, and with all his cleverness he left us penniless. He couldn't be bothered with minor details like that."

"Why were you going to leave him?"

She looks at me, her face tired and worn. "Because I couldn't stand being despised any longer. I deserved better than that."

We sit there in silence then, the clock ticking on the windowsill, the rain still lashing down.

"Bed," says Mam, eventually, standing up. "We have some tough days ahead. Poor Fiona, I hope she's OK. I really do."

I get up too, suddenly exhausted. Upstairs, I brush my teeth and wash my streaky white face.

Mam's standing in the bathroom doorway in her grey dressing-gown. "Hey, Maeve?" She smiles at me.

"Yeah?"

"I love you. You know that, don't you?"

"I love you too." And it's true. I do love her.

There's a shrine for Big at the site of the accident. I've seen these shrines in Limerick before but I hadn't taken any notice because I didn't know the people concerned. It's New Year's

Day, two weeks since he died, and still the shrine grows. There are bunches of flowers taped to the pole. All sorts of bunches from tiny posies to big, colourful plastic sprays. There are laminated photographs of Big with various friends. There's a large one of him aged about ten riding a horse bareback. Others have left nightlights in bright jewelled holders. Fiona left a tiny bear from Harvey that says *Lanzarote* across its chest. There's a mosaic of his name – his real name, Ryan – done in tiny beads and shells. *Love from Nicole*, it says at the bottom.

The Manchester United souvenirs are unbelievable and first I'm amazed that they haven't been stolen. But people still respect death. Nothing has been touched. In fact, someone tidies it every day. Throws away the dead flowers. Lights the little nightlights. Arranges the gifts and mementoes. It's a sad place but a good place too. Like a celebration of his life for his family and friends. A connection to him.

I take the long way home. I do this all the time now because I know if I walk through the park I'll see her. And I can't face seeing her like this. With those people, street people, who drink all day and probably all night. She's even beginning to look like them now. Her blonde hair dark with grease, her clothes dirty. She started right after the funeral and Mam says to give her time, it's her way of dealing with it.

I'm just passing Danahers' shop when I see them. They're sitting on the wall in the car park, bags of cans beside them. There are four of them, including Fiona. She's laughing at something one of the guys has said to her. He has a shaved head and a raw wound over his right eye. She looks over as I pass but she doesn't see me. She's too drunk to see anything.

Twenty-nine

It's Mark's birthday. My phone beeped a reminder to me first thing this morning and I sent him a perfunctory text. Job done. It's a blustery ice-cold Saturday in February. I'm sitting with Harvey on the couch, listening to the wind howl outside, beating and shaking the windows, like it's trying to get in. This morning it felt like spring was coming, a lovely stillness in the air, that sharp cold bite gone, weak heat in the watery sun. Like it's between two seasons. Now it's back to winter. Fiona's out with her new friends – if you can call them that – Mam's in the kitchen tidying after dinner. Cian is probably out partying with Mark. Sophie and Ciara texted earlier – Colin's band are playing in Costello's – did I want to come? It'd cheer me up. Little do they know.

There's a knock at the door but I ignore it. Voices in the hall. Mark comes into the sitting room, hair all over the place from the wind. He grins at me as he sits down on the couch beside me. "Hey."

"Happy birthday."

"Thanks. I got your text."

"Good."

297

He strokes Harvey's face. "He's got so big."

"Yeah. Huge."

"Fancy coming out?"

I shake my head. "I don't feel like it."

Mam has come into the room and flicks the channels on the muted TV in the corner.

"We could go into the gig for a while – listen to the Prophets, hear a couple of revelations – leave whenever you want." He grins at me. The old Mark grin.

"I don't think so, Mark."

"Can't you go out with Mark, Maeve? You haven't been outside the door since . . . for ages," says Mam. "Here, give me Harvey, and you go up and get yourself ready. It'll do you good."

"Please, Maeve? Look, it's my birthday so really you have to go. Your present to me. And speaking of presents . . ." He jangles a set of keys in front of me. "I finally have wheels – an Opel Astra Sport – with L plates, though. That's the not-cool part."

"Wow, your own car. But you can't drive it without a driver with a full licence."

He reaches over and tousles my hair. "I love you, Maevis Ravis – everybody drives on Ls, you know that."

"It's settled so, Maeve. You have a lift and all," says Mam.

I look at their two eager faces, wanting something from me, enthusiasm, happiness, something I don't have to give them. "I'll go."

Mark's car is class. I'll admit that. Sleek, black and sexy, no little Punto or Fiesta for him. We pull up in a perfect space right in front of Costello's. Sexy parking for a sexy car. I can hear the music blasting out as we queue for tickets, and for one mad second I consider running away, just legging it down the street as fast as I can. Everything seems different somehow, like I'm a new version of Maeve, seeing things for the first time.

As we reach the top of the queue we can hear three girls talking to each other in front of us. Did you hear Anna Blake's brother topped himself? Go away, are you serious? Dead serious, excuse the pun. Hung himself – his mother found him in the shed. He was always a weirdo, wasn't he? One of them Goths – do you know the ones who dress in black? They love suicide, that lot . . .

Mark looks from them to me and back again, shaking his head. Understanding and summing up the whole episode with one look. It's one of the things I love about him.

The pub is heaving inside. There's a stage at the far end and the band are in full throttle. Mark drags me to the bar, saluting people as he pushes through the crowd. We order two Cokes, and stand at the bar with them, the crowd pushing us together.

"You OK?" he asks.

I nod. Someone jostles past and Mark gets thrown on top of me. We both laugh and he puts his arm around me and kisses the top of my head. "I miss you."

The minute he says it the stupid tears arrive, but I blink them back quickly. No crying with mascara on.

"I miss you. You're one of the few people in the world I trust – do you know that?"

The band have finished and another band – the Prophets, I think, because I can see the back of what looks like Colin's head – are setting up.

"You can talk to me, Maeve. You haven't really talked to me about it at all."

This time the tears are a little more insistent. There's a golf-ball lump in my throat. I slug back Coke to make it go away.

"That's why I brought you here. Because I know that if I try to talk to you in school or at home you'll just brush me off. How's Fiona doing?"

That question again. Mr Hynes asks me at every opportunity. And nobody really wants to know the answer. She's doing badly. She's hanging out with the street drinkers. Sometimes she comes home. Sometimes she doesn't. Sometimes she stays away for days and we have to go out looking for her. Mam is on sick leave from work.

"She's . . . she's not good . . . she's . . ."

A friend of Mark's pushes between us and begins talking to him, shouting even though the music has stopped. Why do drunk people think everybody's deaf?

The band starts up. Kings of Leon. "Fans". How predictable. Colin's voice is good enough. No mumbling at least. Another crowd push their way past us and we're pressed together, glasses touching. It's like we're in a bubble, locked together by people and an invisible rope, a lasso of understanding. Mark's friend moves on to the bar.

"Sorry about that. So, tell me what's going on with her," he says, his face close to mine.

I want to tell him. I want to tell him all of it. Especially about Big. "I did something, Mark . . ."

But bubbles are made to burst and the needle is a bunch of girls from sixth year, who swallow Mark up in screeches and giggles and birthday hugs and kisses. I move away a little and then Ciara and Sophie are on top of me, hugging me, kissing me, dragging me up towards the stage.

Colin smiles down at me, gives me a wink, and they launch into another Kings tribute. "Knocked Up". The crowd swarms around me, suffocating me. I search for Mark but he's invisible in the mass of bodies. Ciara is screeching into my ear and I'm pretending I can hear what she's saying. I'm sweating now and my Coke is mostly on the floor. I want to leave but I'm corralled by the bodies around me. Sophie's linking me so that every time she laughs or gestures my body is pulled this way and that. At last the set finishes. I want to go home. I extract myself from the girls and battle my way through the crowds, searching all the time for Mark. No sign. Another band are tuning up on stage, their noise making my head pound.

I finally make my way outside, gulping fresh air like I've just escaped from a fire. There's a girl vomiting against the wall of the pub, her friends obligingly holding back her hair while they talk over her head. There's a small knot of smokers at the corner but still no sign of Mark. I walk towards the taxi rank at the bottom of the street, desperate now for the safety of home.

And suddenly he pulls up beside me, beeping the horn for me to get in.

"Bastard. You left me."

"No. You left me – drowning in screechy girls. I'm covered in lipstick."

He grins at me and both of us start laughing. He starts the car and it kangaroo jerks and then cuts out. More laughing. He turns the key again and we move.

"Why didn't Sarah come? I thought you two were still a hot item."

"Sarah? I'm out with my mate tonight – Sarah knows she'd only be in the way." He frowns, concentrating as he negotiates the road. But he's smiling too. We small-talk our way home, the world between us again.

Thirty

So I tell Mr Hynes instead. He asks me the usual question, how are things at home, but I don't give him the usual answer – as good as can be expected. I give him the whole story in all its gory details. The drugs, the life, me setting Big up, the horrible aftermath. I talk in a monologue in the silent classroom. Mr Hynes has his fingers steepled and his head bent. He doesn't move while I speak, doesn't move a muscle. I don't cry at all, not a single tear, just talk in the monotone, like I'm offering a synopsis of a movie or a book. Like I'm not part of the drama at all.

There's a silence when I finish. And then, of course, I want to take it all back.

"That's some story, Maeve," he says finally. "OK – let's try and get a handle on all of this." He rubs his forehead with his fingers, something I've seen him do many times in class when he's trying to explain something. "What you did was dangerous and foolish and irresponsible but ultimately the outcome is not your fault."

"Why don't I believe that? I watch my sister every day

sinking deeper and deeper into shit and it's my fault. If Big was here . . ."

Mr Hynes holds up a hand. "Stop right there. Try to remove the guilt and look at the facts – come on, Maeve, this is your forte, cold hard facts. So, give me the facts if Big was still here."

I look at him, arms folded, like he does when he asks a really difficult question in English. "Well, if he was still here then Fiona . . . then she would be . . ." I struggle with the answer. What would she be? Happy? Safe? What would Harvey be?

Mr Hynes gives me a tiny smile. "You see?"

"Yeah, but I set Big up and she doesn't know that . . ."

"So tell her. Or don't tell her. What are the advantages now of telling her that? It won't bring him back, it'll do no good."

"I was thinking of going to the guards, telling them what I did."

"Why?"

"So that I'd be doing the right thing?"

"OK. Cold hard facts – the things you like. What would the guards do? Nothing. He was a petty criminal, well on his way to a life of crime – Big was never going to live to eighty, grow vegetables and walk the dog."

"Live by the sword?"

"Exactly, Maeve. You feel guilty – and so you should. And telling the guards or Fiona may relieve the guilt temporarily but there's no magic wand to make this better."

"Do you think I don't know that? It breaks my heart to watch Fiona. It's unbearable."

"Fiona needs help, Maeve, help that you or I can't give her."

304

There's a tap on the door. A cleaner sticks her head in, then retreats. Mr Hynes roots in his briefcase and pulls out a packet of wine gums. He breaks it in two and gives me one half. We sit there for a while chewing the sweets.

"I have an idea," he says eventually. "You'll hate it but I always feel with you, Maeve – for the longest time – that if you do this it'll . . . I don't know . . . it'll reconcile the two parts of you that are always arguing inside you . . ."

"So you think I'm schizo?"

He smiles. "Actually, in a manner of speaking – yes."

"That's nice."

He laughs this time. "Let me explain. You're clever – very clever – and you trust that part of yourself completely. Let's call it your brain, for simplicity's sake. But the other part of you, you don't trust that at all – so you ignore it." He stops then, and leans back on his chair, like he's just solved the most complicated maths problem in the world.

I wait a little while for him to continue. He just smiles at me. "So, go on, what is it?"

"You tell me."

And then I know. My heart. I don't trust my heart. And the second it pops into my head the tears come, right there in front of Mr Hynes. Trust. It makes me think of Rodger Taylor and Daddy and Fiona and Mark.

Mr Hynes hands me a tissue. I blow my nose. The cleaner looks into the room again, letting us know she wants us gone. Mr Hynes packs up his briefcase. He puts a hand on my shoulder as we leave the room. "Write it down, Maeve. Don't think it out at all – just write it down. That way they'll stop arguing inside you."

*

I stare at the blank computer screen. Harvey's asleep on my bed, lying on his belly. The TV drones downstairs, canned laughter, murmur of voices. I'll write about Big. About his death. I start to type.

After Ours
Between two seasons we meet
The music between us
in a dark pulse thronged public house
safe in newness I watch
your evening eye rivet on
small talked about big problems
glad you're aware
we dance glass to glass
in agreement almost
braver now your eye on my
well-worded indifference I'm
inside the egg-shelled aloneness
me fighting against the grain
of my own imprint losing ground
only the world between us.

A poem of all things. I think I've just written a poem. A poem about Mark and the bubble. Weird. Harvey stirs on the bed, stretches himself, then settles again. There's the urgent sound of an ambulance in the distance. Muted laughs from the TV. I print it out. Read it once more. Then I find an envelope on my desk, an ancient Hello Kitty one with a coffee stain on the corner. I slip the page in and write "Hynes" on the front. Then I change my mind and add a "Mr". I put it straight into my schoolbag. I feel high, like I just drank some of Mark's dad's champagne. I find my phone and text Ciara. The phone beeps an answer almost instantly. A business card with his number. Before I can think I ring it.

"Colin? How are things?"

Thirty-one

Results 2009

There it is in my hand. Years of work in this brown envelope. Mr Hynes beams at me. A group of girls in front of me scream and jump around, kissing and hugging each other.

"Open it, Maeve, what are you waiting for?" he says, still smiling at me. The principal, Mr Horgan, is standing behind him on the steps of the school, arms folded across his chest, looking expectantly at me. I feel like I'm in a play. The lead actress following her cues.

I tear the envelope open and take out the page. Nine A1s. All in a row. Symmetrical. Perfect.

"Well? Say something!" says Mr Hynes.

"We're so proud of you, Maeve," says the principal. "Fantastic results."

I say my lines: "That's great. I'm delighted."

"You got your A1 in English, Maeve. Fair play to you, brilliant result. I knew you could do it. I'm so proud of you." Mr Hynes hugs me. Then the principal does likewise. Another bunch of students are screaming now, waving their results in the air and dancing in circles.

A photographer approaches, a young woman with a tight blonde haircut.

"So, is this the lady?" she asks.

"The highest marks in the country. We're so proud of her. Off to Trinity to study medicine," the principal says, ushering me up on the step beside him for a photograph. I face the camera, the principal's arm around me.

"Hold the page up, that's it, good girl," says the photographer.

The camera clicks.

"Now, for the next one give us a big smile. You look like you're going to a funeral."

I force myself to smile. The camera whirs again.

"Front page of all the papers tomorrow, I'd say," says Mr Hynes.

I fold the sheet of paper and put it back into its envelope. Another wave of students arrives and the principal goes off to greet them with his stack of brown envelopes.

"So, Maeve, off celebrating tonight? I hear there's a whole gang going to Costello's," Mr Hynes says.

"We'll see. Anyway, I'd better go – my mother's waiting outside in the car."

"Well done again, Maeve. Enjoy college life."

"Thanks for everything, sir."

"You're welcome. It's easy to teach someone like you. Keep up the writing – I'm keeping track of you. Pulitzer, here we come!"

"Hardly," I say, smiling at him.

I walk down the drive of the school for the last time, feeling suddenly nostalgic for the place. The sun beats down, warm August sun, the smell of melting tar in the air.

"Maevis Ravis."

I turn around. "Hey."

"Heard your news. The principal couldn't keep it to himself. You must feel great."

"Yeah. It's great." I consider telling him how I feel. Empty. Detached. Scared. Surreal. How it seemed to matter so much but once you've done it you realise it's not the be-all and end-all. That life goes on anyway. Cheated by the Leaving Cert. A nice neat symmetrical row of A1s, my ticket to Trinity. Not a cast-iron guarantee. Terms and conditions apply. Big-time. "So, how did you do?"

He grins. "Art college. I did a great portfolio so the results aren't really that important . . . So, off to the Big Smoke? Cool – I'll haunt you up there. Heard the nightlife's brilliant."

"How's the summer been?"

"Great. Going InterRailing on Friday with Sarah . . . Anyway, there's your mam over there so . . ."

"Take care, Mark. Stay in touch."

"Goes without saying. Hey, been meaning to ask, how's Cian? I Facebooked him loads but he hasn't replied."

"He's in Australia, in the outback. He's working on a farm."

Mark laughs. "God, I'd love to see Cian working on a farm."

I laugh too. He touches my face. "Maevis Ravis." He kisses me lightly on the mouth and then he's gone, whistling his way down the road. I touch my mouth where he kissed me and watch him as he disappears around the corner.

"Well? I got out of the car even though you ordered me not to – well?"

"Nine A1s."

Mam screams and dances like the girls in the school. Motorists slow down to see what's going on. Mam grabs the envelope from me and rips out the sheet of paper, then waves it at the passing cars. "Nine A1s," she shouts. "Nine bloody A1s – I'm so proud of you." She grabs me in a bear-hug and dances me around the street with her.

"Mam, stop boasting, everyone's looking at us."

"Boasting? You have to boast about something like this. Not that I didn't think you'd do well. I have to phone Linda. And Mary and the book club. I'm so proud of you." She roots in her bag for her phone .

"Look, Mam, let's just go to Fiona's first. I haven't seen her since she came out of hospital and—"

"Yeah, you're right. Oh, I'm so delighted. We'll celebrate tonight – Milano's. Colin isn't working, is he? He'll be able to make it?"

"He wouldn't miss a free meal, Mam, trust me."

She hands me her phone in the car. "You text all my contacts. Nine A1s – you probably came top in the country."

"I did."

She almost swerves the car off the road.

"Mam, you'll crash."

Fiona's house is a new semi-detached in a brand-new estate on the other side of town. We pull up outside. Now that I'm here I don't want to go in. Mam bustles up the drive, carrying a bag of groceries. She rings the bell and waves at me to hurry up.

A pinprick of pain erupts in my chest, a tight little pain that I know will get worse and worse until I get my hands on some Maalox.

I can't see her as she opens the door. I follow Mam into the kitchen. Fiona's sitting at the kitchen table. It's covered in debris from past meals. There are plates with hardened spaghetti and cereal bowls with sour milk piled on top of each other. Mam starts cleaning up straight away. "How are you today, love? Did you get any sleep?" she says, as she bustles around the kitchen.

I sit down opposite Fiona. She has a pale pink dressing-gown on but I can see her bare concave chest underneath. A TV blares from the living room. A football match on full blast.

"Hi," I say, finally making eye contact with her.

Her hair is pulled back in a ponytail but her face is old despite the girlish hairstyle. There are dark smudges under her eyes and tiny broken veins on her nose.

"Well, how did you get on?" she asks, but her voice is uninterested. She's going through the motions. Saying her lines.

"I did fine. I got my course."

"So, off to Trinity? What you always wanted." Her eyes, when you look into them, are empty, like a blind person's.

"Yeah. Dublin. It'll be good, I hope – a change from Limerick anyway."

She listlessly picks at her nails. Mam is doing Mr Muscle on the kitchen worktop.

"You should come up, Fiona, when I'm settled in – and we'll go out on the town . . . Temple Bar." I know as I'm saying it that it'll never happen. She does too.

"Yeah. I might. We could go shopping."

"So where is he? Can I see him?"

She gets up and leads me up the stairs and across a landing strewn with toys and dirty clothes. We creep into the bedroom. He's asleep in his cot. A little angel face, sucking his thumb. Fiona's new baby son. My new nephew.

"Did you decide on a name?" I whisper.

She nods. "Ryan."

"Ryan?" The minute it's out of my mouth I want to take it back. "Ryan. That's a lovely name."

She nods. "Ryan Christiano Thomas."

"Lovely."

We creep out of the room and back downstairs.

"Where's himself?" I ask.

She gestures towards the living room. Mam is filling the washing-machine with clothes. She has them separated into two bundles. Light and dark.

I go into the living room. Kev is sprawled on the couch, a can of beer in his hand. He glances at me, gives me a brief nod, and turns his attention back to the football. He looked exactly like that on the New Year's Day when I first saw him. Sitting on a wall with a bag of cans making Fiona laugh. He still has the shaved head. The only difference is that the wound he had over his right eye has healed into what looks like a hairless eyebrow. Harvey's asleep on the couch beside him but he opens his eyes, like he knows I'm there.

"Maeve, Maeve," he says, rubbing sleep from his eyes with his fists.

I pick him up, kissing his cheek. "My little man, my best boy," I say, blowing bubbles on his neck.

He squeals with delight. "No, no, no!"

But we both know that this means yes, yes, yes.

Fiona's smoking in the kitchen, a thin blue spiral stretching all the way up to the ceiling. Mam's still scrubbing. She's homed in on the sink now, scrubbing with all her might.

Harvey puts his arms out to go to Fiona, but she's texting on her phone. "Down, Maeve, down," he says. I put him down and he toddles over to his mother, his nappy drooping under him. She stubs out her cigarette and Harvey tries to climb onto her lap.

"No, Harvey, Mammy's tired," she says.

I swallow all the things I'd like to say. Swallow them all until I feel the band of pain in my chest tighten another notch. "Can you-know-who come home with us?" I ask her.

"Take him. I might finally get some sleep."

"Harvey, do you want to sleep in my house tonight?"

He stuffs his thumb into his mouth, his brown eyes watching everything. I pack a small bag for him. Some nappies, a teddy and his bird book. The bird book has to go everywhere with him and already he knows the names of all the species.

Kev comes out of the living room, walks to the fridge and pulls out a can of beer. "Do you want one, love?"

Fiona shakes her head. Kev pops the can and takes a long slug of beer. Then it's as if his brain kicks into a higher gear: he takes another can from the fridge and walks back into the living room.

"I'm going to bed, Mam, I'm jaded," says Fiona.

"That's a good idea, and we'll keep Harvey for as long as you want. Just ring me now if you need anything."

Mam hugs Fiona and kisses her on the head. I hug her then, her frail little frame fragile in my arms. Mam watches us together and I can see it in her eyes. How she blames herself. My sister stands at the door to watch us leave. The pain in my chest is a full-blown ache now and I struggle to carry Harvey to the car and strap him into his seat. The tears come as soon as she closes the front door.

Acknowledgements

Thanks firstly to Mary Coll. She drops everything to read anything I throw at her, gives me endless encouragement and makes me laugh out loud every time I talk to her. Thanks to Monica Spencer, Kay Barriscale and Ellie Gallagher – my own personal book club! Thanks to Michelle Reddan for being my Number One Fan – everyone should have one. Thanks also to Emmet for his excellent advice at a crucial stage. Big shout out to Fionn Regan for his kind permission to use lyrics from 'Snowy Atlas Mountains' and 'Hey Rabbit', and to Reverb Music Publishing.

Huge thanks to The Dream Team – my agent and friend Faith O'Grady, my wonderful editor Ciara Considine, copy-editor Hazel Orme and all at Hachette – you are a fantastic crew to work with.

Finally thanks to the usual suspects – my family and friends.